PENGUIN BOOKS

SUGARTOWN

Loren D. Estleman is a professional journalist. He is also the author of four previous Amos Walker mysteries, including *Motor City Blue*, *Angel Eyes*, *The Midnight Man* and *The Glass Highway*, several westerns and one celebrated case of Sherlock Homes versus Dracula.

He lives in Michigan.

Loren D. Estleman

SUGARTOWN

PENGUIN BOOKS

This one is for Carole

Penguin Books Ltd, Harmondsworth, Middlesex, England
Viking Penguin Inc., 40 West 23rd Street, New York, New York 10010, U.S.A.
Penguin Books Australia Ltd, Ringwood, Victoria, Australia
Penguin Books Canada Limited, 2801 John Street, Markham, Ontario, Canada L3R 1B4
Penguin Books (N.Z.) Ltd, 182–190 Wairau Road, Auckland 10, New Zealand

First published in the U.S.A. 1984
First published in Great Britain by Macmillan London Ltd 1986
Published in Penguin Books 1987

Made and printed in Great Britain by
Richard Clay Ltd, Bungay, Suffolk

SHE WAS A VERY OLD WOMAN dressed entirely in black, and when she fumbled open my inner office door the aluminum tubing of the walker she was leaning on gleamed like nickel steel against the black of her dress. I got up from behind the desk to hold the door open against the pressure of the pneumatic closer. She nodded her thanks with that jerky impatience that the very old share with the very young — the poised complacency of age is a myth — but she made no comment, concentrating on the involved business of setting the rubber feet down on the rug and toddling forward and then picking up the feet and setting them down again. Her breath came sibilantly through her nostrils, but apart from that and the way the cords on the side of her neck stood out like telephone cables under her skin, she showed nothing of the strain it took to cross that six feet to the chair on the client's side of the desk.

When she was sitting she closed her eyes and breathed. I walked around the desk and lowered myself into the swivel-squawker and waited while the quarter-size fever spots high on her cheeks faded into their ivory background and her narrow flat chest stopped galloping under the plain black material. I'm very good at waiting, it's the first thing they ask you about when you put in for your investigator's ticket.

I had a nice day for it. It was May, I had the blinds up and the window raised, and three stories below, the cars gliding past on West Grand River caught the sun on their windshields and chrome and the sweetish smell of warm pavement took the bite out of the auto exhaust. Even the horns sounded content. The first decent day of spring will do that, even in a place like Detroit. Pigeons roosted on the window ledges of the apartment house across the way, looking like small animated gargoyles rehearsing for another remake of *The Hunchback of Notre Dame.* Two hours earlier I had been fooling around with the thought of closing up and driving out into the country when the telephone rang and a Polish accent named Martha Evancek asked me if I was for hire. That's as close as I get, the thought.

"You didn't have to make the trip, Mrs. Evancek." I leaned on the second syllable and used a crisp *ch* on the last part, the way she had over the telephone. "I do house calls."

She shook her head. "Everyone tries to save me steps. I must have exercise."

Same voice, same accent. Her face was long and narrow under a black pillbox with a short black veil that hung like Spanish moss to the hump of her thick curved nose, but behind it you could see her heavy lids in the hollows of her eyesockets and below it the deep lines where her cheeks had fallen in. Her hair was very thick, very white, brushed back from her forehead and pinned at the nape of her neck. Fifty years ago it would have tumbled in rich dark waves to her shoulders and had the young Polish blades doing cartwheels to get their fingers in it. At first glance her face had a patrician look; at second glance it was just old. The hands in her lap were blunt and red with skin flaking off the backs. The skin was well scrubbed but there was black dirt older than I was in the creases of her knuckles. There was a thick plain gold band on the third finger of her left hand and a startling red ruby in an antique setting on the corresponding finger of her right. It went with that hand like a silk dress in a steel washtub. There was much to learn about Martha Evancek.

"You are Mr. Amos Walker?" she asked.

I said I was. She said, "I picked your name out of the telephone directory. You are the only private investigator listed whose residence is in Hamtramck. That's why I chose you."

"Not precisely Hamtramck," I corrected. "But I'm so close it might as well be. The boundaries around Detroit are as vague as the mayor's morals."

She made a quick gesture with the hand wearing the ruby that made me feel stupid for even bringing up the subject. "I thought that since you live in a Polish community you might be sympathetic. Are you Polish, Mr. Walker?"

"I can be, if that's what you want."

That wasn't the answer she was looking for, but I watched her think it over and decide it didn't matter. Once someone has made an appointment to see an investigator and then kept it, he either goes ahead or gives up the idea entirely. He rarely shops around. It usually takes everything he has to make the trip the first time.

In her case it took more.

She watched me, the hollows in her cheeks working, sucking at her teeth. I'd glimpsed them when she spoke, white and even as aluminum siding and just as natural. She had sharp dark eyes under the heavy lids. Old people almost always do. Anyone who equates great age with innocence has never looked into an old person's eyes.

"How old are you?" she asked finally.

"Coming up on thirty-four."

"That is very young."

"Not from this side, Mrs. Evancek."

"It is from this one." She might have smiled, tugging the pleating out of her lips briefly. "Your display advertisement in the telephone directory said you look for people who are lost."

I nodded. "I do other things, but most of my business comes from that." It being most of nothing for almost a month, which was why I was sitting there being watched by those sharp dark eyes instead of out picking marsh marigolds.

"I want to hire you to look for my grandson," she said.

I found a pencil and opened my notebook to a page without doodles. "How long has he been missing?"

"Nineteen years."

"I see. Would you mind if I smoked?"

"Cigarettes?"

"Yes."

"Could I have one?"

For no special reason, that rocked me harder than the part about the nineteen years. But I fished the pack out of my shirt pocket and shook out a couple and let her take one and slid the other into the permanent groove in the corner of my mouth and lit them both. She held hers between the second and third fingers of her left hand and filled her mouth with smoke and brought the cigarette away with her lips pressed tight and inhaled. Very little smoke curled back out.

"The doctor says I should not do this since the stroke," she said. "I broke my ankle last year and he said I should not smoke then."

I smiled and slid the big glass ashtray between us and dropped some ash onto the picture of Grand Traverse Bay in the base. I had never been to Traverse City. The ashtray had come with the office and the rest of the furniture. She went on.

"I have been in this country only two years. My husband and I came over when the troubles started in Poland. That was his excuse, but I waited seventeen years to come over and learn what became of our little Michael."

"Your English is very good."

"Thank you. For six years I was maid to an American businessman and his family living in Cracaw. My husband was head chef in one of the largest restaurants there. But the dishes he made were not popular here and all he could get was a job waiting tables in St. Clair Shores, where we lived and where I am still living. It took something out of him. I scrubbed floors and dusted to help us live until this happened." She indicated the walker standing like a big chromium bug next to her chair. "Michael — my husband, our grandson was named for him — died last December. I had sold most of my grandmother's jewelry to pay our way to

America, and I had to sell the rest to bury him. This is all that's left." The ruby caught the light as she waggled that finger.

"Your grandmother didn't get that scrubbing floors."

"She was related distantly to the old ruling family of Poland. When I was a little girl I would sneak into my mother's bedroom and put on the jewelry and pretend I was a princess. Funny little-girl dreams."

I gave up trying to picture her as a little girl and snicked some more ash into the tray. "Your grandson."

"Yes. The business of living, as you call it here, got in the way of our search, but we never forgot our reason for coming. The Hamtramck police were very polite and let us look at their records, but most of them were not there during the time we were interested in, and they could not afford to re-open a case so old."

"Case?"

"I will come to that soon. Our son Joseph came here thirty-two years ago to go to work for the Chrysler Motors Corporation. His father and I stayed behind. No one from either side of our family had ever gone away from Poland. A year later Joseph married an American girl, Jeanine, and bought a house in Hamtramck. The house is still standing, though it is one of those to be torn down for the new plant General Motors wants to build there. They had two children, Michael and a daughter, Carla. I never saw them. Joseph was always going to visit us but he never found the time or the money and we could not afford the trip short of selling my grandmother's jewelry, which at that time I did not want to do."

I watched her take one last careful drag, her hand covering the lower half of her face, and squash the butt in the bay. The hand shook a little. I'd figured her for eighty when she came in but she could have been older. She kept on screwing the stub long after it was out.

"Nineteen years ago this month," she said, "Joseph was let go from his job. He wrote that the Dodge plant was cutting back on personnel, but we found out later he was fired for coming to work drunk and sometimes not coming to work at all.

"For eight weeks he looked for another job, then gave up. On a hot day late in July he got into an argument with Jeanine over his refusal to look for work. He was drunk. The neighbors heard them shouting at each other. Then he went into another room and brought back the shotgun he went deer hunting with in the winter. They heard that too."

She abandoned the shredded butt finally and sat back, looking at me with her sharp dark eyes.

After a long moment I got rid of my own cigarette. It was starting to burn my fingers.

2

A YELLOW OBLONG OF SUNLIGHT draped over one corner of the desk slid off and landed on the floor without a noise. The horns down in the street sounded less content now. I'd have bet the pigeons had flown off too. I turned to a fresh page in my notebook.

"Joseph killed his wife?"

"He didn't stop with her. The police said he used the shotgun on little Carla when she ran in after the first explosion. Then he turned it on himself."

The words came neatly, one on top of another like bills counted out by a banker who no longer thought of them as money. The whole story had the sound of something she'd told plenty of times.

"Michael?"

"He was attending summer school to make up for a failure in arithmetic. If he hadn't come home late he might have been killed too, the police said."

"He discovered the bodies?"

She closed her eyes and nodded. "It was not five minutes after the shooting. The neighbors were afraid to investigate after all the noise. When the police came they found him standing in the middle of all the blood and bodies. He was eleven years old."

"When were you notified?"

"Ten days later. The telephone service in Poland in those days was what you might expect it to be and the cable the authorities sent was delayed somewhere. In the meantime the police had pieced together the entire incident, and Joseph, Jeanine, and Carla were buried and the boy had gone to live with Jeanine's sister and her husband in St. Clair Shores. Jeanine's parents were dead. There was never any question afterwards about our living anywhere else when we came to this country. But at the time there seemed little that we could do. Michael and I argued about it bitterly. He wouldn't let me part with Grandmother's jewels. He said they were the things that kept us from being common peasants. You would have to know the class system in my country to understand such pride."

"We have the same system," I said. "We just call it by different names."

"It wasn't until the troubles came and there was not enough food available to keep the restaurant open that he gave in." She talked right through me. "By that time Jeanine's sister and her husband had moved away and taken little Michael with them. The police had given us their original address but they never answered our letters."

"No forwarding?"

"It was too long ago. The post office stops forwarding mail after a year and destroys its records after two. We talked to the people who were living in their old house but they knew nothing of them. The house had had at least two owners since and we couldn't find the people who sold it to those who are there now."

"If a real estate firm handled the sale you could have traced them through the firm."

"It was sold privately." Her head started to shake. "I don't think these people want to be found."

"Could be. Time has a way of drifting in over your tracks whether you ask it to or not." I tapped the pencil on the edge of the book. "What name did Jeanine's sister and her husband go by?"

"Norton. The Robert Nortons. Her name was Barbara."

I wrote it down. "Occupations?"

She shook her head, deliberately this time.

"Who investigated the shooting?"

"Sergeant William Mischiewicz and Detective Howard Mayk of the Hamtramck police. Mischiewicz was shot to death in a holdup a few months later. Mayk retired four years ago. He still lives in Hamtramck." She gave me the address and telephone number. "We talked to him. He remembered almost everything about the shooting but had no idea where the Nortons moved to."

"Were you satisfied with the official account of the shooting?"

She looked down at her hands in her lap, then nailed me again. Her whole head was trembling now. "I lived through the Nazi invasion. I know that people are capable of anything under certain circumstances. I did not see Joseph the last thirteen years of his life. I can't tell you what kind of man he was in those years."

Outside, the horns were getting nasty. I got up, closed the window, and sat back down. "Do you have a picture of your grandson?"

She had a black crushed-leather purse about the size of an after-dinner mint in her lap. From it she drew a two-by-three snapshot and held it out fluttering in her hand. I accepted it the way I had accepted hundreds of others: too-dark Polaroids with green skies and red spots in the eyes, studio shots with fake landscapes in the background and more touchup than photo, black-and-white poses against cars with big headlights and round fenders long since gone to the crushers, beach pictures with big grins and funny hats and rolls of pale flesh around the middle, school shots with starched white blouses against blue canvas, grainy exposures taken through keyholes of naked white bodies, service photos with neck-high uniforms and visors square over the eyes, vacation shots with tanned faces squinting into the sun and fluted canyons behind, theatrical poses dramatically lit, motel room pictures burned out from the flash, telephotos snapped from across the street, blurred freeze-frames in sixteen millimeter, lightning-clear blowups in bureau-top size, First Communion pictures, bar mitzvah pictures, wedding pictures, clowning-around pictures, candid pictures — you don't really have film in that camera, do you? — pictures you dress up for and pictures you take your clothes off for. Pictures handed over eagerly, reluctantly, in hope and in terror, the act symbolic of breaking open the family circle to admit a stranger. I had handled enough pictures to fill a gallery of the lost. This one, dog-eared and finger-marked, showed a boy with his dark hair wet down and parted on one side, the way no boy anywhere combs it without adult help, with shiny dark eyes tilted slightly toward a large nose and that smile kids have before they learn to show their teeth. Clean plaid cotton shirt buttoned at the throat. The name of a school photo agency was stamped on the back. I memorized those features that counted and gave the picture back to her.

"He'll have changed too much," I explained. "If I showed that around, it would just throw people off. You'd have to be a pro and know what to look for. He'd be about thirty now?"

She looked at the picture for a moment before putting it away. "His birthday's in June. He turns thirty on the fifteenth." She sucked at her teeth a little. "Can you find him, Mr. Walker?"

"I have some tricks," I said, by way of evasion. "If I do, my job stops after I've told you where he is. If he doesn't want to see you I can't make him."

"Why would he not want to see me?"

"I'm just mentioning it as a possibility. Half the time in these things they don't."

She thought about that. Then:

"I want to see him. But if I cannot I will be satisfied to know where he is and that he is all right."

"I charge two hundred fifty dollars per day, expenses extra. First three days in advance. I report daily and put it all in writing at the end." I considered. "One day in advance will be fine."

She was back inside her purse already. She hoisted out a

flat packet and laid it on the desk between us. The bill on top was a crisp new hundred. "Here is a thousand dollars. That is four days."

I left it where it was. When you do see money in my business you usually see it in cash, but there had never been that much of it on that desk all at once. She must have read me, because she said, "I sold my husband's things. Also your public benefit programs here are very generous. I do not require much to live. If you have learned little in four days I can sell the ring."

I split the stack and held out the top five bills. "Two days will tell us whether you're wasting your money."

She hesitated, then took back the bills. There was something behind her face that had not come in with her.

I gave her a receipt and got her address and telephone number in St. Clair Shores and then helped her down three flights to the street. It only took a half hour. She was tougher than she looked. "We'll make it your place next time," I told her, when I had a cab coming our way. She'd taken the bus in. "You must have been all afternoon wrestling that contraption upstairs."

"When you have helped stack sandbags all around your city with shells shrieking overhead, nothing you try to do later is too much." She gave the walker to the driver to fold and put in the front seat while I helped her into the rear. She was as light as pie crust. As I was getting set to close the door she looked up at me. "I feel I have made the right choice," she said.

I swung the door shut and stood back while the cab pulled out from the curb and burbled away. I hoped she was right. I had never stacked sandbags in my life.

Back in the office I dialed the number she had given me for Howard Mayk in Hamtramck. A man's voice, very deep, answered after two rings. Listening to it I saw a big man in a blue uniform with a double row of brass buttons down the front, swinging a stick in one hand and folding deep vertical lines in his cheeks when he smiled.

"Officer Mayk?"

A pause, then:

"That's Sergeant. My last ten years with the department, anyway. Now it's Mr. Mayk. Who's asking?"

"Amos Walker. I'm a Detroit P.I. working for Mrs. Martha Evancek, looking for her grandson Michael. I'd like to come over and talk for a few minutes if you're not too busy."

"I haven't been busy in four years. But I can't tell you anything about what happened to the boy because I don't know. I told her that enough times."

"I realize that. I thought if I knew something about the shoot I might get a better handle on the case."

"Yeah."

"Does that mean I can come over?"

"Yeah."

"I'll be there in forty minutes, then."

He said yeah again and I thanked him and he hung up. This was going to be like pulling nails with my teeth.

Before leaving I broke out some duplicate driver's license application forms issued by the Michigan Secretary of State's office and filled out two of them, one asking for a copy of a driver's license for Michael Evancek, the other asking for one for Michael Norton, including lost Michael's date of birth on both. I stuck them in separate envelopes and addressed them to the Lansing headquarters of the SOS and stamped them and dropped them into a mailbox on my way to Hamtramck. If the stars were all in their places, one of the applications might jar loose a photocopy of the missing party's license containing his present address for a small fee, if he hadn't left the state or taken another name or if he had a license at all. It's a service provided for people who drop their wallets into the sewer while leaning down to pick up a quarter. It can save you steps, but only when you've got a month to spare for the turnaround. I had two days.

3

THERE IS NOTHING SPIRITUAL about Detroit's Poles. They are the supreme property owners of the Western Hemisphere Since the railroad shops and stoveworks and, later, Ford Motors slammed a hole though the immigration laws of the last century and emptied villages in Poland and Italy and Austro-Hungary, the bull-shouldered enemies of Czarist Russia had been coming here with their substantial women, lugging their loaves of hard bread and jugs of thick brown wine, to stake out the half- and quarter-acre lots that remain the sole measure of success in their community. Hamtramck to this day boasts the highest percentage of home ownership of any city in the country.

Driving down Chene through the old village with its tight rows of identical century-old houses painted in peeling colors, you still catch glimpses of the melting pot: old men loitering in front of the old Round Bar where as children they had packed the balcony along with their fathers to watch the struggling glistening naked backs of the wrestlers below; a thick-ankled housewife slitting a duck's throat in her backyard and holding it flapping upside-down while her little daughter catches the warm blood in a bowl for the soup they call *czarnina;* native costumes sagging from a pully-operated line waiting for the Polish Constitution celebration on Belle Isle. But you have to look quick, because it's going, going to eminent domain and General Motors' golden ring in the nose of City Hall, its churches knocked to rubble and kindling, the bricks that paved its medieval alleys piled in heaps for the scavengers.

Chene merges with Joseph Campau north of Grand Boulevard. There doomed Dodge Main warmed its pitted brick face in the sun, considering with blind eyes the spot where the gin mills used to stand in front, the Purple Gang's Lincolns and Caddies barricading the street while the trucks unloaded in the days when the Motor City was Sugartown to every laborer from Montgomery to Budapest. Yellow Caterpillars crawled over hills of naked earth and crumbled pavement in the parking lot. Farther north, the blue street signs that mark Hamtramck proper begin and the housing gets thicker and more modern. It looks like the rest of Detroit and you can have it, except I live there and as bland and monotonous as it gets it still looks like home.

I went past bakeries and butcher shops with names as long as your belt and the municipal tennis courts that turned out this country's best pros before the kids and dykes took over that sport, crossed Holbrook and then Florian, closed off with sawhorses at Joseph Campau for the May Strawberry Festival going on in front of the soaring brownstone of St. Florian's with the lowering sun grazing its stained glass, turned right on Evaline three blocks up and then swung left on Gallagher to a chalk-gray frame house with a high peak and Howard Mayk's number in black wrought iron on the cornerpost. The place shared a driveway with the brick house next door. Michigan cancer was eating through the fenders of a nine-year-old red Ford Bronco parked on Mayk's side next to a spanking green Camaro on the other. I parked on the street and glanced through the Bronco's long rear Plexiglas window on my way up the driveway. A set of rubber waders wallowed on the ribbed metal floor with a long-handled nylon net on top of them. I mounted a concrete stoop and rapped on the screen door's aluminum frame. It was still plenty light out and the room beyond the screen was as black as Martha Evancek's dress.

Heavy feet trod around inside for a little and then the darkness stirred and I was looking at a man in dark trousers and a matching short-sleeved shirt standing on the other side of the screen.

"Mr. Mayk? Amos Walker. I called earlier."

"Yeah. Stand away."

I stepped back and he manipulated a drugstore latch and the door opened out, straining a long steel spring. I stepped up over the threshold and past his long arm into a narrow dank-smelling utility room. A dirty mop in one corner and old mud-dauber wasps' nests under the eaves. There was another door standing open into what looked like a kitchen.

My host let the screen door bang shut and set the latch. My mental picture of the former detective sergeant hadn't been far off. He was a big man, my height, with more shoulder, although what I have is not to be sneered at. His hair was thick, smoothed back from his broad face as if by meaty palms like his, and of that neutral color that can't make up its mind whether to go gray or stay sandy. His heavy jaw was clean-shaven and he had a long upper lip that made his nose look small and a small nose that made his upper lip look long. His eyes were a flat gray under low brows, cop's eyes. He was a very good-looking fifty, but he was fifty. He was wearing a charcoal-gray security guard's uniform with shield-shaped patches piped in red on the short sleeves and one of those Velcro belts that don't need buckles.

"I thought you were retired," I said.

"I am. You think I'd make this a career? My pension's the only thing that hasn't gone up since I left the big blue machine. I was just coming in from the eight to four at Shaw College when you called." He moved a big hand in the direction of the open door and I went that way.

It was a large kitchen like they don't build them now, with a scuffed but clean linoleum floor and a long white enamel sink with a window over it and a gas stove and refrigerator and a table with a sheet-metal top and three vinyl-covered chairs that didn't match drawn up to it. A short wainscoted hallway jogged to the left into an unlighted living room. On the plaster above the wainscoting hung a large crucifix carved from a single block of maple. A Velcro gunbelt lay in a heap on the table with a nickel-plated Colt Python in the holster.

I tilted my head toward the crucifix. "Mayk doesn't sound Polish."

One side of his mouth went up. "It was Maykowski, but not to some civil servant on Ellis Island when my old man came through. My boy went back to it, but he designs machine parts for a living and doesn't have to sign his name as often as I did." He opened the refrigerator and took out a carton of milk, shaking it to find out how much was inside. "This is all I got if you're thirsty," he said. "I been on the wagon since New Year's."

"Milk's fine. Tied one on, huh?"

"Man, I missed most of last year." He got two glasses out of a cupboard next to the sink and put them on the table and filled them, shook the carton again, tilted the remaining contents down his throat, and tossed the empty container into a green plastic wastebasket.

We sat down across from each other at the table with the gunbelt between us and sipped our milk. "How much you jacking the old lady up for?" he asked, whipping away his moustache with a thick forefinger.

"Two and a half yards per," I said. "But I'm not jacking her up. That's the standard rate."

"I figured some cheap shamus would latch on to her sooner or later. I'm just surprised it took this long."

"She came to me."

"You didn't waste a lot of time arguing her out of it, though."

"Turning down paying work takes practice. Look, Mr. Mayk, I'm just poking around. If the trail's too cold I'll give her back what's left of the retainer and advise her to run something in the personals or forget it. Just don't ask me to do my job for free."

"I tried private work after I left the department," he said. "I didn't like the company I was keeping."

Silence stretched thin and tight the enormous length of that kitchen table.

"How was the smelt running?" I tried.

He raised his brows an eighth of an inch — a feat, considering those brows. "What, that bath I took didn't get rid of the smell?"

"I saw your gear in the Bronco. They aren't wearing waders to chase butterflies this year."

"You ever been?"

I grinned. "Once."

He laughed then, a short harsh barking noise, and the air in the kitchen got warmer. "Freeze your ass off all night in Sturgeon River water up to your bellybutton and scoop out little fish till your arms get too heavy to scoop out any more. One man just can't take that much hilarity all at once."

I laughed too. We drank our milk. After a little I said, "The Evancek shoot."

"Didn't she tell you about it?"

"Just what you told her. Cops don't talk to grandmothers the way they talk to people."

He smoothed back his hair with one of his big hands and left it on the back of his neck. When he did that he looked like a big rough farmer.

"It was just about this time on what had to be the hottest son-of-a-bitching day of the year," he said. "Lieutenant Jezewski got the squeal at the station and sent Bill Mischiewicz and me out there. We came to this house where a uniform about twenty-two was heaving his guts out on the sidewalk in front and Bill said, 'I think this is it.' Well, you had to laugh. Anyway, we park behind the black-and-white and go in right past the uniform, which if we were the whole Red Army he wouldn't of noticed us, and, Christ, how can I make you see it? You saw the blood first, on the walls, the floor, Christ, even on the ceiling, orange-red and splattered all over like a pressure cooker full of red cabbage blew up. For a second I thought it was something like that. Blood always looks too bright to be blood till it dries. The bodies looked like bodies, though, not like dress dummies like I bet I heard a million people say. The first two were on the floor in the living room, one a lot smaller than the other, and the only way we could tell the bigger one was a woman was she was wearing a dress. We thought at first the other was a boy because it had on red corduroys and a striped shirt. Their faces — well, they didn't have any.

"Another uniform came out of the bedroom and said we'd find the last one in the kitchen and he had the boy, Michael, in the bedroom. Bill sent him back in to keep an eye on the boy and we went into the kitchen. The third stiff was sitting on the floor with his back propped against the back door and his face all over the wall behind him. He had this twelve-gauge automatic shotgun between his legs and Bill said it looked like he was jerking off. Well —"

"I know," I said. "You had to laugh."

He shook his big head. "Not that time. It almost sent me out front to heave up with the blue suit. I told Bill to shut it. I mean, he was a sergeant and I was just a third-grader then, but the only feelings he ever had were in his holster and in his crotch. No one was all that broke up when some seventeen-year-old punk put a thirty-two slug through Bill's head running out of Svoboda's liquor store later.

"Well, we talked to the boy, but he was in shock and not saying much, and a couple of days later when he'd been collected by his aunt and uncle and we got back to him he said he'd found the bodies when he got home from school. That jibed with what most of the neighbors told us. By then we'd ID'd the stiffs — Jesus, his little sister was just fixing to start school in September — and what we found on the scene and what we knew then about this guy Joseph Evancek and the fight the neighbors overheard just before the shots were fired went with the murder-suicide scenario and we locked it up tight."

"Most of the neighbors?"

"What?"

"You said that what Michael said about coming home from school and finding the bodies agreed with what most of the neighbors said. What did the others say?"

He removed the hand from the back of his neck and waved it in front of his face impatiently. "There's always a nutcase looking to get attention by claiming he saw something nobody else did. An old guy across the street said he looked out his window just as the kid came home *before* the first shot, and then the housewife from next door piped up and said she saw the same thing. You learn to spot them."

"Check out their stories?"

"Departmental fucking procedure. Housewife said she saw the boy coming up the driveway when she went out back to feed the cat. Only there was a six-foot hedge between the houses and when Bill and I went back there neither of us could see the driveway from where she said she was standing, and she was a foot shorter than either of us. The old guy had a clear view but he was a nutcase like I said. There's always some confusion in these things as to who heard and saw what first, but there was enough agreement between the other witnesses to discount his story."

"Would you remember his name?"

"It was almost twenty years ago, what do you think? Anyway, the old guy's dead by now, or if he isn't he's moved. Neighborhood's all tore up."

I drank the last of my milk. It left a slick coating on the roof of my mouth, but in my business you drink whatever they offer you. You never turn it down. "Anything else that didn't fit with the other evidence?"

"I never worked on a case where there wasn't." He frowned, pulling his upper lip still longer. "The blood test, maybe."

"What test?"

"At the autopsy they ran Evancek's blood and the alcohol level tested lower than you'd expect in a case like that. Oh, he was drunk enough to pull off the road, but he had some size, about five-ten and a hundred and eighty, and if a guy with his reputation as a boozer didn't get violent before, it was sort of strange he'd pick then and on so little booze. But it was just one of those things that passes through your head when you're wrapping one up. He did it, all right. We ran every angle and it was the only one that came close to fitting."

I looked at my notebook scrawl. "How much of this did you tell Joseph's mother?"

"She got the Disney version, like you said. That about the blood test didn't bother her any more than it did me when it first went down. She's had a long time to get used to what her son did."

"I guess you don't have any ideas about where the boy wound up."

"If I did she wouldn't of had to hire you."

I passed that one. "I'd like to take a look at the old Evancek place. Could I buy your time as tour guide?"

"Would you charge it to the old lady?"

"Probably."

"Then it's on me." He rose. "I got nothing to do till the wife gets home anyway. Let me get out of this monkey suit and we'll take the Bronco."

"I appreciate it."

"Don't bother. It's for Mrs. Evancek. We Poles stick together."

He went down the hall into the living room and opened a door somewhere on the other side. I got up and leaned a shoulder against the hallway wall and lit a cigarette. "Why'd you quit the department?" I called out.

"I had my twenty in." His voice was muffled, as if through fabric.

"You look like you could have stuck it out till mandatory."

"I could of. I didn't get along with the new skipper and I figured the hell with it."

"Who's the skipper down there now?"

"Same guy. Steve Grabowska."

"What's he like?"

"What's Captain Grabowska like?" He came out tugging an old blue sweatshirt down over the belt of a pair of faded jeans. They nearly matched and he might as well have stuck with the uniform. He would have that look no matter what he wore. "You know the prowl-car cop I told you about, that was throwing up in front of the Evancek place?"

"Yeah."

He went on looking at me. I said, "You're kidding."

"His stomach was a lot stronger when it came to kissing asses." Mayk pulled the Colt Python out of the holster on the table and inspected the cylinder. Then he scooped a couple of rubber bands off the refrigerator door handle where a dozen of them hung like tired brass rings, snapped them around the smooth wooden butt to keep it from sliding, and stuck the gun inside his belt in front, pulling the sweatshirt down over it. "You carrying?"

I shook my head. "I hardly ever need it to talk to an ex-cop."

"Stick close, then." He opened the front door.

"How come?"

"Maybe you'll see when we get there. I'm hoping not."

I followed him out through the utility room and stood on the stoop while he drew the front door shut and locked up. I hate it when they talk like that.

4

"FUCKING COSSACKS."

We were driving through the blasted neighborhoods of old Poletown. The sun was gone and the black squares and angles of houses with rubble all around resembled the ruins of a bombed-out village, with hardly a lighted window to a block. The skeletal boom of a crane with a wrecking ball lolling from the end hung against the maroon sky like the head and neck of a brontosaurus with its tongue out. Mayk had been forced to shout to make himself heard over the wound-up whine of the Bronco's little six-cylinder engine.

"Who?" I asked.

"General Motors and the City of Detroit, to name just two. I grew up here, but I'd need a metal detector to find my way around now. We need another Cadillac plant like the world needs another moon."

"It'll create jobs, the mayor says."

"The mayor doesn't care who's working. He's got a job. And the paper's full of them. But the scroats around here won't step out of the unemployment line for less than fifteen an hour. That's the fairy story of our time, finding jobs for people. What you do is you find people for jobs."

He had it timed so that he banged the shifting cane into a new gear every time he said *jobs*. We bumped over curbs and corners, cut down alleys going the wrong way, jounced and chattered through cleared lots paved with stones and broken bricks. The four-by-four's frame shrieked and rattled.

Don't ever get into a private car driven by a cop if you can help it.

At length we swung around the end of an amber-lighted city barricade and ground to a halt on Newton with gasoline whumping back and forth in the tank. I took my feet out of the floorboards. The street marked the south end of Hamtramck with Detroit pressing in all around like a swollen river parting grudgingly for a rock; on the Hamtramck side a row of houses stood intact, facing a moonscape on the Detroit side with boards and shaggy timbers bristling out of bare stone foundations and big flat sections of shingled roof sprawled on top. It looked like tornado footage on the Six O'Clock News. Three houses stood alone on the corner, two of them dark. Mayk pointed to the one with a light on in a ground-floor window.

"That's where the old guy lived, the one said he saw the kid get in before the fracas. Surprised the electricity's still on. That whole block should have been evacuated by now."

I grunted and we walked up a path of flagstones with dewy grass grown up all around them to the front door of a house on the Hamtramck side, kitty-cornered from the one he had pointed out. This one was a square frame affair with white tile siding that looked blue in the light of a porch fixture fashioned after a carriage lamp. A recent addition on the left did nothing to relieve the boxy look of the turn-of-the-century construction. Mayk pushed the bell. The ratchety ringing sheared a hole through the stitching noises crickets made in the yard, but after a pause they started in again.

A face came to the diamond-shaped window in the door, then vanished before I could fix on the features. The door came open and a small man in a sleeveless undershirt and workpants with knobby muscles in his skinny arms pointed a small automatic pistol at our feet.

"Yes?"

The word hung in the air between us like an angry bee. Mayk said, "Mr. Stanislaus?"

"Yes?"

No change in inflection. Mayk said, "I'm Howard Mayk, a former detective sergeant with the Hamtramck police, and this is Amos Walker, a Detroit investigator. We'd like to talk to you about the shooting that took place here nineteen years ago."

"I don't know nothing about that."

"I believe you. Mr. Walker —"

"You wouldn't believe the burnouts I boot out of here a couple times a year, wanting to get their pictures taken in front of a murder house, tromp all over the wife's roses and spoil my new grass."

"We don't want to do anything like that. Mr. Walker just wants a look inside if it's all right. Just to see where it happened. It has to do with a case he's working on."

Stanislaus thought that over. He was in his late thirties, with dark wiry hair arcing over his forehead but cropped very close at the temples so that his ears seemed to stick out, small bright eyes like new nailheads on either side of a substantial nose, and a heavy dark moustache that turned up at the ends. The gun in his hand was a .25. Its bore was no bigger around than a pencil, but like the man said, no one really wants to get shot with anything. "You got ID?"

"Thought you'd ask." Mayk produced a worn leather folder from his hip pocket with his picture on a card behind a window and RETIRED stamped diagonally across the card in purple ink. There was a place on the other half of the folder where a badge should be. I flashed my photostat and the honorary sheriff's star. Stanislaus' little eyes spent a lot of time on each item. Then he stepped back and lowered the automatic until the barrel was in line with the seam of his trousers.

"Sorry," he said, as we stepped inside. "There's been a lot of vandalism around here lately."

"So I heard." Mayk closed the door behind and pointed at the pistol. "I hope that's registered."

"It's one of about three in this city that are." He set the weapon down on a table near the door. "At least we got some police protection on this side of the line. Punks set fire to a place across the street last week and the cops and fire department was a half hour getting there. They rode the family over to the Perpetual Mission on account of they didn't have a house no more. Sometimes they don't show up at all. You hear the police commissioner on TV the other day when the reporters pumped him about that?" He looked at me.

"He said it was the homeowners' fault for not vacating when they were told."

"Bullshit. Their time ain't up yet."

"How long you got?" Mayk asked.

"Till the end of the month. We're moving in with my wife's folks till I find a place near work. Know what the city's paying me for this place? Fifteen thousand. It's worth forty. I paid twenty-two for it twelve years ago. It's worse in Detroit. Those people won't be able to buy a trailer for what they're getting."

Mayk said, "Government's required to offer full market value."

"The assessors work for the city. Just like the judge we took the complaint to in the first place. My grandfather would of been better off keeping the family in Poland."

"I thought it was a federal judge the property owners went to," I said.

"What's the difference? His office is in Detroit."

"Funny, all those vandals popping out of nowhere," Mayk said.

Stanislaus said, "You don't hear me laughing."

"Who was it, Thad? Oh."

We were standing in a small square living room with flocked wallpaper and a rug that was starting to show some wear and pink slipcovers on the chairs and sofa. A young brown-haired woman with tight birdlike features, wearing a pullover and stretch slacks that showed off her slight paunch, had come in from another room and backed up a step when she saw Mayk and me. I took off my hat.

"Just some men who want a look at the place," Stanislaus explained.

"From the city?"

"No, it's about the Evanceks."

"I hope you told them that was long before we came."

"They know that."

"We wouldn't have bought the place if we knew there was a murder in it. They didn't tell us that when we bought it."

"They wanted to sell it," said Mayk.

She looked at him. "Isn't there a law or something that says they have to tell you about that kind of thing before you buy?"

"They're supposed to mention bad pipes and a leaky furnace. I don't think they have to tell you someone got whacked there unless you ask."

"Who would think to ask?"

Mayk shrugged. Stanislaus said, "It's been a good place to live. You talk like there's flies in the sewing room or something."

"I'll just be glad to be out of here." She went back into the other room, rubbing a hand up and down one arm as if she were chilled. A television set was playing in there. A cop show, from the sirens and gunplay.

"I got a thousand knocked off the asking price on account of the murder," Stanislaus told us in a low voice. "Don't tell her."

Mayk asked him if we could look around.

He jerked a thumb in the direction his wife had gone. "You ain't going to have to go in there, are you? We built that on ourselves. Call it a rumpus room. We don't hardly use this one anymore. My boys are in there."

"It's just the old part we're interested in." Mayk waited. When Stanislaus made no move to go, he said: "We'll try not to steal anything valuable."

The homeowner showed white teeth behind his moustache. "You find anything like that here, be sure and tell me and we'll split it." He picked up his gun and went into the addition.

"You know how many Polacks it takes to fire an automatic?" Mayk asked me.

I stared at him.

He made that dismissing gesture with one of his big hands. "Skip it. I know lots more funnier ones. I went through the academy course in Detroit and you get to be a connoisseur."

"This where you found Jeanine Evancek and little Carla?" I asked.

"This is it. Looks different."

"New wallpaper, I guess."

"New everything. But a room with a stiff in it looks and feels different. It's bad enough in a funeral home when they're all scrubbed and dressed and made up like a whore on Cass. When they're spread all over the walls like —"

"Red cabbage," I said. "I know."

He paced off a quick twelve feet from the front door. "They were about here, the little girl laying next to her mother, like she was standing over her when she bought her own load square in the face. They both got it in the face, the M.E. said. Bill thought it —"

He stopped talking. With his back to the room's only lamp, his own face was a blank slab of shadow. "Funny what you remember when you come back to a place," he said then.

"That being?"

"Well, like I said, I wouldn't trust a setup where everything clicked. The parents' bedroom was down there, next to one the girl and boy shared with a partition between them." He tipped his head in the direction of a short hallway running parallel with the front of the house, with doors on both sides. "That's where the shotgun came from, the parents' bedroom. We found a coloring book open on the floor of the girl's place and some loose crayons, like she might of dropped everything and run in here after the first shot, the one that killed her mother. Only a shotgun makes a hell of a loud wham indoors and if I was a little girl I'd run the other way."

"She could have come out during the shouting match and been here when Evancek fetched in the gun."

"Yeah. Also there's no predicting a person's reaction under

stress, especially a kid's. It's just one more of those things that can go six ways when you try putting a thing together backwards. Killers don't write scripts neat like you see on TV. The kitchen used to be this way." He went down the hall and turned left.

It still was, a fairly modern room about half the size of Mayk's kitchen, with the usual kitchen stuff plus a microwave oven and blue stylized flowers on the floor tiles and that symbol of our times, a woodburning stove, all black iron and white enamel with a warming oven overhead. There was a door at the back with a square window looking out on a shallow back porch. Firewood was stacked to the overhang with syrupy blackness beyond.

"The porch is new," Mayk said. "Different appliances and paint job. Jesus, you wonder who'd have the stomach to scrub the place down after a thing like that. That's the door Evancek was sitting with his back against when we found him."

"Was he sitting when he pulled the trigger on himself?"

"We figured he stood with his feet braced and his back against the door and slid down afterwards. There was a good five feet between where the top of his head would of been if he still had a head and where the blood started."

"What'd he trigger it with, a stick?"

"We didn't find one. You can do it with a toe, but he had his shoes on. The gun was a Marlin and short, just barely legal. He could of held it out in front of him with the muzzle to the bridge of his nose and triggered it at arm's length."

"Awkward."

"There's no textbook way to blow your face off," he said.

"You ran the gun for prints?"

He nodded. "We got a clear thumb off one of the shells in the magazine. It was Evancek's. The rest of the prints were smeared the way they always are coming off a gun."

"That just proves he loaded his own shotgun."

"Don't look to go unraveling no mysteries from the past, Sherlock. They buried the killer with his victims years before you got your first lay."

"Who buried him?"

"How the hell should I know? The Nortons, I guess. Jeanine Evancek's sister and brother-in-law."

"Damn generous of them."

"Maybe the space was paid for already and they didn't want it going to waste." He grinned suddenly. "Why did the undertaker fire his Polack gravedigger?"

"He dug the hole too deep and didn't have enough dirt to fill it back in. Thanks for the tour."

"Old times," he said, moving a shoulder. "Not that they were that good. In the department we used to call Bill Mischiewicz the original six-foot Pole you wouldn't touch anything with. You get anything out of this?"

"Not really. If there are vibes here I've got a tin ear."

We went back into the living room. I leaned through the doorway into the addition and rapped on the frame. "Thanks, Mr. Stanislaus."

He folded his copy of the *News* and got up from a worn green La-Z-Boy to see us out. His wife was sitting on a swaybacked sofa watching television, and two boys of about seven and nine with dark tousled hair and bright black eyes were pretending to do their homework on the rug over the slab concrete floor in front of the set. The same cop show or one just like it was howling and banging away onscreen.

"Find anything valuable?" Our host chuckled.

"Just a typical American home, Mr. Stanislaus," I said. "I guess it doesn't get any more valuable than that."

"Oh, please." He looked pained.

I said, "You wouldn't know anything about where the old man went that used to live in the house across the street. He was there at the time of the shooting."

Mayk said, "He's dead or in a home. Got to be."

"Old Stash?" Stanislaus was looking at me. "Hell, he's still there. They'll have to peel him off the big iron ball."

"Christ, he must be ninety." Mayk's tone was hushed.

"Nearer a hundred. But you better watch him if you're going over there. That old man's crazy."

5

IT WAS A COOL NIGHT. A low ceiling had rolled in and the lights of the city rinsed the clouds' bellies in cold pale light. A horn sounded out Woodward way like a lone goose on the water. The rushing sound underneath might have been wind through pines, but it was Goodyear rubber on damp asphalt. Our shoes slithered through the overgrown grass in Stanislaus's yard. The crickets had gone back to bed. My winter suit was at the cleaner's being scraped and damp air found its way through my imitation seersucker without any detours. Mayk seemed comfortable enough in just his sweatshirt and jeans. He was big enough to provide his own heat.

"Think your wife will mind my borrowing you a little longer?" I asked him when we reached the street. With barricades at both ends we stood in the middle like idiot dogs.

"She can wait. She's the one wanted the part-time job."

We went on across the street and up a narrow walk that was going back to jungle. Senile weeds hung in clumps like old men's chins over the edges, obliterating the bread-colored concrete in places and slobbering on our pantslegs as we walked through them. The house had been painted white once with red trim, but the red was curling away from the door and window casings in long slashes and the white was rubbed down to leaden-hued board beneath. The gutters had begun to secede from the cornices and the city light reflecting down off the clouds showed through the rust-perforated iron. Up close some of the window panes were fresh naked plywood. Blunt advice of a scatological nature decorated the

front of the house in spray-painted loops. The paint still
smelled.

We mounted the porch. A rake and a garden spade caked
with orange rust and dusty Coke bottles left over from the
days of the two-cent deposit lay on the seat of a long wicker
bench there. No young lovers or anyone else had sat on it in
a long time. The name s. LEPOSAVA was embossed in white
letters on a strip of cracked blue tape on the mailbox.

"This was a nice place nineteen years ago," Mayk said.

"Everything was nicer nineteen years ago." I pushed the
button. It made a grating sound in its scabbed socket but
there was no answering ring or buzz from inside. I put my
knuckles to work.

A brief pause, and then a loud flat bang and a silvery tinkle
from the back of the house.

Mayk was already off the porch, tugging his Python out of
his belt. "You take the front," he barked.

I tried the knob. It wasn't interested in turning today. But
the lock was strictly Calvin Coolidge and I shattered it in two
kicks. The door sprang inward and I hit the floor.

No one shot at me. I was crouched in starting position on a
thin rug from which most of the leaf pattern and all of the
color had been trodden years ago, with feathery balls of dust
darting about in the current of air stirred by the open door.
In front of me were the claw foot and heavy turned leg of a
massive oak table, and in the electric light leaking from another room a ring of dark paintings in swollen gilt frames of
bearded faces so hostile-looking they had to belong to saints
glared down at me from the walls. It was a brown room with
tired umber paper on the walls and ceiling and bronze-
colored curtains without luster over the windows and dirty
beige baseboards with mouseholes in the corners, and Mayk
would have said it felt like a room with a stiff in it.

It wasn't. I got up dusting my palms and looked around the
room and at a long sideboard with a row of religious pictures
painted on flat wooden rectangles the size of paperback books

propped up on top. Several of the pictures had fallen or been knocked over and lay on their backs or faces. My toe nudged one on the floor and I picked it up. It was an exquisitely detailed rendition of a blond beach boy wearing a sheet and holding a flaming sword high over his head. The colors had the rich patina of age. For a century anyway its artist would have known the Archangel Michael by sight.

I stood it up on the sideboard and walked through a door into the room with light in it. If they wanted me they could have me. I was through with floors.

This one was a front bedroom, with an eight-drawer chiffonier scraping the comparatively low ceiling, more brown wallpaper and disapproving saints in frames with gilt cupids carved into the wood, a painted nightstand holding up a tarnished brass lamp with a yellow paper shade, and a high bed with a painted iron frame. By the window a candle the size of a big toe burned with a pale orange fixity of purpose in front of another pocket-size painting like those in the other room on a varnished stand. The room smelled of hot wax.

Some of the parched furniture and all of the artwork were antique. The rest was just old, like the man on the bed.

In the light shed by the lamp his head was large, yellow, onion-shaped, and as bald as a thumb. There were blue veins in his closed eyelids and his eagle's profile had been cut with an engraving tool out of tough old ivory without a line or a crack in it except for those that seemed to have been drawn by the weight of his moustache. It was the size and shape of an inverted horseshoe and as white as virtue, as white as bones in the desert, as white as an old man's moustache under electric light in a house in Poletown after dark. It made the pillow his head was resting on look dirty. He lay on his back in an old-fashioned cotton nightshirt with a thick brown sweater over it and his fine long yellow hands with the blue veins in them resting on a pink quilt drawn over his stomach.

His eyes snapped open. It was as if a pair of shutters had been flung wide on the dawn. They were gray with a bright sheen and I could see my reflection in their pupils.

"All Christian czardoms have come to an end," he said, "and have been gathered together into one czardom of our sovereign, according to the book of the prophets, that is to say the Russian czardom; for two Romes have fallen, but the third stands, and a fourth there will not be."

"Okay," I said, drawing it out.

"The seeds for Constantinople's destruction were sown by the Latin heresy, the belief in immaculate conception and the trinity, over the true faith of just the Father and the Holy Ghost. In the patriarch there is continuity and power."

He stopped talking suddenly and his eyes became slits. I felt them rake my face. "You're not Father Olszanski," he accused.

"I never have been." I said it a little too loud. His voice was little more than a cracked whisper, but there was in it the memory of strength and I was trying to match it. He rolled his consonants ponderously in an accent that was familiar but not precisely Polish.

"No need to shout," he said. "I'm close to blind, but my hearing works perfectly around the middle register. I thought you were the priest come to continue the argument. He smiles at everything I say until I get to the Pope. That's when he leaves. Otherwise he's harder to get rid of than a cataract."

"I thought most Poles were devout Roman Catholics."

"He's Ukrainian," said Howard Mayk, coming in. "Some of them are Russian Orthodox."

The former detective sergeant was carrying one of the small religious paintings in one hand and his Colt Python in the other, although it wasn't pointing at anyone. Even then he didn't handle it the way Stanislaus had his, like a closed umbrella. You find firearms in the hands of two kinds, gun people and people with guns. Mayk was a gun person.

The old man squinted at the newcomer, then at his weapon. His big head sank deeper into the pillow. "You won't need that to rob me. You're welcome to everything in the house. I'd rather see it in a thief's hands than under rubble."

"We're not here to rob you, Mr. Leposava. That's already happened once tonight." He looked at me. "The guy broke the window in the back door and let himself in. He went out that way when we knocked on the front door. What we heard was the rest of the glass going when it slammed behind him. He dropped this in the yard." He held up the painted item.

This time it was a woman in the sheet, no sword, but the same many layers of existence on the dark reds and glazed blues.

Mayk put away the gun. "It's an icon. Magdalene, I think. Their version of a plaster saint. He's got them all over the house; no telling how many our friend got clear with, or what else."

"The converted whore," acknowledged Stash Leposava, narrowing his eyes to bring the painting into focus. "That's appropriate, for this town. I must have slept through it. One thing I do well now is sleep."

"Are they worth a lot?" I asked Mayk.

"Some stay in families a couple of hundred years. Collectors go pretty high on the better ones. Bill and me traced a hundred grand's worth once through a fence that used to specialize in religious articles in Hamtramck. He pulled eight to twelve in Jackson."

"What we need is some law."

"No police," put in the old man. "They won't come anyway, and if they do they'll just have me committed. It will save serving me with sheriff's papers."

"You've been hit before," I suggested.

His translucent lids slid down and up, reptile fashion. "I never was until the city condemned my property. I kept picking bricks up off my floor until I got tired of replacing broken glass. In a few weeks it will all be dust anyway. Me too."

I said, "Someone should stay with you till the lock on the front door gets fixed and the hole in the back door gets plugged. Do you have any family?"

"Not since the October Revolution."

"What about the priest, Father Olszanski? Would he stay?"

"Until the conversation swung around to His Eminence," he said, shifting the ponderous weight of his moustache. "If you must, his number is in the book on the table in the dining room. But they turned off the telephone last month."

"I'll use the Stanislauses'." Mayk laid the icon down on the nightstand and went out.

Leposava closed his eyes again and left them that way. I listened to the house sounds: timbers settling with fat men's sighs, a gust of wind chattering a loose pane, the furnace cutting in. Outside of the felony tank in any jail in this country there is no place quieter than an old man's bedroom. This one had a medicine smell, sweetish under the burning-wax stench, and a skin of dust on the furniture. I stepped around the bed to where the candle was still glowing determinedly on the wooden stand in front of the window and peered at the icon it was illuminating. A Madonna and Child, with the gloss of youth shining out of their big wet hound-eyes across a gulf of time that encompassed powdered wigs and Valley Girl T-shirts, muskets and ICBMs, Napoleon and the Ayotollah, Abbott and Costello. I was punchy. I straightened up and got out a cigarette and smoothed it between my fingers. I glanced at Leposava. His eyes were open and on me, icon-bright with the candle flame squirming in their centers.

"Who are you?"

I told him. "I'm looking for Michael Evancek, the boy whose parents and little sister were killed across the street nineteen years ago. That's Howard Mayk who just left to call the priest. He was a detective in Hamtramck then. According to him your account of the shooting didn't go with the other witnesses'."

When he heard the name Evancek, his face set like cement.

"Was it that long ago? Yes, it must have been. It would take that long for things to get this bad. Who's paying you to look for him?"

I told him that too. He moved his bald yellow head from side to side slowly. "Foolish old woman. I hope for her sake you don't find him. It would be grotesque."

"Does that mean you won't help me?"

"How much can it matter? I can't tell you where the boy is."

"Where a person goes often depends on why he left," I said sagely.

He was still looking at me. I don't know how much he was seeing. Probably more than he let on. "Do many people believe that?"

I grinned punchily.

"Some. I'm just fishing, Mr. Leposava. Looking for a place to start."

He stared across the years, and I knew then that those old artists had used Ukrainians for their models.

"It was hot," he said. "The air was very thick, the way it never was on the steppe and the way I could never get used to. I had every window in the house open. I worked then, translating news from the Detroit press into Russian for the local Ukrainian paper. I couldn't concentrate in the dining room because of the shouting across the street."

Here his moustache twitched. "It wasn't the noise; I could work in a boiler factory. If it really bothered me I could have closed the windows on that side or moved to another part of the house. But it is difficult not to listen when two people you don't know are shrieking out each other's faults. I'm telling you things I never told the police. For some reason it was important to me then not to be thought a — what's the word?"

"Busybody."

"Busybody." He tasted it. "A good word. The American idiom is very close to Russian. We are much the same people after all."

He seemed to have lost the thread. "They were shouting at each other across the street," I said helpfully.

"I said that. I was just organizing my recollections. Why is it that what you ignore in people your own age you automatically consider proof of senility in anyone over sixty? Yes, young Mr. and Mrs. Evancek were shouting at each other and what they were saying wasn't nice. Don't ask me what that was. Her poor housekeeping, perhaps."

"I understood it was over his refusal to look for work."

"I don't remember that. That could have been behind it, but people rarely argue about what's really bothering them. It's the inconsequential things that set them off. I translated a story once about a brother and a sister who shot their father because he wouldn't let them smoke marijuana. In any case, the fight stopped when the boy came home."

"This was *before* the shooting?" I fought the tug to lean forward.

"Definitely before. I know what the others said, but they were wrong."

"You're sure it was Michael?"

"I saw him go in the front door. I knew the boy well enough by sight. We waved when we saw each other, his parents too. I was and am not the visiting type."

"How long between when he came home and you heard the first shot?"

"About five minutes."

"Your memory for time is very good," I said. "After almost twenty years, a lot of people wouldn't be able to say if something took five minutes or a half hour. Generally they shorten it."

"You forget I worked for a newspaper. I wrote up the incident later and you tend to remember something you've written down."

"How many shots were there?"

"Three. Very loud."

"How close together?"

He thought about it. "I can't tell you. I'd just be guessing. I'm not sure I could have remembered the sequence at the time. It seems to me the police asked me about it and I said the same thing."

"You had me worried there for a minute, Mr. Leposava," I

said. "In my business when you get gold in every pass it's time to get a new pan."

The moustache moved.

I smoothed the cigarette some more. It was plenty smooth. I stuck it in my face and left it there without lighting it and was thinking up another question that would make me sound like a detective when Mayk got back for the cross-examination.

6

THE FORMER DETECTIVE SERGEANT looked large and martial in his blue shirt and pants and his gun was an obvious growth on his flat stomach under the shirt. "He's on his way," he said.

The old man on the bed had closed his eyes again and showed no reaction. I told Mayk what he had told me.

"What's it, a hundred yards between the front of this place and what was the Evanceks'?" said Mayk, loud enough for Leposava to hear.

"About that," I said.

"That's damn good seeing for someone who thought you were a priest the first time he looked at you."

I said, "I think I resent that."

"I had twenty-twenty vision the first seventy-five years of my life," put in the Ukrainian. "Are you as good a man as you were two decades ago?"

"We're not talking about me." Mayk approached the bed. "Why is it you're the only one saw the boy get in when you say you did?"

"Perhaps I was the only one looking."

"You remember that so good, how come you can't remember how close the shots came together?"

"A boy coming home from summer school is a normal occurrence. Shotgun blasts are not, or were not, in this neighborhood in those times. It's difficult to think of timing with something so unexpected."

"Got all the answers, don't you?"

"You have all the questions."

I set fire to the cigarette finally, trying not to grin.

Mayk circled back. "Six witnesses swore the boy came home after the shots were fired."

"Did they see him come home?"

"You're the only one claims you saw that."

"Interesting. That they'd swear to a thing they didn't see."

"Yeah, there seems to be a lot of that here."

They went back to the subject of the argument and I lost interest. I wandered to the open doorway where my smoke could find its own way out and leaned against the frame. From there I had a good view through the front dining room window of the house across the way, where on a sweltering afternoon in a time of relative innocence three loud crashes had carried across the world to the other side of Europe.

Father Olszanski came in twenty minutes later. A lean six feet, he brushed his iron-gray hair back from his widow's peak in twin wings that kept wanting to slide down over his forehead and he trimmed his white beard so close it looked like stubble until you looked again. His eyes were a flat sad blue behind spectacles whose gold rims winked when he jerked his hair out of his eyes. The clerical collar under his light black topcoat was blue-white against the brown of his throat.

"Have you grown weary of your graven images?" Leposava greeted him, once Mayk and I had introduced ourselves and taken the priest's clean corded short-nailed hand in ours.

"You old pagan, what are you doing in bed? You've played the crippled ancient so long you've begun to believe it yourself."

The banter proceeded in this fashion for another minute or so. Olszanski's accent was as American as french fries.

Mayk said, "He won't let us call the police."

"Once they got the address they'd just file it under the blotter," the priest said. "*Now* will you move, you old Tartar?"

"I did all the moving I intend to in the fall and winter of

nineteen seventeen." He lay as calm as a boulder in the sun.

This was where I'd made my entrance. I pinched out my second butt and parked it in my jacket pocket next to its uncle. "We appreciate your time, Mr. Leposava. Good luck."

"I won't wish you the same. The young man should stay lost."

Olszanski escorted Mayk and me into the front room. He slid an aluminum tube out of an inside pocket and broke out a greenish cigar without a band, went through the ritual of passing it under his nose and licking the seam and never did light the thing.

"Stash is a remarkable man," he said in a low voice. "He fought the Bolsheviks, you know. There's Cossack in him and the Lord God knows what else. He speaks six languages and could have been a fine writer in any of them if he didn't insist on translating the work of men of lesser talent. He worked until he was past eighty. Lately, though, his mind —" He waved the cigar. "He has no family. When he says he'll be here to greet the wreckers he means it. There are some good nursing homes up north; as the one closest to him I can go to court and sign the papers. He'll have clean quarters and round-the-clock care and even a counterfeit of love, plastic smiles and girls one-fourth his age who will call him by his first name in tones the rest of us reserve for dogs and children." He smiled in his beard with his sad eyes on the expensive unlit cigar. "I'll miss our talks."

"Where do you preach?" Mayk asked.

"Immaculate Conception."

"Oh."

"Yes." The sad smile was unchanged. "Some of the parishioners feel we will save it yet. I admire their faith. At election time the politicians all have their pictures taken going to church. I haven't seen them since the condemnation papers came. I regard this as a sign."

"I was asking Mr. Leposava about the Evancek shooting across the street," I said.

He nodded, licked the cigar. "Yes, there was some gossip about it when I came here from Our Lady in Boston. It was before my assignment."

I asked him about the Nortons. He didn't know anyone by that name. We thanked him for coming.

"Thank you for calling me. Though I would rather it were anyone else."

Mayk and I got out of there. On the porch, the ex-dick filled his lungs with a long draught. "Next time *you* be bad cop."

"What do you think of Leposava's story?" I asked.

"I think he's an old guy that once he gets his choppers into something won't let go if you hit him in the head with a trombone."

"What *was* the sequence of those shots?"

He shook his head. "We never got two people to agree on that."

"You nearly had me," I said. "It was a sweet act."

"I just sort of slipped into it."

We started down the walk.

"Witnesses can be wrong," I said. "Even six of them."

"Don't I know it. My last year with the department we trashed a guy on an attempted six-two-seven. Eight people who were in the bar when this steelworker bought a thirty-eight slug in the neck ID'd our man from the book and nailed him in the lineup. Then the steelworker came out of his coma and took one look at the mug and said, hell no, that ain't him. Detroit snagged the right fish for CCW a week later and he spilled his guts under questioning. But that was different."

"Yeah, the victim was still breathing."

He stopped walking and turned toward me. The Stanislauses' porch light was off now and we were beyond reach of the glow through Leposava's window. But I felt Mayk's cop's-eyes on me in the shadows.

"It isn't like that," he said. "We don't tie up a case the soft way just because there's nobody left to raise a squawk. Once you get enough dots strung together to see the trunk you don't need to connect the rest to know it's a picture of an elephant. The only mystery in these domestic beefs is who gets stuck with the report."

We didn't say anything in the Bronco during the demolition drive back to his place. There was a light on in the house when we swung into the driveway and stopped behind a battered blue Pinto with panic stripes on the rear panel.

"My wife." He killed his headlamps. "Uses a fork to fish a piece of toast out of a live toaster and she's scared a truck will rear-end her and flame her out on the E-way."

"You've got to laugh in its teeth somewhere." I put a foot outside and stuck one of my cards on top of the visor. "If you ever have a keyhole that needs looking through."

He was watching me with his hands still on the wheel. "We went together kind of smooth in there. Where were you ten years ago?"

"Protecting my best side in a Cambodian jungle."

"Yeah? Korea here."

"Same war," I said. "Different people. Good night, Sergeant."

"That's Mister. But good night anyway."

In ten minutes I was home. Just three rooms, a garage, and a dandelion patch with some grass in it, but the surrounding houses were still standing with lights on and when you woke up in the morning it was to the sound of the neighbor's power mower or the Doberman down the block yapping its head off at a lost hubcap on the front lawn and not a two-ton ball punching holes in the brick house across the street. So far General Motors hadn't whistled at the mayor and pointed my way.

There was nothing in the mailbox but a religious pamphlet. I had had enough of religion that evening. I left it for seed and let myself in. The place needed dusting, but not as badly as Stash Leposava's. I determined to do something about it before it did. I hung up my hat and climbed out of my jacket and necktie, wound the clock my grandfather bought for his mother, went into the kitchen and got a tray out of the freezing compartment of the refrigerator and ran some water on it in the sink. Scrod, with a side of corn and little round potatoes the size of marbles in compartments like you see in a cash box. I hate scrod, but it had been on sale and I had four more trays of it. There was a time when I cooked, really cooked, but it seemed like a lot of trouble to go to for just me.

I took down a bottle of Scotch three-quarters full, or one-quarter empty, from the cabinet over the sink and wet a glass from it and cut it with water. While waiting for the hoarfrost to melt off the TV dinner I looked at my reflection in the night-backed window and wondered how I would look with a white moustache.

When the scrod was in the oven I took my glass and went back into the living room and sat down and looked at the dust on the blank television screen.

People move all the time. They can't find work at home and go where the jobs are, they get transferred, they grow tired of shoveling snow in April and go west or south, they get sick of waking up every morning to the same face on the next pillow, they go to find themselves, they go to lose themselves, wives run to Bermuda with exterminators, husbands head for Vegas with little blonde numbers from the secretarial pool, kids light out for anywhere not home with just their thumbs and a nylon backpack with something by Kerouac in it. Mommy's gone away, son. No, Daddy doesn't know when she'll be back. Eat your cauliflower. What was he wearing when he left, lady? I can't understand it, Dad. He's never been away this long without calling. She was an A student until she met this boy, Officer. Jim, Brian's an hour late getting home from school and I'm worried sick.

Sometimes they get snatched and then you wait for the call

from someone talking through a handkerchief, telling you where to bring the cash or from a cop asking you to come downtown and take a look at what they found jammed into a culvert in Redford Township. Sometimes they go into hiding and then you have to work backwards to find out why. Sometimes they just move and forget to leave a forwarding address. Those are the hardest, because people forget a lot more thoroughly than they cover up.

You get a cramp filling out duplicate driver's license application forms and wear your tongue out licking stamps, you bribe postal clerks to go into the basement and rummage through the obsolete change-of-addresses for information that's supposed to be free to the public, you ruin your eyes reading old personals on microfilm at the library, you say sir and ma'am to people you wouldn't wipe your feet on otherwise, because they might remember the name of a moving van parked across from the house they were casing on a certain afternoon. Sometimes people don't like your questions or the tie you're wearing and bounce things off your skull, and that might not be so bad except they call you names while they're doing it. Then the cops call you names because you didn't run to them with information you didn't know you had about felonies you weren't aware took place and shine lights in your eyes and shove tape microphones up your nose and tank you for forty-eight hours on suspicion without a telephone call or a lawyer. They can do that and to hell with what you saw on *Adam 12*, all bets are off when you get sucked up into the big blue machine. All to keep the bloodsuckers off your back and your belly from scraping your spine, or so you answer on those not infrequent occasions when you find yourself asking why you do what you do.

Every morning is your last. You'll put in one more day and then hang up the shoulder holster, ditch the forms, let your dues lapse in the Snoopers and Sleuths Union and get a real job with a place that has a bowling league and a company picnic and every other Friday a check you can almost raise two-point-five kids on with a wife who thinks she really ought to have a facelift, you make that decision and then the telephone rings or the door opens and the devil enters disguised as an old lady in widow's weeds with a thousand dollars and a picture of a new missing face and you bite the apple. You're hooked, you're an addict. You've got the call.

The oven timer made a rude noise and I drank off what was in my glass and went in and ate my dinner standing up at the drainboard. It saved washing dishes and wiping up afterwards. I don't know why I bothered. It was too late to reserve a table at the Rooster Tail.

When that was done I mixed some more Scotch and water and sat back down in front of the set and dialed Martha Evancek's number in St. Clair Shores.

"Hello?"

It was the voice of a young woman without a foreign accent. After a pause I asked if I had the right number.

"Yes, that's correct. Is this Mr. Walker?"

I said it was and asked if she was related to Mrs. Evancek.

"I'm her companion. She's gone to bed. May I take a message?"

"It can wait till tomorrow," I said.

"Wait, Mr. Walker. Hello?"

"I'm here."

"I'm in Mrs. Evancek's confidence. I know she's hired you to locate her grandson and I'm familiar with the circumstances surrounding his disappearance. You can talk freely." The voice was fresh and cool, like an ice-green mint.

"I'm sorry, Miss —?"

"McBride."

"I'm sorry, Miss McBride, but you're not in my confidence. No one ever is. I have one or two more questions I'd like to ask Mrs. Evancek. I'll swing by in the morning if that's all right."

The voice got a little cooler. "Any time after nine o'clock would be acceptable."

I thanked her and cradled the receiver.

There was nothing on television and I sat up for a while smoking and trying to read a paperback mystery I'd picked up in a drugstore once while tailing someone. It was about a private eye back East who wore expensive running shoes with everything and squawked so much about the things he wouldn't do that you had to wonder what people hired him for in the first place. His partner was a professional killer and if there was a mystery to it at all I couldn't find it and gave up. To hell with P.I.'s with codes they have to keep hauling out and looking at like pocket watches and to hell with cool fresh voices in women's mouths. They never match the faces. I put down the book and looked around the room in the light of the one lamp I had burning. It needed dusting, all right. She probably had pinched nostrils and fuzz on her chin.

I went to bed and dreamed I was a Cossack who got his head lopped off bending down to tie his expensive running shoes in the middle of a battle.

7

IT WAS A CLEAR FRESH MORNING with the sun rum-colored on the grass and the smell of a lakeshore at dawn in the air. Birds were singing for the pure hell of it and if you listened hard you could hear the sound of convertible tops coming down all over the city. I showered and shaved and shook the butts out of my almost-seersucker and got my gray Olds rolling northward along the scenic route. I cranked the window down on the driver's side. A convertible it isn't.

As you hit the rolling country above Eight Mile Road and swing east, you pass through a series of suburbs, none of them as old as this century, with names like Hazel Park and Warren and East Detroit and Harper Woods, and if you miss the YOU ARE ENTERING signs you're lost, because you won't see anything like a Roseville Dairy Queen or a Centerline Bait & Tackle Shop. That's too small-townish for the city folk who came up here to get away from the ethnics. You pass low brick schools and churches built like service stations and sudden glass-and-steel blisters that call themselves civic centers and the vast sterile fenced enclosure of the GM Tech Center, where college lads in white coats tinker with everything from genetic engineering to ashtrays with little fans in them that smoke your cigarette for you. You drive through block after block of nice residences, not too large, with all-weather driveways and lawns the size of money clips, skirt brief business sections with two-car parking lots, and never catch a green light all the way. The cops are all eighteen and wear sky-blue uniforms with short sleeves and cruise in pairs in cars painted the chief's wife's favorite color with discreet emblems on the doors. If you blow a tire and don't have a jack they won't lend you theirs but will call the wrecking service the city has a contract with and if you go two miles over the limit they will nail you. They are nice places to live but you wouldn't want to visit there.

The pioneers who founded St. Clair Shores didn't speak French or Spanish. They preferred tight overcoats to doublets and instead of Toledo steel they carried Chicago typewriters whose workmanlike chattering became as much a part of the lakefront as the foghorns' belching when the soup drifted in from Canada. They set up a winch to unload the boats from Windsor during the dry time and sold the stuff to the Capone organization in Chicago. Jews and Italians and Poles and even a few Greeks from down Monroe Street, they moved in their families and built homes and schools and churches and synagogues and rented themselves a police force and when Prohibition ended they all sent their kids to parochial school to get a good education. Today it looks like any other upper middle–class community of retired schoolteachers, with a noise ordinance and speed bumps in the residential section and no marble stands erected over the places where the founding fathers shed blood over cases of Old Log Cabin. But in the venerable dock pilings are holes that weren't made by worms, and if the older buildings there could talk they'd speak with the bitter accent of the eastern slums.

The house was a white frame duplex on Englehardt with faded awnings over the upstairs windows. Martha Evancek's number belonged to a door in the el at the end of the driveway that went on to become the garage. My knock got an invitation from inside and I opened the door and climbed three steps and turned left and climbed another two.

"Mr. Walker? I'm Karen McBride."

The voice was even cooler and fresher in person, and for once it went with its owner. She was in her late twenties, short, but well-proportioned — very well-proportioned — so that I didn't realize she was short until I was standing in front of her and could look down on top of her head. It was a nice head, covered with dark brown hair that could be called chestnut if you cared. I was admiring it when she smiled and gave me her hand. Her grip was firm but feminine. I could take her two falls out of three any day in the week.

"Carrying Mrs. Evancek up and down those steps must be what keeps you in such good shape," I said.

"She manages them quite well. She told me she managed the three flights to your office without help. Let me take your hat."

"Sorry. I forgot I had it on." I took it off and gave it to her.

She opened a door to the left of the entrance and got rid of the hat. When she turned I saw that her hair was caught behind her neck and spilled into a loose sort of ponytail down her back almost to her waist. Her front was covered by a white pullover with the straps of her brassiere showing underneath and she had on a dark gray skirt, slightly flared, that hung to the tops of brown leather boots wrinkled around her ankles. She had a high round forehead and a small nose that turned up a little at the end and large brown eyes and her mouth was just a little too wide, so that when she unzipped it to smile, the dimples went clear down her cheeks. The boys would have called her Monkey-face when she was little and bought a black eye for their trouble. I liked her face fine. So far I liked all of her.

"Martha didn't tell me she was going to see you or I wouldn't have let her go alone," she said, closing the closet door. "I think she deliberately waited until I left for the day because she was afraid I wouldn't have let her go at all. When I came by last night to help her into bed and saw how tired she was, I got the story out of her. They can be such children at that age."

"She's a grown woman," I corrected. "Would you have?"

It threw her for a second. She stopped smiling and wrinkled

her smooth brow. "You mean let her go to see you? I couldn't stop her. She has rights."

"But you don't love the idea."

"Are you always this penetrating this early?" she demanded.

"It's the detective thing. Sometimes the switch gets stuck on. Do we go in to see the lady or does she come out here?" *Out here* being a narrow entryway with a linked rubber mat on the floor and on one wall one of those framed portraits of Christ screened in Day-Glo on imitation black velvet that K-Mart sells next to posters of Loni Anderson.

Karen McBride's expression changed. "I'm sorry you came all this way. Mrs. Evancek had a scare early this morning. She was taken by ambulance to the hospital. I just came back from there. I tried to call you but I guess you'd already left."

"Is she all right?"

"Her doctor thinks so. She was calling for me when I got in this morning. She was shaken and very flushed, disoriented. Her pulse was racing. It may have been a minor stroke. They're holding her for observation, but it looks like the danger is past and there doesn't appear to be any major damage. It was brought on by yesterday's physical and emotional strain, I'm sure."

Her tone was reproachful. I said, "She didn't tell me her medical history when she called or I'd have come to see her. The trip downtown was her idea."

"Of course. I'm sorry. It's just that I've come to like Martha a lot. You get protective."

"She's like the grandmother you never had."

"You're impertinent," she blazed.

"Aw, go on. I had my shots."

For a moment a smile and a snarl wrestled for her just slightly too-wide mouth. The smile won. You could lose your car keys in one of her dimples. "You might as well come in," she said, standing aside. "I try never to throw anyone out until I've given him coffee."

We walked into a spotless living room with a carpet like a

mutt's coat and floral print covers thrown over everything that wasn't a table. Someone had painted the brick fireplace white and stood a potted geranium on the grate. No one was going to start anything as messy as a fire in there, by God. There were the usual shiny copper long-handled implements that had never touched ash next to the hearth and on the mantelpiece some cheap plaster saints.

I was starting to think someone was out to convert me.

She kept walking, through a door bright with sunlight into a well-ventilated kitchen. "The coffee's on already. Make yourself comfortable."

"Okay if I smoke?"

"If what you've been hearing the past ten years hasn't convinced you it isn't," she said, "why ask me?"

"Does that mean I can light up?" I had one out.

"Go ahead. I haven't been able to make Martha quit in a year. I don't expect to have better luck with you in five minutes."

I rolled it along my lips but didn't set fire to it. I was standing in the doorway watching her fuss with the makings at a linoleum-covered counter but didn't go in. I was sick of kitchens. This one was very clean and traditional; the most modern things in it were the coffee maker and Miss McBride. I asked her if she worked for Social Services.

"No, I'm on the night shift at the hospital. St. John's. I'm a registered nurse. Martha hired me to care for Mr. Evancek when he was dying of cancer."

"And when he was gone?"

"I stayed on. I help Martha out of bed in the morning and do the heavy cleaning and help her into bed at night. I don't charge her. Aside from that she's pretty independent. Does her own shopping and fixes her own meals. She's a wonderful cook."

"I guess you have to be when your husband's a chef. Black."

She made a face, spooned some powdered creamer into one of two cups, and handed me the other.

While she was putting things away I went back into the living room and set my cup and saucer down on a low glass-topped coffee table. A big brown scrapbook flabby with pictures lay on the corner. I hinged open the cover and turned the pages idly. Faded oval sepia prints of serious-eyed children in baggy white sailor-dresses, boys as well as girls; a wedding picture of a young man in a high starched collar, his dark moustache waxed into sharp points and his hair parted in the middle and plastered down with pomade, his bride beside him in ivory lace, dark eyes in a grave pretty face that I recognized with a start as Martha Evancek's fifty years ago; washed-out wartime shots, uniforms and rubble; a snap taken on a visit to some Eastern European city with a postwar look to its spires and minarets under repair and a hefty, smiling young man standing in the foreground; the picture I had already seen of an eleven-year-old boy, newly returned to its corners and the reason the book was out; a little towheaded girl, probably Carla, in a wading pool; and, toward the back, page after page of jarring color Polaroid photos of an emaciated old man gasping out his life, naked to the bedcovers. His eyes were huge in a face whose hollow cheeks and temples and outward-curling earlobes had nothing in common with the sternly confident young bridegroom in the wedding shot.

"I took those."

Karen McBride's voice almost made me jump. She had come in carrying her cup and saucer, looking not at all like a young maid at tea in a Gibson print.

"Martha insisted," she went on. "She said it was family tradition to maintain a complete photographic record of each life. I thought it was ghoulish, but Mr. Evancek agreed with her and I used my own camera. Funny people, those Old Worlders. Their threshold of shock is a lot higher than ours."

"Watching your friends and neighbors get blown to pieces in artillery barrages will do that." I flipped back through the book. "You've seen this?"

"Martha shows it to me often. She has a story to go with

each picture. They aren't all the kind of stories you'd expect a sweet little old lady to tell."

"They don't get to be old wearing blinders. She tell you about this one?" I showed her the beefy lad in the fairy-tale city.

"That's Joseph at eighteen. He looks like a good-natured ox. Not at all like someone who would do what he did."

"I think they can arrest you for looking like that."

I closed the book and sat down. She balanced her coffee stuff on her knee in an upholstered chair with a straight back and antimacassars pinned to the arms while I fought to avoid being swallowed whole by the sofa. There's a company that makes those specifically for private investigators to sit in while visiting the homes of little old ladies.

"Nice place," I lied.

"It's horrible. I always feel like a little girl having to keep quiet at her grandmother's when I sit in this room. She rents it furnished from the people on the other side of the wall."

"You're right, it stinks."

Her mouth tried for a prim look. "I see. It's a funny detective."

"I'm glad you think so. There are those who wouldn't agree. But the heck with them. Are you married?"

The snarl took another fall after a little struggle. The smile had her face now. I'd been rooting for it since its first victory. She sipped some coffee. "What did you want to ask Martha? She's told me a lot about Joseph's — tragedy and about little Michael. Who I guess isn't so little anymore. Maybe I can help."

I pulled myself out of the morass of horsehair and printed flowers and balanced on the edge of the sofa's frame. I picked up my cup, remembered the cold cigarette between my lips, and put it away before drinking. "I'm in a delicate position here," I said.

"So I noticed."

I forced a grin. "I bet they love you down in Intensive Care.

There's a little matter of client privilege riding on just how much you do know about why Mrs. Evancek hired me and how much more I might be telling by asking you questions."

"You're a very careful man," she said.

"Impertinent too. Don't forget impertinent."

She passed that one. Her eyes were almost amber in the sunlight streaming in from the kitchen. "I'm careful too. After Martha told me she'd hired you I checked up on you. I called the police. They referred me to a lieutenant in Homicide. I forget his name."

"Alderdyce. John Alderdyce."

"That's him. From what he said I couldn't make up my mind whether he likes you or wants to charge you with something. But he said you were honest enough. If I could ignore what you thought passed for a sense of humor, he said, we'd get along fine."

"John's a great kidder."

"Now I guess it's my turn." Talking, she tapped a short glossy-pink nail on the handle of her cup. "You're looking for Michael Evancek, aged about thirty, whom Martha lost track of nineteen years ago when her son Joseph, the boy's father, went berserk and murdered his own wife and daughter and then committed suicide. She offered you a thousand-dollar retainer and you gave back half. You also promised to report daily."

"Nothing to report, except that what she told me checks out so far. You always waste a little time in these things jumping up and down on the information your clients give you to see if it stands up. The lies come thick and fast in my corner. Okay." I sat back carefully, sinking a little. "What I want to ask, does Mrs. Evancek have any letters her son or grandson sent her in the last year or so before the blowup?"

"I don't know. I could look. Why?"

"If I knew that I wouldn't have to ask. So far I've got two pictures of the Evanceks, American branch, an old lady's and the cops'. They're a mile apart. The letters might bridge the gap. Also I'm stuck, which is nothing to get hopped up about. I get stuck a lot."

"Not for long, I bet."

"You smooth-talker," I said. "Let's elope."

She parked the cup and saucer and rose. "I think I know where she might be keeping those letters. I'll just be a minute."

She went through another doorway. I took advantage of her absence to get something burning in my face.

8

IT TOOK LONGER than a minute. It always does. While I was waiting I got up and looked at some pictures in gold frames on a corner of the mantelpiece not occupied by brittle martyrs. Mr. Evancek — grayer than in his wedding picture but healthy — standing, thumbs in his vest pockets, before a commercial building with Cyrillic characters on the sign. I figured it was the restaurant where he had worked in Cracaw. A family shot of an older Joseph in a sport shirt with one hand on an ordinarily pretty blonde's arm and the other resting on a nine- or ten-year-old Michael's shoulder, the boy in a red sweater with his white shirt collar spilling over the neck and his dark hair tousled, next to his sister, beaming in a pink dress, all golden curls and shiny red cheeks. Another picture, very old, of a young Martha Evancek with a couple in the styles of another century, their faces faded to blank ovals. Her parents, probably. Four generations pictured and only one member known to be still living. You start out playing solitaire with a crisp new deck full of promise. Sometimes you win. Oftener you get all the aces out and still run dry. You mount pictures lovingly in the family album and someday someone will turn the pages and wonder who the people are.

Karen McBride came in carrying a thick sheaf of yellow curling envelopes with a faded brown ribbon tied around it. "I just looked at the return address," she said, holding it out. "They all came from the same place in Hamtramck. She had them in one of Mr. Evancek's old cigar boxes in the bottom drawer of the bedroom bureau."

I accepted them. Her fingertips grazed mine accidentally. This close she smelled of soap that would be pink, but she wouldn't choose it for the color. I couldn't decide if she used perfume. The sheaf felt like a stack of dried leaves.

"I'm hoping these will tell me something of Michael's interests," I said. "Sometimes you can track a person down through them."

"Young boys have a lot of interests. But they change them like socks."

"Maybe one or two stuck." I looked at my watch. "I missed breakfast this morning. Can we go somewhere and eat? I guess you'd call it brunch up here."

Something glinted in her eyes. "Is this business or a pickup?"

"I guess that depends on how far your cooperation goes."

"Its tongue is silk," she said. "I promised Martha I'd keep an eye on the place until I leave for work. Also I'm sort of involved with someone at the moment."

" 'Sort of.' " I tapped the bundle of letters against my open palm. "That falls somewhere between 'I'm pinned' and 'What color should we paint the bedroom?' Which is it?"

She smiled the smile. "Your switch is stuck again."

I didn't have a topper. I collected my hat and got away from her while I still owned a watch.

I caught a ham sandwich at the counter down the street from my office and let myself into the thinking room. No one stopped me on the way through the little room where the customers cooled leather. There was no one to stop me. My mail on the floor inside the slot all had little windows in it. I picked it up and carried it reverently to the desk and filed it in the top drawer next to the whoopee calendar from the police supply house where I'd bought my first set of handcuffs five years ago. Loyalty, you take it where it comes in my business. I sat down and got the bundle out of my inside breast pocket and undid the ribbon.

Some of the letters were in a thick, jerky hand with Joseph's signature at the bottom. They were in English. The first one was dated two and a half years before the shooting; it would be the language he was most comfortable with by that time. The last had been written a full month short of it. The letters got fewer and the dates got farther apart as months went by, as they will the longer a son stays away from home. Others had been written by his wife Jeanine with easy open loops and cheery circles over the i's. Joseph got a raise, little Michael put a caterpillar in his pocket and forgot about it, the new furniture came, Jeanine fell and fractured her wrist on the icy sidewalk in front of the house. Michael joined Little League. Joseph had him batting 297 and fielding flies like Horton; Jeanine had him unable to get out of his own way. In May the boy was into collecting coins. By August he was chasing butterflies and then he got burned by a magazine advertisement offering a bag of rare stamps for a dime that turned around and billed him afterward for eight-fifty. In November he was back to coins. There were hand-drawn holiday cards from Michael and Carla to their grandparents and how-are-you-I-am-fine letters scrawled in blurred pencil on ruled lines half an inch apart, Michael going on about iron Lincoln D pennies and asking the old folks to send him Polish coins.

The family was planning a vacation trip to Arizona, Jeanine thought she was pregnant again but it was a false alarm, the snow was up to the sills, the sun was shining, it had rained six weekends in a row. By the second spring most of the letters were Jeanine's. Late in May Joseph was laid off from Dodge Main. They blamed it on the bum economy. In June there was one more letter from Joseph, a short one, blotched and nearly illegible, assuring his parents he would be called back anytime. It was the last letter in the stack.

Reading the letters from this side of that explosive July, you wondered why no one had smelled the fuse burning. Then you went back over them in the frame of mind in which they must have been received and they were just letters, and damn boring ones at that. Thousands of people had written hundreds of thousands of letters just like them and then gone bumping along like the rest of us without ever killing anyone.

I put them back in their envelopes and stacked them in their original order and retied the ribbon. I sat back and smoked and looked out the window at the pigeons fiddlefooting along the splattered ledge of the apartment building. Filthy birds. Carried lice and ticks and the noise they made in their throats sounded like mugging victims gurgling through slashed windpipes in stinking alleys. I disinterred the office bottle from the file drawer in the desk and blew dust out of the pony glass and oiled my gullet. As the heat expanded from the base of my stomach I recapped the bottle and put it away and looked out at the pigeons again. It was okay now. They were just birds.

I made a brief field trip to a drugstore around the corner, a department store really, with shelves of electric razors and wristwatches and garden gadgets and if you looked long enough a prescription counter at the back, and returned with a magazine for coin collectors. There had been three on the rack, all published by the same firm in Cedar Rapids, Iowa. Long-distance Information gave me the number. I dialed it and a switchboard operator with banjo strings for vocal cords got me someone in Circulation.

"My name's Walker," I told the guy. "I'm a Michigan State Police licensed investigator trying to track down a witness to a murder. I think he may be on your subscription list."

"Which title?"

"Any or all of them. He collects coins."

"Sec."

I parked the receiver in the hollow of my shoulder and lit a cigarette. I was just stringing popcorn. For all I knew, Michael Evancek hadn't touched a coin except to feed a meter in nineteen years.

The voice came back on. "I checked and the lists are in the data bank. I'll just punch them in here and have them on your screen in ten minutes. What system are you using?"

"Underwood and Noggin. I don't have a computer."

The pause on his end was just long enough to tell me I blew it.

"You're with the Michigan State Police and you don't have a computer?"

"I'm not with the state police," I said. "They just issued my license. I'm private."

"So why mention them at all?"

"Mainly, to avoid conversations like this."

"That changes things some. Our subscription information is confidential."

"Bull. You sell it to every mail-order advertiser that comes along."

"That's business." He paused again. "But a subscription to one or all of our magazines entitles you to some things."

"I'm not a collector."

"Suit yourself, Jack."

"I could be, though," I said, before he could hang up. "Which one would you recommend to a beginner?"

"*Numismatics Monthly.* It runs fifty dollars per year."

"How much for six months?"

"We don't offer six-month subscriptions."

"What do the others run?"

"Fifty dollars."

"Uh-huh."

"Listen, you want the list or not?"

"I'm just interested in two names," I said. "Why don't you tell me if they're on any of the lists and if they are I'll get a check off to you."

He laughed. It wasn't a very nice laugh. "You must think I'm a philatelist."

I said, "Okay, one way or the other you get it."

"How do I know you'll come through?"

"How do I know you'll tell me straight?"

"I guess we just have to trust each other," he said. He didn't like saying it. It lay like alum on his tongue. "Okay, shoot."

"His name's Michael Evancek." I spelled it. "He might be going by Michael Norton."

I heard keys rattling. After a minute he said, "No Evanceks. We got two Nortons, Philip in San Francisco and a B. Norton in Dayton, Ohio."

"Barbara?" I jumped on it. Barbara Norton was Jeanine Evancek's sister.

"Just the initial. Sec." More keys rattled. "We got a kill on it. Subscriber moved a few months back without filing a change-of-address."

I asked him for the old number and wrote it down, along with Philip's San Francisco address. They might not have liked the name Michael any more than they did Evancek.

"I don't see how you function without a computer," Circulation mused.

"It's tough. I'm like a musician without a saddle. Who do I make the check out to?"

"Albert C. Moss."

The publishing firm's name was entirely different. I wrote down Albert C. Moss and said I'd get the check off by the end of the week.

"Where should we send the magazine?" Albert asked innocently.

I laughed nastily and pegged the receiver. They grow them funny in Cedar Rapids.

I looked at my watch. Then I looked at the bathing beauty on the calendar on the wall. Then I looked at my watch again to see what time it was. I was going to have some fun explaining fifty dollars for a magazine subscription on the expense sheet. Especially when neither of the two names and addresses it bought, one of them obsolete, probably had anything to do with Michael. I wondered if Karen McBride was really sort of involved with someone or if I was using the wrong aftershave. My mind was starting to wander. I called Long-distance Information again and asked for the main branch of the U.S. Post Office in Dayton, Ohio. A clerk there looked up B.

Norton in the change-of-addresses and gave me a number on Gilbert in Detroit.

My heartbeat accelerated a little. There was probably nothing in it. There was no B. Norton in the Detroit directory. I called Local Information. They had it under New Numbers and I worked the plunger and dialed it and got a busy signal. I hung up and smoked a cigarette and tried again. Same thing. Well, when you flush two birds you're supposed to go for the far one first anyway.

San Francisco Information put me in touch with Philip Norton. He had a high affected voice that made me hold the receiver a little away from my ear. He said he was 45, owned a coin shop off Golden Gate, and had never been in Michigan in his life. But if I was ever in the Bay Area I should look him up.

B. Norton's line was still busy. I wasn't very nice to it. I wanted to get that one out of the way and start shaking loose some real leads. There were a million Nortons in the world, probably a hundred thousand B. Nortons, and anyway if Michael was still into coins why would the magazine be going to his aunt? Write off the fifty and go find some real detective work to do.

From the top drawer of the desk I took a Smith & Wesson .38-caliber revolver, the one they call the Police Special, with a checked ball-rubber grip and a four-inch barrel. I looked at the cartridges, then slid it into its stiff leather holster and strapped the works on my belt with the butt snugged into its permanent dent in my right kidney. Then I locked up and drove to B. Norton's address on Gilbert. It was a good neighborhood. The very best people were found dead there.

9

You CAN DRIVE back and forth to work every day along Michigan Avenue and never know the street. The Michigan Avenue that cuts in at an angle on that undigested lump of real estate alternately called Cadillac and Kennedy Square in the heart of downtown Detroit is not the Michigan Avenue that squeezes rush-hour traffic in and out of Cadillac Main where the old Grand Trunk crosses or the Michigan Avenue that takes you past a solid bank of hookers displaying their legware at Livernois when the lights come on. It starts at the base of the old Grand Circle among weathered brown skyscrapers and slashes straight as a knife westward through where the city becomes horizontal, refusing to crimp until it becomes US-12 just east of Dearborn. The bad areas don't look that much different from the relatively good ones, and unless you're familiar with the street's changing moods you don't know until you cross the wrong alley and suddenly find yourself walking in a very quiet block with invisible eyes watching you from doorways that you've come too far. You can trust John R and the Cass Corridor to be treacherous, but you can never be sure about Michigan. If it were in a bottle it would carry a warning label.

A city barricade stood across one lane of Gilbert at Michigan with a blue-and-white parked in the other and a uniformed black cop in short sleeves leaning on the car. He signaled for me to stop and came across, swaggering a little the way cops will when they're wearing the belt with a gun and a walking radio and cuffs swinging from it. He came to a stop just behind the open window on the driver's side with the post between us.

"Good afternoon, sir," he said. "May I see your driver's license and vehicle registration."

I got them out and handed them over. He had smooth cocoa-brown skin and a black Fu Manchu moustache, which was as much of an impression as I got of him behind that post. They're trained to stand just there because its harder to turn and shoot them that way. Some people manage to do it regardless.

"What's up?"

"Just a routine check, sir. What is your business here today?"

"I asked you first."

A white cop who had been sitting in the prowl car monitoring the radio came over and joined him. My guy gave him my license and registration and he carried them back across the street and leaned in through the window and hooked out the mike and started reading.

"We're just following up some citizen complaints in the neighborhood," said the black cop evenly. "Your business?"

"Oh," I said. "Princess patrol. Why didn't you say so? Your watch captain must have it in for you."

His brow bunched under the visor of his cap. "You plain-clothes?"

"Private. How's the murder rate?"

"Up twenty percent over this time last year. But the commissioner says snag hookers so it's hookers we snag. We're hitting the johns this week."

I told him I was chasing down a lead on a missing persons beef.

"Yeah," he said. "My old man was a house painter. Took his paint can with him everywhere and nobody asked him what he thought he was doing because he always looked like he was working."

"Does this look like a face that has to pay for it?"

"You're asking the wrong person. All you folks look alike to me."

We grinned at each other like two strange cats in an alley. The white cop returned with my papers. "He's clean."

"You won't recognize the block next visit." The black cop gave them to me. "We'll have all the girls out of their mini-skirts and banging typewriters in offices downtown."

"Or something." I started the engine and waited. The uniformed pair stood clear and I cranked the Olds around the end of the barricade and cruised on. In my rearview mirror the cops swaggered back to their parked prowl car and got ready to dig another hole in the Atlantic Ocean.

The place was a three-story apartment complex with outside stairs leading to iron-railed balconies, the lower of which was a long porch to the people on the ground floor. It would have started out with a trumpeting THIS IS THE FUTURE SITE OF sign and had all its apartments rented out before the foundation was poured, and there would have been a swimming pool in the courtyard and automatic washers in the basement and a window-cleaning service, but somewhere along the way things would have gone sour. The tenants would have gotten together and bought the building and yanked out the laundry to make room for storage and save on water and maintenance and put the window cleaning on a pay-as-you-go basis, and no one would use the pool anymore or skim the top and the water would have seeped down and the green scum have dried on the bottom and cracks would have appeared and the tenants would have had it filled in so that the courtyard resembled nothing so much as a giant air shaft with balconies all around for no better reason now than to look down and see how the concrete was doing.

Then as the city's complexion changed, as burglars and rapists turned commuter and building security went the way of the laundry and the window-washers and the pool, those tenants who could afford to leave would have left and either rented their old apartments to whoever had cash or let them stand empty. The aluminum siding would grow pockmarked and the picturesque ivy matting the front wall would run wild and pry shingles loose from the roof and the rosebushes along the base would overgrow and strangle all but a few lean ugly city-bred buds. The iron railings would be scaly like dead skin to the touch and there would be brown curled leaves in the cobwebs in the porch corners. As a rule you find a better class of slum there on the west side, but a sty is a sty.

I drove around behind the building and parked in a circular lot that would be about as easy to get out of as a bulldog's mouth and walked back around to the front, where a sign reading OFFICE was screwed to the door of a corner apartment at ground level. On the strip of lawn in front of the place a middle-aged black man in a cap and green workclothes had a hose in his hand from a tank with training wheels, spraying industrial-strength weedkiller over a lone dandelion.

The woman in the office, also black, wearing white-framed glasses with an oriental tilt and a red wig, directed me to Twelve and put the door in my face before I could ask if B. Norton was a woman and what the B. stood for. She had something in the oven that smelled like a fire in a plastics plant. I thought about using the little brass knocker again, shrugged, and turned toward the outside stairs. The gardener or whatever was still bombarding the dandelion when I reached the second row of apartments. Well, he had all afternoon and a full tank.

The door to Apartment Twelve was standing open, as were several others in the summery warmth. A woman's voice floated out.

"Sir, I was just asking if you were bothered with peeling and flaking paint. I did not mean to imply . . . No, sir, I did not accuse you of living in a dump. Sir, I'm just asking the questions my employer wants me to . . . Well, then, you can take your peeling and flaking paint and shove it up your ass."

I poked my head through the door just as she banged the receiver into its cradle. She said, "Creep," and took a pencil out of her hair to draw a line through something written on a yellow legal tablet on the table in front of her. She was in her fifties and running a little to fat, with a shadow under her chin and dewlaps over the corners of her small mouth. Her hair was done up in a kind of hive and tinted a bright brass. She had on a man's gray cotton workshirt with flaps on the pockets. I couldn't see what she was wearing under the table but it wouldn't be chiffon. Her small eyes had a pink, naked, crowded-together look on either side of a nose that was just a nose and when she glanced up and saw me in the doorway she tipped down a pair of glasses with big round lenses and bows with a dip in them like racing handlebars. She peered at me through the lenses and said, "Well?"

"I'm looking for a Barbara Norton," I said.

"I'm Barbara Norton."

I narrowed my eyes a little. She looked like she could be related to the ordinary blonde in the family picture with Joseph Evancek and the kids. Then she didn't. I said, "The Barbara Norton I want took in her nephew Michael after he lost his family in Hamtramck nineteen years ago this July. It's him I'm really looking for."

She didn't scream or run up any walls. All she did was put the pencil back in her hair. Maybe for her that was the same thing.

"Michael's dead," she said. "He's been dead almost two years."

10

I STEPPED INSIDE. There seemed to be an invitation in what she'd said about Michael. It was a fairly large apartment with a hallway leading to other rooms farther back and a sliding glass door opening onto a balcony overlooking the courtyard that told me I'd been right about the pool if there had ever been one. The place was halfway clean. It would always be halfway clean while she was living in it. The rug had been vacuumed within memory, but feathers of dust clung like frightened children to the legs of the table. There were stacks of magazines and old newspapers solid enough to sit on in the corners. Shirts and dresses and slips were flung over the arms of the chairs and sofa. Dust made little hammocks in the corners of framed pictures of sailboats and windmills on walls that were scrubbed sometimes but not as often as the rug was vacuumed. The sliding glass door was streaked enough not to need a brightly painted butterfly stuck to it at eye level, but it had one. The butterfly looked as if it would rather be out pollinating flowers the gardener hadn't poisoned yet. I knew how it felt.

I had spent a lot of time in private residences in this case. I was starting to feel like an insurance agent. You've a lovely home, Mr. and Mrs. Fosslethwaite. What kind of fire protection are you carrying at present?

Barbara Norton had a cigarette burning in a pile of butts on the table that might or might not have had an ashtray under it. She broke the cigarette free of an inch and a half of ash and stuck it in her face without taking her eyes off me. They

looked larger and less naked behind her window-size lenses.
"Who are you?"

I told her, flashing the bona fides. That has an official touch
that works with some people, but I could see it meant as much
to her as someone else's baby picture. I put the wallet away.
"I'm working for Martha Evancek, Michael's grandmother.
She's in this country and she wants to know where he went.
I'm sorry he's dead. How'd he get that way?"

While I was talking she got a fresh cigarette going, using
the butt of the last. She did this with the concentration of a
watchmaker replacing a jewel the size of an ant's cufflink,
then smashed out the old butt in the pile.

"Close the door," she said.

I closed the door.

"Have a seat."

I had a seat. This time I chose a padded rocker with a brassiere slung over the back. The sofas of the world could swallow air for a while.

"Excuse the condition of the place," she said. "When you
work at home you don't get much chance to pick up."

"What do you do?"

"Whatever doesn't burn gas. Stuff envelopes. Type up student papers, only my machine's in hock just now. Mostly telephone work, surveys and advertising." She indicated the
Metropolitan Detroit directory lying open on the table and
the legal pad with names and numbers scribbled on it, many
of them scratched out. "Just now they've got me selling vinyl
siding."

She mined a thin stack of colored plastic strips out of the
general clutter and fanned them out expertly. They looked
like insoles with a phony wood grain.

"What are you supposed to do," I said, "describe them over
the telephone?"

"They came in the same envelope with the list of questions
I'm supposed to ask prospective customers. I guess they're for
inspiration. I'd sure hate to have this stuff on my house,
though. I'd feel like a foot in a plastic shoe." She dropped the

strips back to the table. "You should see my phone bill. The manager sent the cops up here yesterday; she thinks I'm a call girl."

I grinned and lit a Winston. "Michael."

"He drowned in the California Gulf a year ago last August. He and a friend were standing in water just over their waists off Cabo San Lucas when the undertow got them. Someone in a boat rescued the friend. Michael's body was never recovered."

There was a deliberate deadness in her tone.

I said, "What was he doing in the Baja?"

"He was on vacation. He worked for a package design firm in Ohio."

"Is that where you went after you left St. Clair Shores?"

She nodded, leaking smoke out her nostrils. "Dayton. My bastard husband Bob ran out on both of us six weeks after the move. Couldn't stand having a kid in the house. What was I supposed to do, stick him in an orphanage after that filthy son of a bitch Evancek —"

"Mrs. Evancek and her husband wrote you after the shooting. You never answered their letters."

"I wanted Michael to forget all about his father's side of the family. I wouldn't even let him write his grandparents. It was the right decision. He grew up normal."

"The authorities in Cabo San Lucas investigated the drowning?"

"You can check with them."

"Was Michael married?"

She shook her head. "I used to nag him about it. But his opinion of the blessed state couldn't have been high, and who could blame him? So you can tell the old lady to forget about great-grandchildren."

"Of course, you could be lying about that," I said.

"You could find out easy enough."

There was an ashtray rounded over with butts on the end table next to the rocker. I tipped some ash on top of the pile. Thinking. "What brought you back here?"

"The rent's cheaper than Dayton. I just moved back the first of the year."

"You collect coins?"

She raised her eyebrows at that. They were tweezed very thin and gave her an owlish look behind the glasses. Then she laughed, an abrupt, harsh sound with no enjoyment in it. It ended in a coughing fit. She ground out the butt. "Yeah, I should have guessed that's how you found me. I started subscribing to that magazine for Michael at least ten years ago, when he was still at home. Because my name was on the check they sent it to me. I never got around to canceling it for sentimental reasons."

She seemed as sentimental as a wrecking ball. I said, "How did you and Joseph get along before the shooting?"

"We didn't. I never liked the idea of Jeanine marrying that dumb greasy Polack and I don't guess I hid it too well. I only visited her when he was at work. I didn't see much of her after he got canned and started hanging around the house all the time getting drunk."

"How do you know that if you weren't around?"

"Jeanine told me. We talked on the phone when he was passed out or busy tanking up at some bar. She was miserable. The kids were the only reason she stuck. My sister was runner-up for homecoming queen her senior year in high school. She could have had her choice of anyone. Ah, shit." She picked up a disposable butane lighter and got another weed burning. "That night, when the phone rang, and it was the police, I think I knew what they were going to say before they said it. I didn't feel anything but tired. Even when they called me down to the morgue — I don't know why, there wasn't anything to identify —" She let it hang and looked at me. "I guess you think I'm just another burned-out bitch."

"What I think won't change my underwear."

She made the noise again, this time without coughing. "All you good-looking guys got tact. Bob had tact. That's why he ran out on me."

"Do you remember the name of the friend Michael was swimming with?"

"Fred something." She thought. "Florentine. Fred Florentine. They worked together. The company was Buckeye Industries in Dayton. He might still be there."

I finished my cigarette. I had run out of questions. I thanked her and got up. "I'll let you get back to work now."

Her eyes followed me. "What are you going to tell the old lady?"

"The truth. It's paid for."

"It better be, for your sake. It's not a thing you'd buy after you heard it."

"It almost never is."

She had the receiver in her hand and was dialing another number from her list. I left her to that and the bitterness that was like another person in the room.

The dandelion was still on the lawn when I came out on the stairs but there was no sign of the gardener. He was probably on the telephone to the National Guard. Tough little weeds, dandelions. They ought to be licensed and bonded. They could tell a sick old lady that the grandson she'd never met had been dead as long as she'd been looking for him and never blink a leaf. I got into my crate and pried it out of the little parking lot and drove back to the office at the approximate speed of a funeral procession.

The telephone was ringing when I let myself in. I took off my hat and pegged it and sat down behind the desk and it was still ringing. I picked up the receiver. "Walker."

"This is A. Walker Investigations?"

It was a woman's voice, clipped and businesslike, ageless and almost sexless. You hear a lot of voices like it these days. I said it was.

"I represent a party who might be interested in engaging your services. Would you be free to discuss it at the Westin Hotel this afternoon?"

I said, "I'm just wrapping something up. Could we make it this evening or tomorrow morning?"

"Mr. Alanov has a speaking engagement this evening. One moment." A hand went over the mouthpiece on her end. Presently: "Mr. Walker? He will see you in his suite tomorrow morning at eleven-thirty."

She gave me the number of the suite. I wrote it down. "This wouldn't by any chance be Fedor Alanov, the Russian novelist?"

"Mr. Alanov is Russian and a novelist. To say that he writes Russian novels could be misleading."

It sounded like banter, but the tone of the voice hadn't changed. I wondered what it would take to change it and if it would ever be worthwhile. Aloud I said, "Could you give me a hint of what I'm seeing Mr. Alanov about?"

"Not over the telephone. We'll pay your expenses to and from the hotel, with an added inducement regardless of the outcome of the interview."

"An inducement of say how much?"

"I believe your consultation fee is two hundred fifty dollars."

I confirmed the time and suite number and got off the line before her mind changed.

I thought about it. I hadn't read Alanov; I could never sort out all the *viches* in books from that part of the world. But I'd heard about him plenty at the time he left Russia to stay ahead of the gray suits that didn't care for the liberal tone of his writing. Someone had told him the press was free here. I played with it a little, then put it away for later. For the next hour anyway I was still on salary to Martha Evancek.

A female switchboard operator answered at the number Long-distance Information gave me for Buckeye Industries and told me to hang on when I asked to speak to Fred Florentine. Florentine was the young man who according to Barbara Norton had been swimming with Michael Evancek the day he drowned. He wouldn't still be working there.

"Hello?"

"Hello," I echoed. "I'm trying to get hold of Fred Florentine."

"You can stop trying."

"You're Florentine?"

"Years now. Who are you?"

He sounded young and confident, a lad with his own office. I told him who I was and what I was after and what Barbara Norton had told me. It took longer to tell than it did to know.

He blew air. "Mike. God, I haven't thought about him in months. That was a bad day. I hope it's the worst I'll ever see. One second I was standing there talking to Mike and enjoying the water and the next I didn't know which direction the surface was. I thought a shark had me. First thing I did when they plucked me out of the water and pumped out my lungs was check to see if everything was still there. And Mike — God, it was like he was never here, he was gone just that fast."

"I guess you two were pretty close."

"He was my goombah. I was a long time getting over it. Maybe I'm not over it yet. Maybe you never are. Who'd you say you were working for?"

"I didn't. But it's Mike's grandmother, Martha Evancek."

"Really? I never knew he had one. He never mentioned her."

"They didn't know each other. What did he do at Buckeye?"

"Worked in the catalogue department, same as me. 'Lightweight, durable, one-twentieth-inch cardboard, ideal for storage and shipping.' We wrote that. It was our most successful collaboration."

"What kind of a guy was he?"

"The best. If you got run over by a bus he was there and if you just needed five bucks till payday he was there too, making you think you were doing him a favor to take it. Guys like him are so rare I guess God figured he shouldn't stick around any one place too long."

"Getting dead does a lot for your social standing," I said.

"I'm not just saying these things because he's dead. Mike was the best friend I'll ever have."

"He must have had something wrong with him."

"I don't know what it would be, unless he was too quiet. You know, I never even thought about that till he was gone. I tried to remember things he'd said, the way you do, and couldn't think of a one. Oh, he talked, but it was almost always in answer to something you said. Maybe that's why I liked him. He was a good listener. He made you feel as if everything you had to say was gold. I guess it's not so strange I didn't know about the grandmother, close as we were. He never talked about himself."

"Did he ever mention the shooting?"

"What shooting?"

"Something he had no control over," I said quickly. "Listen, I'd like to give your name and telephone number to the old lady. She might want to talk to you about Michael."

"Sure. I'd like that. Just having talked to you about him makes me feel better."

I wrote down his home number and we stopped talking to each other. I got Information again, which put me in touch with someone who could give me the number of the authorities in Cabo San Lucas, Baja, Mexico. The telephone rang fifteen times there before a Sergeant Cristobal answered. The line was thick with static and his voice was even thicker with Spanish accent and something else, but I finally got through to him what I was after. His English improved quite a bit after I mentioned fifty dollars American. He asked if I was the man who had come to ask about the drowning before.

"What man?" I asked. "When?"

"A man. Months ago. I will send you a copy of the full report in a few days." Just before hanging up he bellowed at someone named Elena. I could almost smell the tequila on the sergeant's breath.

I tried Barbara Norton's number. Busy. Then I spent some

more money and called Fred Florentine again. I asked him if he knew anything about anyone going down to investigate the accident.

"No. But that's not unusual, is it? Insurance companies don't get to be big trusting their clients."

"I've worked for enough of them to know that. Thanks."

I poured myself some Scotch, nodded to the looker on the advertising calendar, and drank it off. Then I poured some more and didn't toast anyone. I filed the bottle again and got my hat. It was heavy. They had gotten the material from a quarry and lined it with lead.

The sun was somewhere west of Southfield and shadows were clotting on the lawns of St. Clair Shores when Karen McBride met me at the top of the steps in Martha Evancek's house. She had her nurse's uniform on now and looked crisp and white enough to make me feel wilted and sallow. I had a head start on it. Her smile of welcome saw my face and dangled.

11

"How IRONIC. To survive murder-suicide and grow up to drown in water waist-deep."

"If it's wet you can drown in it. I could tell you stories."

But I didn't. Instead I closed my mouth and knocked almost half of my cigarette into a glass ashtray on the arm of the sofa. I hadn't wanted it, my throat already felt like a chimney in need of sweeping, but it was something to do with my hands. For some reason I had told her the whole thing. I had started with what she already knew, the old lady hobbling into the office, and gone straight through what I had scraped up from Howard Mayk and the visit to the old Evancek house and everything else, finishing with Fred Florentine in Dayton. Stash Leposava fascinated her most of all. She had asked me a dozen questions about the old Cossack and sat on the edge of the upholstered straightback chair with her hands between her white linen-covered knees and her face thrust forward to hear the answers. When it got too dark to see each other she got up and snapped on a lamp and sat back down for the rest of it. Soft shadows brushed her cheeks and the hollow under her full lower lip and made her look like a little girl playing dress-up in front of an attic mirror.

"Do you want a drink?" she asked.

"I had one. Two. They didn't help."

She looked down at her hands. "I'll tell Martha. She's stronger than you'd think. She'll handle it."

I killed my stub, shaking my head. "That's why I took the money. It isn't like it hasn't bought bad news before. I'm an old hand. If my car had a mast I'd keep black sails in the trunk and run them up at times like this like Ulysses."

"I thought it was Jason."

I looked at her. She shrugged an apology. "I know her better," she said. "You can give her the details later."

I got out the envelope and held it out.

"What's that?" She didn't take it.

"The second half of her five hundred, less expenses. I tied it up in one day. The time I spent checking out her story last night doesn't count. It would have if she'd lied. I'll type up a full report and bring it around in a few days."

She took the envelope. "She'll say you earned it anyway."

"Maybe at first. The more she stewed on it the less she'd think so. In the end I'd be out a reference. I'm not nearly as noble as I look. I have to work in this town."

She got up and put the envelope in the drawer of a sidepiece with a lace shawl on top and pushed the drawer shut. Her skirt rustled that way you can hear clear down a hospital corridor. She turned around and looked at me.

"Does that brunch offer hold for dinner?"

I said, "I thought you worked tonight."

"It's the middle of the week. I can get someone to cover."

"Is it my good looks or are you sorry for me?"

Her face took on a clinical cast, studying mine. "You'd look okay, if you let your hair grow over your ears and didn't shave your upper lip so close. But I'd have to say in this case it's pity."

"Good enough. Let's go." I rose.

She smiled the monkey smile. "Let me make a call and climb out of these whites."

One good thing about the slow retreat of jazz before soul's groaning, sliding advance in Detroit — the only good thing about it — is you can get into a downtown jazz club in the middle of the week. We had a fifteen-minute wait at the bar of a place on Gratiot, then a hostess in a ruffled blue blouse and a floor-length skirt with peonies on it escorted us to a table across a murky hangar from the stage, where a fat black man in an orange-and-green plaid sportcoat leaned on a saxophone case smoking behind mirrored glasses. We ordered, and when our waitress withdrew with the hem of her skirt slurring the floor we sipped at the drinks we'd brought over with us.

"You're not satisfied," Karen said.

"I haven't tasted the prime rib."

"No, I mean about Michael. You don't think he died the way they say?"

"He probably did. It's the shooting that bothers me. I believe old Stash."

She laced her fingers under her chin. She wore no rings, or jewelry of any kind. She had on a black shift of some sort with no sleeves and a scoop neck that quit where it started to get interesting. Her hair was pinned up in back. Candlelight from the thick orange cut glass on the table winked in the glossy waves. She watched me and said nothing.

"A gang of witnesses is always suspect," I said. "They get together and start comparing notes and there's always one or two that saw something better than all the rest, and then the others get to thinking that what they have isn't so interesting after all, and by the time the cops show up they've all seen the same thing. But the old man didn't hang around with the rest of the neighbors. He saw what he saw and it didn't matter to him that none of the others saw it. He just reported it and didn't try to glitz it up with stuff he thought the cops would like to hear."

"But he's senile."

"Now, maybe. Not then. Maybe not now either. You can be young and stubborn and they call it muleheadedness. When you're old and stubborn they say you've got space to rent upstairs and stick you in a home. I think the old man saw Michael get in before the shooting. Remember that none of the other neighbors saw the boy come home at *any* time.

They would have had no special reason to be looking out their windows until the shotgun blasts drew their attention. The cops just wrote down what Michael said days after the fact. Chances are he was still in shock. You can be for a long time and not show it."

"Barbara Norton would know that better than anyone," she said.

"Probably. But she's as soft as an abutment and I don't have the six months it would take to wear her down."

A thought came into her face. She raised her chin from her hands. "You don't think Michael —"

"No," I said. "Though it wouldn't be all that unthinkable. There's nothing you can dream up that someone hasn't done, and recently. But the official record's probably right so far as it goes. Say what you like about them, most cops are reasonably honest and usually right. But thorough they can't always be, considering their tight budgets and workload. I think Michael saw something that would nail down some of the loosest ends. But he's fish food in the Pacific and it doesn't much matter any more."

The waitress came with our dinner and we didn't talk again until she'd emptied her tray and gone. Then Karen said, "I've never known a private eye before. I thought they were mostly flat-nosed thugs who spend their evenings bouncing people off the walls of alleys. You're kind of nice."

"I've bounced my share. Tonight you're looking at my St. Clair Shores face."

"What's that?" She picked up her fork.

"Restrained and polite. It's like my Grosse Pointe face, only there I put a little weasel in it. You know, that smooth panting look. Here it's regular John, get-a-load-of-those-gams. I save the flat nose for Cass and Mt. Elliott."

" 'Gams'?" Her eyes crinkled.

"Sorry. When I'm tired I talk dirty."

"How about Iroquois Heights?"

"Up in Iroquois Heights I just try to get in and out with

any face at all. There they push them in just for something to do, like a mean kid de-winging flies when he ought to be looking up the Congress of Worms."

"I was born in the Heights," she said.

"A lot of nice people were. It's the cops and their pet prosecutor you don't show your back to if you're fond of your head."

The entire band, a five-man combo, had gathered on the stage and climbed into "Ebb Tide" for horns, bass, piano, and drums. She glanced that way, then nibbled at her gin and tonic. "That wasn't your St. Clair Shores face this morning."

Grinning, I pushed aside my empty plate and picked up my drink. I'd demolished a prime rib and all the options and hadn't tasted a bite. "That was your fault. You went stiff old maid on me, which always brings out my thirteen-hundred face. That's the one I show the cops at thirteen-hundred Beaubien, police headquarters. It generally gets me a lift out the back door and my hat tumbling along afterwards."

"I was on the defensive this morning," she said. "I didn't know you. I'm still a long way from knowing you. What makes a halfway intelligent guy with a flashy line of gab and a nice face — this one, anyway — peek at people's underwear for his living?"

"What makes a girl who should be a model empty bedpans for hers?"

"I get to see a lot of naked men. But I asked you first."

"A friend died and left me the business. I don't get to see nearly as many naked women as I'd like."

"No, really."

I sat back and toyed with a cigarette. "I ask myself that eight times a week. Twice on Mondays when I'm still hung over from Saturday's sapping. A bright young fellow like me should be in high tech, except my distrust of computers borders on the pathological. I could go out West and become a cowboy. But the only time I was ever on a horse I got tossed and had the sense not to remount. You don't get back on a hot stove. I could run for mayor only I'm not black enough or slippery enough. Law —"

"What about police work?"

"Next question."

She ran the edge of her fork along the rim of her plate. "You're a riddle, all right," she said. "I'm just debating with myself whether it's worth the trouble to solve."

I let that one drift. The waitress came back to ask if everything was all right. I ordered a bottle of something with a cork in it and she went away. The band was playing "Stars Fell on Alabama" — slow, with the trumpet up front, the way Red Nichols used to. It was a better band than the place deserved. A few couples were prowling the floor. We watched and listened.

"Swaying to music like primitives in a *National Geographic* special," murmured Karen. "Kind of dumb when you think about it."

"Dumb." I got up and held out a hand. She took it.

Our feet made no noise at all on the layers of varnish on the dance floor. She was wiry under a padding of deceptively soft flesh. Her head came to my collarbone. "It dances, too," she marveled. "My father taught me, back when everyone I knew was shaking his arms and snapping his head like someone trying to swim backwards up a waterfall. Where'd you learn?"

"The hookers in Saigon only did one other thing."

We danced some more. She felt warm.

"What's this?" she asked.

"Don't be naive."

"This." She patted the Smith & Wesson on the back of my belt under my jacket.

"I thought I might have a use for it earlier. I didn't. I forgot I was still wearing it."

"I hate guns."

"They're not a thing to love or hate. They're just so much steel."

We danced. Her hair smelled sweetly of soap and female musk.

"Listen, I'm worried about this guy you're sort of involved with."

"Don't be. I'm not."

"Involved?"

"Worried."

When we were through dancing we drank some wine and then I took her home. She had an apartment on the second floor of a brick house on Lake Shore Drive, one of the big ones that would have been built by someone named Phil the Camel or Charlie Blue Eyes, with a bay window looking out on the smoked-glass surface of Lake St. Clair with the lights of Windsor strung like sequins along the far shore and the broader glittering sheet of Grosse Pointe Woods and Harper Woods farther down on this side, and beyond that Detroit. I was looking at Detroit with the lights off behind me and my tie undone and my jacket draped across a chair when Karen handed me a glass of something and slid her arm around my waist, laying her head against my upper arm. She was tiny with her shoes off.

She said, "I like it at night. I like to stand here and look out and wonder what's going on behind each lighted window."

"A murder behind at least two," I said, "if the stats hold up."

"We're cynical tonight."

"We're tired. Why is it always 'we' with you nurses?"

"What've you got against the place?"

"It isn't what it was. Don't get me started."

"We've got all night."

"You're doing it again." I drank. It was good bourbon, with a slight char. "When I came to the town it was like a big dumb hunky with a neck like a beer keg and a big wide stupid grin. It worked hard, got dirty, swore, told off-color jokes, and laughed a lot and loud. Then the riots came and after them the murders and then this new gang took over and threw up those silos on the riverfront and called it the Renaissance City. Now it's like a hooker that got religion, avoiding its old friends, won't laugh at the old jokes. But at night it still opens its thighs to whatever comes along. I guess it's the holy attitude I don't like."

She said, "You expect too much of a pile of bricks and steel."

"Maybe. I miss that old hunky."

She turned her face up then and I kissed her. It started out friendly and wound up self-defense. I had to bend my knees to keep strain off my back. She was pressed against me from breastbone to thigh and her tongue darted and one hand found my shoulder blade and the other went prowling down my spine to the small of my back and found the revolver and recoiled. I let go of her with one hand and reached around behind and unsnapped the holster and fumbled it, gun and all, onto the window seat. All this was very awkward entangled as we were, but we never broke formation. She was at once as pliant and as sinuous as a young ocelot and her lips were like crushed wild berries, untamed and smoky-sweet with her teeth like thorns in the center of the sweetness. I did some biting of my own and plunged deeper into the jungle.

I dressed quietly in the dark. The bedroom had a smaller version of the bay window in the living room, and as she stirred atop the tangled sheets and drew one slick leg up its mate the city glow lay blue-white on her naked skin. She lay with her hair fanned out dark across her pillow and watched me buttoning my shirt.

"Why not hang around for morning?" she asked sleepily. "I fix a mean breakfast. Never go near the hospital cafeteria staff."

"I don't eat much in the way of breakfast."

"There are lots of other good reasons to hang around."

"Better than good," I said. "But tomorrow's for working. I can't get someone to cover for me like you."

"Also mornings are yours and you don't share them."

I looked at her. All of her. Sighed. "She's smart too."

"I live alone. It goes with the territory, like talking to yourself and eating on your feet."

She got off the bed and slipped on a red kimono that wasn't any longer than it had to be. In it she saw me to the door of the bedroom and went up on her toes for a kiss. I made it a quick one. I patted her silk-covered backside and grinned. "This is where we got into trouble last time."

She smiled, but it wasn't the wide monkey-smile. It was that tight one even the best ones get, that says no matter how far you go in this world or what you do, some part of you belongs to them. "Call me tomorrow?"

I sighed again. "Uh-huh." I kissed her again.

Later I picked up my jacket and tie in the living room and got the gun and holster from the window seat and strapped them on behind my right hipbone. The weight felt at home, a lot more than I did standing in that living room. For all that it was a nice room to read a morning paper in. I left with my jacket over my arm, tiptoeing like a second-story man.

12

I CAUGHT SIX HOURS' SLEEP and a shower and a shave and was looking at myself in the mirror over the sink when the front door buzzed. It was the boy from the cleaners with my good blue suit. I paid for the cleaning and tipped him and took the wire hanger off his hands. "Would I look better with my hair longer and a moustache, do you think?"

He looked at me appraisingly. He was a young Arab with smooth brown skin and a striped necktie on a plaid shirt. "Maybe," he said. "Maybe not. Where I come from they throw you in jail if you don't have a moustache by thirteen."

"Where would that be, Iran?"

"Highland Park." He showed very white teeth under his own neat black Clark Gable.

When he was gone I got out of the robe and unpinned a new pale blue dress shirt and put it on and chose a black necktie with a silver diamond pattern and put on the fresh suit. I tried a display handkerchief, looked at it in the mirror, didn't like it and took it out. I brushed my teeth and my hair and frowned at the blue shadow on the lower half of my face that no razor designed by man had been able to do anything about. A new gray hair glittered among the thick brown at my temples. Gray temples are for solid men. I figured there had been some mistake. I wiped off each shoe with a towel and used the front door. I hoped I looked good enough for a Russian writer.

The sun wasn't shining today. There was a thin silver layer of cloud overhead and the raw-iron smell of rain in the air. I threw a raincoat in the back seat for luck.

The Westin Hotel, built only a few years ago as the Detroit Plaza, pierces the sky at 740 feet surrounded by the cylindrical towers of the Renaissance Center. The city needed the hotel accommodations for conventions, so tore down a bunch of older hotels to put up this one, along with a concrete-paved festival square that is sinking into alluvial river soil and a covered sports arena with a ceiling too low for football and a leaky fountain designed by a Japanese architect, that looks like a big steel slobbering tarantula. I parked in the city lot next to the Center and rode the elevator up to Fedor Alanov's floor. There was no one in the quiet carpeted circular hallway when I alighted. Like every other hallway in every other expensive hotel in the world it felt like the anteroom to the chamber where they lay out the dead.

"Good morning, Mr. Walker. You're punctual. Please come in."

Her voice didn't sound in person the way it had sounded over the telephone. It wouldn't, any more than an art masterpiece looks the same in the gallery as it does in a magazine. I stepped inside and let her hang my hat in a closet and took a hand that was soft and cool and made for taking and pressing and then letting go. She smelled faintly of something that if it wasn't jasmine should have been.

"I'm Louise Starr, Mr. Alanov's editor. We spoke yesterday."

Here was a blonde. Her hair was brushed back behind her ears to curve out at her shoulders, but left to its own it would fall over her right eyebrow, and even in its present fettered state it threw off soft sparks in the lamplit room. The tan of her face was even enough to be her natural complexion except for the telltale white of her eyelids. Her eyes were blue, like Lake Superior is blue under a violet sky. She wore some make-up but I didn't pay much attention to it. It would be the right shade for her and she would know where to go to learn how to apply it. She had amber buttons in her ears and a cream blouse and a tailored jacket and skirt of that rich brown that is supposed to say all business and no sex, but the guy who figured that out had never met this lady. She was a few inches shorter than I, in flat-heeled maroon shoes cut low on the sides.

"Come meet the premier artist in our stable," she said.

I got my tongue unstuck from the roof of my mouth. "I thought the only thing you kept in stables wore iron shoes and blankets."

"It's just an expression. As I keep telling Mr. Alanov."

I was following her through one of those rooms that are just rooms you walk through to get to other rooms. It had a salt-and-pepper carpet and some chairs no one ever sat in along walls with paintings no one ever looked at. Louise Starr's hips switched a little in the snug tailored skirt.

We went into another room twice as large, with more of the same carpet and paintings plus some green chairs and sofas with high humped backs and long spindly legs of dark wood that gleamed. Windsor lay in muted colors outside a big window in the right wall with the Detroit River slicing steel-blue in front of it. A drink cart full of bottles and polished shakers stood next to one of the sofas, where a bearded man sat topping off a stemmed glass with deep red liquid from one of the bottles. A younger man, also bearded, turned from the window as we entered.

"Mr. Alanov, Mr. Walker," said Louise Starr.

The older man finished pouring and set the bottle back on the cart before looking up at me. He was thickset but not fat and wore his black hair shaggy and swept back without a part like windblown grass. His brows were thin for a Russian but absolutely level across eyes with lashes as long as a woman's. His nose had a deep dimple where the bridge should have been, as if someone had laid a stick across it years before, and twin bands of silver swooped down through his beard from the corners of his mouth and up toward his ears as if he'd drooled them. He had very coarse skin with pores you could stick your fingers in.

He looked at me for a moment that was as long as the walk across Mussolini's office. Then he drank some of his wine and topped off the glass again and said, "I don't like you."

I got a wolfish grin on my face and peeled the cellophane off a fresh pack of Winstons. "For a minute there I was worried we'd never break the ice," I said.

"There's no smoking in here." He turned large black eyes with no shine in them on the Starr woman. "Didn't you tell him there's no smoking in here?"

"Mr. Alanov has an allergy," she explained.

I put away the pack and looked at the younger man. He was about six feet tall and well built, with a dark mariner's beard fringing a square face. His eyes were dark and pretty and spaced evenly from his straight thick nose. They would have given him a feminine look if not for an ugly puckered jagged scar that blazed the right side of his forehead. In contrast to the older man's printed short-sleeved shirt that left his furry arms bare, this one wore a neat black suit and a red figureless tie. Louise Starr introduced him as Andrei Sigourney, Alanov's English translator. He smiled and said something polite and offered his hand. When I gave it back to him he didn't wipe it off or anything. Here was a lad with manners.

Neither he nor Alanov had a Russian accent. The writer spoke with a British inflection and Sigourney might have been from Big Sur.

At the woman's invitation I took the sofa opposite Alanov's. This one felt like a two-by-four with a handkerchief spread over it. Hotels discourage unpaid-for guests sleeping on the furniture. She took a chair and crossed her trim ankles the way no one seems to have time to teach them anymore. Her legs were tanned too, very smooth. I couldn't tell if she was wearing stockings, but she would be. Sigourney remained standing, with one hand resting on the back of Alanov's sofa.

"You're English." The writer was leveling the contents of his glass again. He never took a sip without replacing it immediately.

"A couple of greats and a grand back, on my father's side."
I swallowed. I hoped my throat sounded dry.

"Frosty people, the English. I went to Cambridge."

"I keep urging Fedor to try writing in English," the woman
put in. "Andrei's translations are excellent, but something is
always lost when a man's vision changes hands."

"Mixed metaphor," grumbled Alanov.

"Sorry."

"I will never write as well in English as I do in Russian. I
write on smoke and the wind currents change between
languages."

"Someone was telling me just yesterday that American and
Russian are very close," I said.

He frowned thoughtfully. His beard was designed for
frowning and he looked like a bear. "It's a good theory. But
it requires fluency in both idioms, and *that* requires a lifetime, or more likely two. I'd rather blame the inevitable failures on Andrei."

Sigourney smiled politely. He was a polite boy was Sigourney. I wondered what he was like away from Alanov. Whoever had given him that scar could tell me.

I uncrossed my legs and crossed them the other way.
Cleared my dry throat.

Alanov, who was pouring again, picked up on the signal
this time. He gestured with the bottle before putting it back
on the cart. "My doctor has directed me to drink wine before
and after meals. I can't tell you how many doctors I went
through before I found one that would prescribe wine. In any
case that's why I'm not offering you any."

"You have an allergy," I said.

Louise Starr changed the subject. "Mr. Walker, are you
familiar with Mr. Alanov's background?"

"Russian, isn't it?"

"Do we need this man?" demanded the writer.

"He's Russian," she said, sidestepping the whole thing
neatly. "He was famous in his own country as a poet and the
editor of its leading literary journal years before he wrote a

book titled *The Window on the Baltic,* which captured the attention of the world and resulted in his exile from the Soviet Union. It was mainly through the urging of our firm as Mr. Alanov's American publisher that the U.S. State Department offered him asylum. Which, incidentally, is the title of his forthcoming book."

"Tell him what it's about," Alanov said.

"The title, like all of Fedor Alanov's writing, is double-edged. Although fiction, the book is a sociopolitical autobiographical treatment of his defection that attempts to show the disparity between America's pose of democratic freedom and the internal prejudices that make such freedom impossible."

"Tell him the plot."

"The hero is a poet —" Belatedly she caught the sarcasm in the writer's prodding. She settled back a little, waving a slender hand wearing an amber stone in a delicate gold setting. "Well, it's poor form to discuss a work not yet finished. Let's just say that it will be an important book, as well as one that will infuriate authorities on both sides of the so-called Iron Curtain. There are people who would prefer that it not be written. Unpleasant people."

"Ours or theirs?" I asked.

"Ha!" Alanov struck his knee with a hairy paw, almost spilling his wine. "Excellent question. I'm beginning not to not like this young man so much after all."

I smiled thinly.

"We think theirs," Louise Starr said, answering my question. "Specifically, a man named Rynearson, whom we suspect of being an agent for the KGB."

"Oh," I said. "That kind of case."

"Well, we don't know that he's a foreign agent. But he runs a large shop on East Jefferson that sells goods imported from eastern Europe and does a lot of business with representatives of Communist-bloc countries and is under federal investigation for suspicion of espionage. This much we know from our contacts in Washington." She paused. "I should add that this is confidential information and shouldn't leave this room."

"Maybe we should ring down the cone of silence."

That surprised a smile out of her, liquid white teeth sliding between pink-glossed lips. "I suppose it does sound like a plot recycled from *The Man from U.N.C.L.E.* That doesn't make it any less true."

"There are a couple of things wrong with it," I said. "The book is fiction, and who cares what an exiled poet has to say about politics in a work of fiction? Also, if there were ever any danger of Mr. Alanov's writing about things better left out of the public stalls the Soviet government wouldn't have let him leave the country in the first place."

She nodded, glancing at young Sigourney, like a mother approving her daughter's choice of suitor. "That's what the people at the State Department told us when we applied to them for protection. They're too busy trying to woo Soviet scientists and engineers to our side to worry about one writer, and a writer of fiction at that. That doesn't change the fact that men in the employ of Eric Rynearson attempted to kidnap Mr. Alanov last week."

"No smoking," snapped Alanov.

"Sorry, habit." I put away the pack again. "Go on, Miss Starr."

"It's Mrs.," she corrected primly.

13

"FRIDAY NIGHTS Andrei drives Mr. Alanov to their favorite restaurant in Ypsilanti. It's the only one in the area that serves authentic Balkan cuisine."

" 'Balkan cuisine.' " Alanov poured again. "I love what this country does with language."

Louise Starr ignored the interruption. "Last Friday night, a big station wagon was parked across the end of the exit ramp off US-23 at Washtenaw Avenue in Ypsilanti. It was drawn up at an angle, as if the driver had lost control and stalled it while fighting the wheel, but its flashers weren't on and Andrei had to do some fancy driving to avoid hitting it."

"I pulled a sharp U," put in the young man, grinning shyly. "Just like we used to do it in the street in front of the high school."

"I've guaranteed Fedor a movie sale if he'll write the scene into his book." Mrs. Starr smiled.

"We'll get Burt Reynolds to play me," said Alanov.

Sigourney said, "There was something wrong about that car's being there just when we were. After we got pointed the other way I kept going the wrong way up the ramp. I sideswiped a car that had been behind us but I didn't slow down or stop. Luckily it was after rush hour and we didn't meet any more cars until we were back on the expressway and going the right direction. I pulled off at the next exit and called the police from a service station. But by the time they got there and went back to the other exit, both the station wagon and the car I had hit were gone. So far no one's come forward to report the sideswiping."

"Maybe they didn't want to make waves with their insurance company," I suggested.

"Or maybe they were working with whoever was in the other car," said the woman, "and were there to slam the back door. Tell him the rest, Andrei."

He put his other hand next to its mate on the back of Alanov's sofa. "There was lettering on the side of the station wagon that showed up in my headlamps as I swung the car in that U-turn," he said. "It was a delivery wagon belonging to Eric Rynearson's shop on Jefferson."

I said, "That was bright of him."

"Rynearson is strictly an information man." Mrs. Starr recrossed her ankles the other way. "He would make such mistakes in an active operation. Naturally he told the police that neither he nor the wagon was anywhere near Ypsilanti that night. We didn't file a complaint. Mr. Alanov hadn't seen the lettering and it was just Andrei's word against Rynearson's. The State Department was of no more help than the police."

"What makes you think he was out to snatch Mr. Alanov?" I asked.

"We're giving him the benefit of the doubt. He might just as well have meant to kill him. Chances are, though, he would want to get his hands on the *Asylum* manuscript first."

They were all looking at me. Even Alanov had sipped twice from his glass without replenishing the contents. I inclined my head toward the cart loaded with bottles. "Is that for everybody, or just Mr. Alanov's allergy?"

"Andrei, please fix Mr. Walker whatever he wants," said Mrs. Starr.

He stiffened. "I'm a writer, not a servant."

"Oh, for heaven's sake," she said.

"Thanks, I'll pour my own." I got up and walked around behind the cart and tonged some ice out of a cooler into a moderate size tumbler. There was a jug shaped like the head of a Phillips screwdriver on the cart and I transferred some of its contents into the glass along with a squirt of seltzer without bothering to look at the label. Anything in a pinch bottle was good enough for me.

I glanced at Sigourney, busy looking down at his hands on the tight green sofa fabric. They were corded and heavily calloused for someone who got most of his exercise sitting at a typewriter. "I'd have hollered too," I said.

He said, "I'm sorry. I just think I've earned better."

"You look it. What were you before you turned translator?"

"Fisherman. My family fished the Black Sea for six generations. I was eight when my parents brought me here and we settled in California. I worked as deckhand for a charter boat service in Long Beach before coming to Detroit. I guess I'm just tired of taking orders."

"I didn't mean it that way," Mrs. Starr told him. "Mr. Walker is our guest and you were the only one on his feet."

"Get that on the boat?" I indicated the mark on his forehead.

He touched it with his fingertips. "Marlin spike. I was landing a beauty when he tore loose."

"We're going to hear the fish story again," Alanov said.

Sigourney grinned and said nothing.

"It's a mess," I said, stirring the ice with a swizzle stick from a glass of them on the cart. "I don't guess that the KGB is any more efficient than the CIA, but assuming that Mr. Alanov's book is important enough to keep out of circulation it doesn't soak that they'd send an amateur like Rynearson to do it in a car with his name splattered all over the side and get out-maneuvered by someone who put in his driver training laying rubber on the way to the soda fountain."

Mrs. Starr's eyes were sapphires in the light coming through the window, gray as it was getting. "Ordinarily, no. Which is why we're convinced that Rynearson is acting alone, with civilians in his employ. He's got it in his head that stopping the publication of the book will win him points in Moscow."

"Rynearson doesn't sound Russian."

"Most KGB agents operating in this country are Americans in the pay of the U.S.S.R.," Alanov said. "Foreign accents are counterproductive. He has apparently been useful to them for some time and like the rest of us is hoping for something better in his old age."

"Hot dogs come in all nationalities." I sat down again and inhaled good whiskey. "Who pointed you at me? James Bond I'm not."

"That was Andrei's idea." Mrs. Starr smiled at him. "Since he was driving that night he spent more time with the police than anyone else. They made the recommendation."

"Not cops," I said. "Not me."

"Louise was being kind." The translator's tone was only mildly malicious. He was getting over almost being demoted to bartender. "After she flew in from New York, we got in touch with the State Department. As you know, they weren't encouraging, but after some stalling they came through with the information on Rynearson. I found out that the state police issue investigation licenses in Michigan, and since it was state troopers who answered my original complaint I went to them and asked who was best in the area. They were reluctant to recommend anyone. I had no idea there was so much hostility between the two professions."

"We fill in cracks they don't like to admit exist," I said.

"They finally gave me a list of names. I immediately eliminated all the ex-policemen — not that I have anything against them, but chances were they were just trying to throw business toward old friends. Whenever I asked for someone who could lean hard when he had to, wear a tie where it belonged, keep his tongue in his mouth, and who was not a former cop, your name came up."

I swirled my ice around. "I still don't know what it is you want me to do. Bodyguards always shoot second and my exploding Scripto is in the shop."

"My department," said Mrs. Starr. "Mr. Alanov is delivering a series of lectures at Wayne State University. He'll be in

Detroit two more weeks, and while he's within reach I doubt that Rynearson will be able to resist making another attempt on him. Fedor says he needs that much time to complete his book." She looked at him.

"I'm not leaving until it's finished." He emptied the last of the wine into his glass, shaking loose the drops. "It takes me a month to get settled into a place before I can even think about writing, and I'm just reaching my stride now. I'll not delay my work one day for a bauble merchant with Stalinesque delusions."

Mrs. Starr looked at me, raising and dropping her slim shoulders. "That being the case, and since Rynearson is an amateur and an old man who is likely susceptible to a — how shall I put it?"

"Threat," I said.

She considered it. "A warning, let's say. Given all this, my firm is prepared to engage you to deliver that warning and, if necessary, and within the bounds of ethics and legality, carry it out. We are prepared to pay you a thousand dollars for delivery, with an additional amount to be negotiated should it become necessary to follow through."

"In other words I sweat him."

She nodded.

"What part of the budget does that go under?"

"Promotional expenses, I should think. For the book. Do you accept the assignment, Mr. Walker?"

"He'll think the Kremlin fell on him." I drained my glass.

14

IT HAD STARTED TO RAIN, big drops the size of glass beads flattening out like women's breasts against the big window and melting down, streaking the cityscape of Windsor. It couldn't last. Louise Starr made out a check for a thousand plus my day rate for coming down, signed it, and handed it to me.

"This one's on my personal account," she said. "I'll put in a voucher for it later. Probably get it back by Christmas."

"Things that bad?" I folded the check and put it away in my wallet. It felt good against my heart, like a woman's head. I remembered I was supposed to call Karen.

"You only see the tip of the iceberg. Americans have more leisure time than ever before, but are they reading? They're fooling with computers and videogames and colored puzzles designed for bored executives. Until recently the line in publishing was to put out best sellers in order to subsidize more important works that didn't sell so well but added to the industry's prestige. Exxon and the other conglomerates have changed all that by gobbling up most of the good publishers. Now every book has to pay for itself and preferably be a best seller or the author and his editor go down the road muttering to themselves. They think you can sell literature like toothpaste and motor oil. So editors are afraid to touch anything not tested and won't tamper with a word written by the few good old masters left for fear of losing them to another publisher and their jobs with them. As a result, even the good writers don't write as well as they did. Yes," she said, "things are that bad."

Fedor Alanov applauded silently, fluttering the fingers of his right hand gently against the palm of the one holding his glass to keep from spilling what remained of his wine.

Mrs. Starr flushed slightly. We were standing next to the table where she had made out the check. "Of course, Fedor needn't worry. There will always be a place for his titles in our line."

"Ha!" He inhaled some of the red liquid.

"You ought to save that for the ladies' Sunday afternoon tea and book socials," I told her. "They'll lap it up."

"And I'll be out hunting for a job in a typing pool somewhere. The current line is to push this as the most literate generation ever." She made a little shuddering movement and gave me a smile I could feel in my shoes. "We're having lunch sent up. Won't you join us, Mr. Walker?"

"Thanks, I better get on this. I'll want a look at Rynearson before I make my approach. What's the address of his place on Jefferson?"

She gave me the number. I wrote it in my notebook. "When can we expect a report?" she asked.

"In a day or so. Keep an eye on Mr. Alanov meanwhile. You might hire security, but like I said, bodyguards just finish what someone else starts. Can I reach you here?"

"I have a room on the next floor down. Fourteen-oh-six."

"Just a room?"

"Suites are for Russian expatriates. I'm just the help."

I grinned and she lent me her hand. I shook Andrei Sigourney's firm one and said good-bye to Alanov, who grunted back and sipped his wine. Mrs. Starr saw me through the other room to the door and handed me my hat.

"I'm afraid you weren't my first choice," she admitted. We were out of the others' earshot.

"I hardly ever am, Mrs. Starr. I come at the end of a long line of better alternatives."

"The police offered protection, but I could see they didn't believe Andrei's story and it would be casual at best. Also Mr. Alanov has an understandable distrust of authorities."

"Is he that good, or just money in the bank?"

"He writes powerfully, if a bit mannered. It's hard to tell in translation and I don't read Russian. And yes, he's one of our biggest-selling authors. The front office has made it clear that if we lose him, the firm can get along quite well without me."

"I can't get a handle on Sigourney. Except for his name and looks he comes off about as Russian as one of the Beach Boys."

"He wrote a marvelous novel based on his experiences as a professional fisherman and sailor, but because he doesn't have a name I couldn't swing it with the editorial board. That will change. I went to the wall to get them to agree to have him translate *The Window on the Baltic* for us and Mr. Alanov was so pleased with the result that Andrei was the first person he asked to meet when he arrived in this country. They've been close ever since. He has an apartment here in town."

"I think that'd be bad all around," I said. "If you got fired, I mean. I have an idea you're a good editor."

"Thank you. But you can't know that. You haven't seen me edit."

"These days beautiful women don't get where you are unless they have something to go with their looks. The apprentice letches are all running scared."

Her eyes glittered when she crinkled them. "Well, I've seen your satin side. I don't suppose it's the one you plan to show Eric Rynearson."

I leaned against the door and tapped a Winston on the back of my left hand. "It wouldn't be Mrs. on the way back to Miss, would it? Just for future reference."

"No, I'm happily married." Her expression didn't change.

"Just asking." I straightened up and got the door open. She hadn't moved. The current from the hall drew her jasmine scent or whatever it was my way.

"Of course," she said, "we're in Detroit and my husband is in New York. The geographical situation has possibilities."

Backing out into the hall, I made a try for my right eyebrow with the tip of the unlit cigarette in my lips. She laughed and closed the door on me. Her laugh had music in it, like a climbing chord on a harp. It stayed with me all the way down to the lobby.

The rain was over by the time I made the sidewalk. There had been just enough to darken the pavement and raise the smell of concrete dust. It was cool enough to turn on the car heater to get the damp out of the seats. For all of that it was a fine day. One week you're thinking of boiling the wallpaper to get the flour from the paste and the next everyone's standing in line waiting to throw a thousand dollars at you. I looked around for a decent restaurant, but in the end I had lunch at the same diner down the street from my building. Overdue bills came off the top. I didn't care. It was spring and the world was full of beautiful women.

Before going upstairs I went back to the car and got out the raincoat. The temperature was sliding down the way it does only in Michigan in the spring when it's rained.

The office had a stuffy smell. No one was using the waiting room. My private tank had mail in it but it was the throwing-away kind. I did that and tossed my coat and hat onto the customer's chair and got the window open for a minute. Then I parked a hip on the corner of the desk and dialed the number Karen had given me for her place. There was no answer. I hung up and shut the window and sat down behind the desk and found the number of Eric Rynearson's Eastern Imports shop in the city directory. A recording came in on the second ring to tell me the place didn't open until four. The tape sounded almost as old as the man's voice.

I pegged the receiver and had my hand on it to try Karen again when it rang. It was herself.

"You didn't call."

"You didn't answer the first time," I said. "Hi."

"Hi. I'm on duty at the hospital, paying for last night. Which was worth it."

"I can get next to that." I sat back and rolled a cigarette

around in my fingers. Muted thumps and shuffles and a tiny intercom voice floated over the line from her end.

"I told Martha about Michael," she said.

"How'd she take it?"

"She didn't tear her hair or run around the room. You'd have to know her to see how hard it hit home. But she's stronger than she looks. She wants to see you."

"Tell her I'll be around to her place after they release her."

"No, she wants to see you at the hospital. Can you make it today?"

"Sure. I'm not exactly swamped."

"Ask for me at the desk."

"Maybe we can check into a room or something."

"Don't be lewd." She hung up on me, not hard.

The air outside had a wet-metal edge to it. I belted the raincoat and ground the starter a couple of times before it turned over. I took the Edsel Ford Freeway through neighborhoods like slick gray stone to Moross and parked in the St. John's lot. It was a hospital. They paint the walls in Baskin-Robbins colors now and don't wash them down with carbolic anymore, but the halls are still full of whispering rubber soles and they still boil burlap and call it breakfast.

The nurse in charge at the circular desk in the main lobby had artificially black hair skinned back and knotted behind her head and her face had an unnaturally shiny look without wrinkles. Any she might have had would have wound up in some cosmetic surgeon's scrap bucket. She used a microphone to page Karen McBride. While I was waiting I smiled at a younger nurse thumbing through cards in a long gray metal box on a shelf in front of her swivel chair. She smiled back. She had a face like a horse but it was a nice smile and she wore an engagement ring on her left hand. Both nurses had on mannish-looking uniforms of one of those pastel shades that have just about replaced hospital whites everywhere.

"Hi. Shopping around?"

I turned. I hadn't heard her coming. She looked fresh and efficient and anything but old-fashioned in her crisp whites. I thought there was a flush to her cheeks I hadn't seen before, but it could have been just the light in the lobby. Her eyes were tawny.

"For shame," I said. "You talk like a nurse in a burlesque sketch."

"The stories I could tell would curl your toes. Well, maybe not yours. Her room's two floors up; the elevator's this way."

We walked away from the two goggling nurses at the desk. She held my hand in the elevator, but aside from that she might have been taking any visitor to any room. She smelled very clean in the enclosed space. She didn't wear a cap but her hair was pinned up and the light gleamed softly on the chestnut waves. The elevator stopped on the next floor. She let go of my hand just as the doors slid open and a young doctor or intern in a white lab coat entered. They nodded at each other. We all got off at the next stop.

"That was nice last night," she said, after the young man had passed us, walking swiftly.

"We aim to please."

She smiled monkey-fashion. We walked. Banks of tall windows broke up the pastel walls at intervals, looking out on a sweep of green lawn two floors down.

She said, "Martha's out of danger, but she tires easily. You'll have to be gentle."

"I left my gun home and everything."

"What's that, your thirteen-hundred face?"

"Sometimes it slips into gear without warning. This it?" We were slowing down near a corner room. The hall took a sharp turn ten feet up and we were alone in our stretch.

"This is her room. I won't be going in. She wants to talk to you alone. I might not see you before you leave."

"Then we'll say good-bye right here." I gathered her up.

She struggled a little. "Someone might come around that corner any second."

"We'll say you were trying to resuscitate me."

"Standing up?"

"We could lie down."

"Never mind."

We kissed. When we came up I said, "I met a blonde today who makes you look like a boy."

"So go to her. Who's stopping you?"

"She'd swallow me whole. It was that kind of blonde."

"Not you."

"Thanks — I think. This guy you're sort of involved with; is he a doctor?"

"He's studying to be. He's two years younger than I am."

"Horrors. What do you do with your cane when you're necking?"

She nodded. "I guess I deserved that. I was daring you to object."

"Uh-huh."

We were still entangled. She put a hand against my chest and tilted her head back to get a better look at me. "What's that supposed to mean?"

"Just uh-huh. It's something I say when I can't think of anything to say."

"His name's Tim."

"Nice name. I don't like him."

"Nobody asked you to." She got loose and straightened her uniform. Just then a white-haired male patient in a robe and pajamas turned the corner and passed us trailing an odor of pipe smoke. We kept silent until he was out of range.

I said, "Funny how you have to hide this sort of thing."

"It's called being civilized."

She had cooled about two degrees below professional. But the flush was still there, in different light this time.

"Busy tonight?" I asked.

"Double shift, remember?"

"You get off when, four A.M.? We could have a cup of coffee."

"I need my sleep. Tim doesn't have classes tomorrow. He's taking me sailing on St. Clair."

"Uh-huh."

"Uh-huh."

We said good-bye. I watched her walk back down the hall and press the button for the elevator and wait. When the doors opened she went through them without looking back. I scratched my right ear. Then I changed faces and stepped through the open door into Martha Evancek's hospital room.

15

THE ROOM WAS SEMIPRIVATE, dim gray, and as noisy as fingers in a felt glove. Mrs. Evancek had the bed nearest the door, with a folding screen standing between it and its mate. I peeped around the edge of the screen. Vertical blinds were drawn over the room's only window and what light there was fell on a mop of dirty-gray frizz showing over a humped blanket.

"She's quite deaf, Mr. Walker. Fireworks in the room wouldn't awaken her."

I turned. Mrs. Evancek was half sitting up with two pillows bunched behind her back and a thin green cotton blanket drawn over her lap. She looked less aristocratic, more peasant-like without the veil, and some strands of her white hair were loose, but the bold nose and heavy lids were still arresting, and dramatic shadows lay in the many hollows of her face. She wore a gray flannel nightdress that tied at the neck and had long sleeves and a rufflled bodice that probably embarrassed her. Her strong rough hands were folded on the blanket.

"They tell me you had a scare." I hung my coat and hat on the edge of the open door to the bathroom.

"Very little is left that can frighten me. Please sit down."

The only chair on her side of the screen was a tricky tan vinyl number with an attached footstool that slid out when you leaned back. I didn't.

"You are good at what you do," she said. "You learned in twenty-four hours what I could not in nineteen years."

"I got lucky. My fist went through the wall in a spot where

I usually just bruise some knuckles." I paused. "I wish the news could be better."

She shifted her position on the bed and reached across to open the drawer in the nightstand. Her hand rummaged around inside for a moment and then she sat back again, breathing heavily. "They've hidden my cigarettes again."

I gave her one of mine and lit it without taking one for myself. She inhaled smoke in that odd way she had, holding it in her mouth and then seeming to swallow it, letting what was left find its way out her nostrils. She looked at me. "What is the Norton woman like?"

"A hard egg, we used to call her type. She thinks everything she does is right once she's done it and no one can change her mind. Not a bad woman. Just tough."

"Tough." She ate some more cigarette, her hand covering the lower half of her face. "It's an important word over here. I'm not sure I understand its meaning."

"You're not alone. Some cops think it has to do with getting someone in an interrogation room with badge muscle all around, and in the corner poolrooms downtown it seems to mean who has the loudest gun. You can be born tough — the kind of tough that lets you watch German bombers roaring roof-high over your backyard and not blink — or you can acquire toughness like callus from what life bounces off you, like Barbara Norton. We set a lot of store by it here ever since a small group of misfits in Boston stuck their tongues out at King George and made him like it. That's what tough is really all about, bucking the odds and coming out with all the important things you had going in. It's one of the reasons so many Americans support what another small group of misfits are up to in your country."

"That's all very democratic and inspiring, but the people who make speeches here wouldn't invite the people who are fighting there into their houses to use the bathrooms. And in most cases they'd be right not to."

"Nice people don't make revolutions," I said. "Being tough

doesn't have a lot to do with knowing which fork to use at a dinner party."

"I think you would know, or make those who do know appear superficial. And yet I think you are tough."

I said nothing. The ruby on her right hand glistened like a drop of fresh blood in the room's dimness.

"Tell me about Michael," she said.

"He had a friend, Fred Florentine, in the place where he worked. He was the one who was with Michael at the time of the accident. I spoke to him on the telephone. He said Michael was the best kind of friend to have, the kind that's there when he's needed and good to have around even when he isn't. The kind of friend I've been looking for all my life. He collected coins," I added. It seemed important. None of it was enough, for a life.

"That's comforting. But of course you only hear good about the dead. I would like to talk with this Fred."

"I have his number. It'll be in the report."

The woman on the other side of the screen stirred. There was a rustling of bedclothes and a thin old voice like a parrot's said something to someone named Caroline.

"Her daughter," Mrs. Evancek explained. "The nurse said she died in childbirth thirty years ago."

I nodded sagely.

"There is something else," she said.

Her eyes moved to the door of the room, which remained open. I got up and closed it and sat down again. She moved her head approvingly.

"It is a religious artifact, a silver crucifix trimmed with semiprecious stones. It has been in my family as long as this ring and was cast by the jeweler to the court of Sigismund Augustus in the sixteenth century. Its intrinsic value is not great. Its historical value is greater, though not enough to make the difference between a poor man and a wealthy one. I gave it to Joseph when he left Poland. He was to keep it as a family trust and not to part with it unless his life were threatened. I don't know what happened to it after his death. I would like to know now." ·

That spilled me as much as anything about the old lady had spilled me from the first. Her case had seemed complete without a holy relic. I took a deep breath and leaned back and the footstool licked out. I used it.

"Why didn't you mention this before?"

She tipped some ash into a saucer that was trying hard not to look like an ashtray on the nightstand. "It was not as important as finding Michael. There was the possibility it would be found when he was, but if not I would have been content to have my grandson returned to me. It is different now, you see. Also, the crucifix would be considered a national treasure and illegal to remove from Poland. I did not know you well enough before to trust you with the story, which might mean deportation if it reached the immigration authorities here. I feel that I know you well enough now. Also the possibility of being made to leave this country has lost its terrors."

"You want it back."

"It belongs to my family, not to the Russian puppet government in Warsaw."

"I can ask Barbara Norton. If she has it she'll want something for it."

"It isn't hers to sell," she said sharply. Then she closed her eyes and rested the back of her head on the pillows. Lying that way she reminded me of Stash Leposava.

"Do you have proof it's yours?"

"Of course not." She opened her eyes, smoked. "You may offer her five hundred dollars. In the nature of a reward."

I nodded. "She might bite, if I offer cash."

"You will do it?"

"I'll do that much. If she doesn't have it I wouldn't know where to begin looking."

"Karen has deposited the rest of the money I gave you. I have that and the five hundred dollars you returned Tuesday and a little more."

"It'll keep till you get out of here. What's the cross look like?"

"It's silver, as I said, about seven inches by three. The largest stone is a lapis lazuli, deep blue, perhaps a third of an inch across and set in the center. There are smaller red garnets set in each of the four points. The inscription on the back is in Cyrillic characters and means 'Glory and Eternity.' "

I wrote it all down and kicked the footstool back under the chair. "I'll get back to you with her answer."

"Karen is not to know anything about this," she said. "If she asks what we talked about, tell her it was about Michael."

"Sure." I got up. Her eyes followed me.

"She has it in her mind that I am an old immigrant woman with nothing to live for but her memories. I'm afraid she'll think me grasping if she hears of the crucifix. Do you?"

"You aren't paying me to think, Mrs. Evancek. But if it's grasping to want what's yours we're all just as bad as one another. She won't hear it from me."

"They say that material things mean less the nearer we get to death. I think that those who say that are very young."

She ground out her cigarette in the ashtray and lay back. She was having trouble keeping her eyes open. I told her again I'd get back to her. She might have nodded. I got my hat and coat and left. The hallway seemed bright after the gray colorlessness of that room.

There was no sign of Karen on my way out of the building.

16

BARBARA NORTON had moved some since my last visit. I could tell, because this time the door to her apartment was closed. I knocked and she barked and I opened it to find her sitting where I had left her, wearing the same gray man's workshirt, with the telephone receiver screwed to her ear and what might have been the same cigarette burning in her face. The pile of butts on the table was half again as big as before and the fluffy dust on the rug scurried in front of the stirred air like pigeons in the park.

I sat in the chair I'd occupied earlier and tipped my hat back on my head and waited while she finished talking about peeling and flaking paint. At length she rang off and flipped down her cheaters and looked at me.

I said, "I'm back."

"I noticed right away." She waited.

"It's an object I'm looking for this trip. A crucifix, more properly referred to as a cross, as this one doesn't have the figure of Jesus on it. Seven inches by three, silver, with a blue stone where the crosspieces meet and smaller red stones at the points. It belongs to Martha Evancek's family. She'd like it back."

She laughed the laugh with the dry cough in it. The cigarette bobbed in the corner of her mouth and dropped ash on the front of her shirt but she didn't brush it off. "Now it's a search for the holy grail. What's she paying?"

"Couple of hundred. Mostly sentimental value. It disappeared at the time of the shooting and it looks like it came out of the house with Michael."

"Just a couple of hundred?"

"It's not even worth that, really. Silver drops a little every time gold goes up and the stones are nothing."

"Hardly worth your coming down here, is it?"

I lit a Winston. "Family stuff."

"I wouldn't know anything about that. I never had one, exactly, though I tried to do what I could for Michael after that bastard Bob took off and Joseph, that son of a bitch —"

"I heard this. What about the cross?"

"I don't have it."

"She'll go five hundred," I said. "Tops."

"If I had it I'd sell it. I didn't let him take anything out of that house but the clothes on his back. I even made him leave his coin collection. He howled about that, but it was the right decision. He grew up normal."

Her conversation had all the fresh spontaneity of her telephone spiel. The more I heard her the better I thought of Bob Norton.

"Where would such a thing be if Michael didn't take it with him?" I wondered out loud.

"How the hell should I know? Still in the house, probably."

"Not after all this time. It'd get sold or —" I thought. The ash on my cigarette grew. I got rid of it and stood up. "Well, thanks again. I hope you sell a lot of siding. One more thing. Did you have an insurance policy on Michael?"

"Are you kidding? Who could afford the premiums?"

"Who else but an insurance company would send someone down to look into the drowning?"

"I'm sure I wouldn't know."

It was three o'clock when I got back to the office. Howard Mayk would still be on duty at Shaw College. I looked up security there and got a voice like a smashed windpipe who switched me to a call box across campus.

"Yeah?"

It was Mayk, all right. "This is Walker. Remember me?"

"Who could forget? The wife and I had a honey of a fight

that night over me not being home when she got in from work nor leaving a note. The hell with her. Find the kid?"

"More or less. He's dead. Accident."

A pause. "Jesus, I'm sorry. How'd the old lady take it?"

"Better than someone who never stacked sandbags during a shelling. I'm looking for something else now, a religious item Joseph Evancek took with him out of Poland. What's the procedure in Hamtramck when no one comes forward to claim the deceased's personal effects? Hello?"

"I was just remembering," he said quickly. "There wasn't a whole lot, just some cash and clothes and furniture and the usual house clutter. Some Church stuff, not much. Evancek's wife was Protestant. The Nortons took the cash, and our cable to Poland about the rest of the stuff never got an answer. It would of gone on the block. What kind of religious item?"

"A large silver cross. Too big to wear."

"I don't remember it. I think I would if I'd seen it."

"I didn't think you had. If the department sent an itemized list to the Evanceks in Poland it would have been on it. The reason I called, I got to thinking about the jam Evancek was in before the blowup — unemployed, drinking up what was in the bank. He might have hocked the cross for whiskey money."

"Could be."

"When I thought of that, I remembered the fence you said you and Bill Mischiewicz put in soak, the one that specialized in religious articles. This cross is one of a kind. If Joseph came to him he might remember, or know if it was in circulation at all. Is he still around?"

"He was when I left the department, but we could never get anything on him again. Now, I don't know. He'd be pretty old. Name's Woldanski, John Woldanski. He ran a shop on Trowbridge; you could check it out."

He gave me the address. I wrote it on the telephone pad and tore off the page. "Thanks, Mr. Mayk."

"Yeah."

*　　*　　*

Power shovels reared like glutting beasts against a mildewed sky, their yellow iron jaws drooling dirt and rubble and vomiting their loads into big piles. The air throbbed with engine noise and the grinding creak of mashing gears and peep-peep-peep of heavy machinery backing up. It wasn't doing much backing up. It was creeping uptown with the unstoppable inevitability of glaciers on the move. New barricades had been erected farther north that had nothing to do with strawberry festivals. The scene played like evolution in reverse; civilization had had its day and the dinosaurs were taking over, leaving only naked earth like droppings in their wake.

I made enough detours to get lost in a town I knew like my tongue knew the inside of my mouth, but came out on Trowbridge eventually and pulled up to a meter with some time left on it in front of a square brick building with a charred front and department-store windows on the ground floor. There was junk in them, porcelain lamps shaped like women's legs and dirty-faced reproductions of famous dead artists' masterworks in plaster frames and "antiques" you can buy brand new in any hardware store, here rescued from barns and garages with some of the rust knocked off and showing evidence of half-hearted attempts to clean them up. Young smartly dressed married women with credit cards in their purses would buy them for living rooms with old barn siding on the walls. Yes, this is an original panel from a two-seater outhouse that once belonged to a German pig farmer in Mecosta County. I simply stole it from this grubby little shop in Hamtramck. Don't you think it makes a lovely coffee table?

The place had a half-finished look inside, as if someone had started to clear it out for some other business and then given up and walked away from it, leaving exposed wires and junk stacked in corners and trestle tables holding up dusty glass insulators and dented silver sets and tin cigar boxes and square brown bottles of Dr. So-and-So's Horse Linament and Bunion Cure with the contents a thick hard layer of varnish in the bottoms. Someone had put a lot of time and effort into that half-finished look. You can call a ten-year-old enema tube a hookah and charge three times as much for it if the place has ratholes in the corners. One of the fluorescent tubes in the ceiling spat and flickered like a moth caught in a screen door.

The counter was another trestle table running along the right wall with a group of Philco radio shells and a fairly modern cash register standing on it and a forty-year-old black man sitting on a stool behind it, bald to his crown with scimitar-shaped sideburns and a moustache and whiskers that looked like a coal-smear around his mouth. The sleeves of his stained sweatshirt were cut off to show the lumpy muscles in his upper arms. He had a dragon tattoo on his left bicep that looked as if it had been done by a drunk with a rusty razor. Another black, younger, with an impressive natural and a long loose look under a ragged denim jacket over a black T-shirt and jeans, slouched in a sprung overstuffed chair at the end of the counter with one leg hooked over the grimy arm, watching me through the smoke of a cigarette in the corner of his mouth. He looked half asleep.

I figured he was the one to watch.

They had been talking about bikes when I came in, breaking off when I walked straight up to the counter without pausing to browse. The one with the tattoo and smear of beard looked at me the way some animals in the zoo look at the people who come to their cage, the ones the keepers are told to keep an eye on when the shift changes. I speared my lips with a weed and let my eyes wander over the place while I got a match out of its folder. The three of us were alone.

"You fellows are a ways north of Grand, aren't you?" I lit up.

"It's the land of opportunity," said Tattoo. He sat with his hands on his thighs and his head sunk between his shoulders like a fighter, looking up at me from under his brows.

I shook out the match, grinning. "Hamtramck?"

"I said it's the land of opportunity. I didn't say anybody had to like it. You're just the second customer we had in all day. Folks up here sure can hate."

"They've had four hundred years to practice. Woldanski in?"

"Woldanski who?"

So that's how we were going to play it. "I was told he owns the joint."

"The name ain't Woldanski today."

"You're the owner?"

"Cash on the barrelhead. Nothing down and no easy monthly payments."

"Cash?"

"Green on one side, gray on the other. Lots of little pictures of presidents."

"Must be nice. Being an heir."

He said nothing. I blew a plume of smoke. "Know where I might start looking for Woldanski?"

He kept on watching me from under his brows. I glanced at the lean lad in the overstuffed chair, who moved his bushy head from side to side slowly, watching me. I felt watched. The younger man fanned smoke away from his face with a narrow and oddly beautiful left hand.

Without taking his eyes off me, the other picked up a package of Pall Malls from the counter and shook one loose and got it between his lips and left it there, without lighting it or touching it. Just three boiled birds standing and sitting around with plugs in our beaks.

The seal on top of the pack was unbroken. He'd opened it on the bottom. I reached out and nudged it with a knuckle.

"Milan or Jackson? Or some slammer out of state?"

He smiled then without front teeth. "Hell, why didn't you say you was with the cops to start?"

"I'm not Nero Wolfe. If you don't want people knowing you're from the neighborhood you'd better start smoking from the right end of the pack. They only open them that way in places where if they fall out of your pocket and roll loose they start a brawl. So how about Woldanski?"

"I don't know no one named Woldanski," he said. "I'd

throw Woldanski at you if I had Woldanski so you'd get out of my face. My name is Roland DePugh. Does that sound like Woldanski?"

"I think I'm getting it. You don't know Woldanski."

The man sprawled in the chair chuckled, a low, rippling sound like a panther's purring. I looked at him.

"No Woldanski," he said sleepily. "Roland's had the paper on the place, what, two years?"

"Three come September. Bought it from the boys that own the block. Before that they rented it out, I don't know to who."

"Whom," I said.

"Huh?"

"Forget it. I've been hanging around too many writers lately. A thing like that can ruin you. Who owns the block?"

DePugh gave me the up-from-under look. "You ain't no city cop. They'd know that."

"You said I was a cop. You never heard it from me."

He punched the NO SALE button on the cash register, lifted a Colt Detective Special with a two-inch barrel out of the compartment where he kept the twenties, and clunked it down on top of the counter, keeping his hand on it. "You done wore out your honeymoon here."

"It's guns," I said. "After the first ten have been jammed in your kisser the thrill's all gone."

He thumbed back the hammer.

I said, "That's not necessary with a double-action."

"Easier on the finger, though." The man in the chair held up his thumb, studying it like an artist. "I'd go, mister. That fall Roland took was for ADW knocked down from assault with intent. Shot off a brother's left earlobe."

"Nice shooting."

"I was aiming between his eyes," said DePugh. He drummed his fingers on the revolver's cylinder.

I dropped some ash on the plank floor. It wasn't its first "Well, I'm gone. I don't need any stuffed mooseheads today.

Or whatever else you've got in the back room that the owners don't know is for sale."

"I run a legitimate business here."

"The place reeks of it." I nodded to the other man, who gave me a cat's smile back and the smallest nod that could be nodded. I left.

The investigation business has more dead ends than a magician has pockets, and as many other ways to go. From there I drove back across the line and on downtown to Lee Horst's office in one of the bank buildings, never mind which. Lee is an information broker. Whenever you need brain fodder that the Detroit Public Library can't supply — legitimate, shady, borderline, just plain illegal — you go to see Lee Horst. He specializes in information of a personal and sometimes embarrassing nature, but he's no blackmailer. He won't do business with known squeezers or reporters or cops. If he doesn't know you or your references he's polite, he gives you the glad hand and the warm smile and takes you on the grand tour that always ends with you standing alone in the hallway wondering just where and when you dropped the ball. Most of his information comes from servants and repairmen and delivery boys, the so-called invisible people who pass in and out of people's homes attracting data like lint, and who meet Lee in parking garages and shopping centers to sell what they have. He buys almost everything about almost anyone, and if you've spent any time at all in the Detroit area, chances are he has something on you. His business is by no means a rare quantity in today's fishbowl society, but he is one of its few scrupulous practitioners. He's also one of the twenty wealthiest men in the city.

The gold lettering on the frosted panel of the door to his outer office read HORST RESEARCH ASSOCIATES. That was window dressing. So far as I knew he was the entire company. A buzzer went off when I opened the door and went on buzzing until it closed behind me with a pnuematic hiss. A couple of chairs and a sofa upholstered in yellow fabric stood on a yellow carpet with yellow-painted walls all around and fresh magazines arranged in a fan on a yellow library table. Lee likes yellow. I was alone in the waiting room.

A door marked PRIVATE opened and Lee strode out, a huge soft smiling man with a lot of creamy yellow hair arranged in waves and a broad ruddy face with a dust of freckles across his cheeks and bright little eyes like shiny steel buttons with little cracks at the corners. He was sixty-eight years old then and still looked like an overgrown boy. He had on an ivory-colored suit that moved with him and a yellow silk tie on a pale yellow shirt with the collar buttoned down. The whole rig had to be built especially to his scale; he was six-seven anyway and tilted the scales at four hundred pounds. He took my hand in both of his moist warm flippers.

"Amos, Amos," he said in his high, soft, chiding voice. "I never see you anymore."

"Lower your rates and you'll see me more often. How are you, Lee?"

"Just fair. I don't know where next month's rent is coming from." He held open the door to his private office. A diamond stud the size of a horse pill winked on his shirt cuff.

I hung my hat and coat on the hall tree and made myself comfortable in a chair covered with yellow leather. It was a corner office, with windows in two walls opening on the brown skyscrapers and jammed streets of downtown Detroit. The automobile horns blatting six stories down sounded remote, like Canadian honkers flying high overhead. Lee walked around behind his big bare-topped desk and lowered himself into a swivel chair with a tall winged back that was big enough for two men, but it was just big enough for him. The superstructure creaked but it held.

"I need the address of a man named John Woldanski," I said. "He used to run a shop on Trowbridge in Hamtramck, where he fenced valuable religious objects until a few years ago. Two cops named Mayk and Mischiewicz there busted him a long time ago and he went to Jackson for a hard stretch.

He's not listed in Hamtramck or Detroit or any of the suburbs. I don't know that he's still in the area, or even if he's
still alive."

He confirmed the spelling, then turned in his chair and
slipped a vinyl cover off a screen and keyboard on a stand
where a typewriter would be ordinarily.

I said, "Not you, too."

He made a wry face. "It saves time. But I'm still paying rent
on a warehouse full of files in case a stray bolt of lightning
knocks out this bastard's memory."

"That happens?"

"So the guy that installed it told me. Also power failures
and nylon undershorts and a good stiff sneeze."

He turned it on. It didn't make any more noise than it had
when it was off. I got bored watching him click keys and lit a
cigarette. I hoped that wouldn't bother its memory. After a
while he sat back and gave me an address on Denton in Hamtramck and an unlisted telephone number.

I wrote them down. "When I was a kid only rich people
weren't listed."

"It's the telephone solicitors," he said. "Why look for other
salesmen's marks on picket fences when you can just stab a
finger and dial?"

"People don't want to have to buy plastic siding. What's the
damage, Lee?"

"For you, seventy-five."

I jumped a little. "Dollars?"

"No, Cadillacs. Of course dollars."

"Just for tapping a few keys?"

"I have to pay for the machine. Listen, you're getting a
break on account of we're old friends."

"Buy yourself some enemies." I slid four twenties out of my
wallet and pushed them across his desk. He gave me a five
from the metal cash box in the top drawer and wrote out a
receipt. I put it in the space vacated by the twenties.

"Stay and talk?"

"Not at these prices." I got up and reached for my hat.

He patted the computer console's sky-blue hull, not unlovingly. "You know, if I were you I'd worry about one of these things turning me into a buggy whip."

"Until they start making that shell out of solid bone, no way."

I said good-bye and drove back to Hamtramck. It was the paddle, I was the ball, and the elastic string between us wasn't an inch longer than it had to be.

17

THE HOUSE WASN'T TEN years old, a low brick ranch job with a green slate roof and one of those big picture windows in front that you have to buy eight hundred-dollar drapes for unless you want the neighbors to know what you look like in your Jockey shorts. It had been built so close to the bigger older frame house next door that you could skin your nose trying to squeeze between them. Both lawns needed mowing. They would continue to need it until the dozers trundled in and tore them up.

It would be a quiet street normally, but the quiet now was of desertion. There were no other cars in sight when I parked on the street. No curtains moved in any of the windows as I went up the walk to John Woldanski's front door. I felt like the gunslinger in the story who rides into the ghost town only to be shot down by the shades of the men he's killed. Even the doorbell made that unmistakable hollow sound of chimes ringing in an empty house.

When no one answered five minutes after my second ring I tried the door, shielding the movement with my body. It was locked. The door was tight to the frame and anyway it was a dead bolt lock. I walked around to the back.

A spreading oak as old as the Crusades took up most of the tiny backyard with a weathered redwood fence around its huge trunk. A white picket fence in need of painting separated the yard from the backyard of the house facing the next street over, which had no windows on this side, and a garage stood between me and the place on the opposite side of Woldanski's from the too-close frame building. I seemed to be the only thing stirring in the neighborhood.

I opened the screen door to the enclosed back porch and walked across a fairly new concrete slab with a rubber mat on it and looked at another dead bolt lock on the back door. Just for fun I tried this knob too. It turned and the door opened.

I didn't like anything about it.

I left the door standing partly open and went through the porch again and back around to my car and got my spare gun out of the special compartment under the dash. It was a Luger without a history or papers and if I was caught with it, it was worth a stiff fine or a jail sentence or both from a judge who probably had an unlicensed firearm of his own strapped on under his robes. But my legal piece was still at home and you get a thing about empty houses once your head's been bounced off the floors of enough of them. So I was strolling back around to the porch with nine millimeters of German automatic in my hip pocket when the screen door hit me in the face.

Somebody's shoulder was behind it. Lights flashed. I pivoted on my left foot to catch my balance and grabbed for the wall of the porch with both hands and missed. I went down on one knee, scuffing my shoulder against the wall. By the time I scrambled up and clawed the gun out, my screen door man had hurdled the back fence. I glimpsed movement between the houses facing the next street, did some hurdling of my own, waltzed with a young maple that leaped in front of me without warning, and cleared a four-foot passage between houses in time to see a taillight flicking around the corner. I heard the engine hesitate, then take off shrilly.

Somewhere a dog started barking. I realized I was standing on a public sidewalk holding an unregistered Luger. Well, officer, there was this screen door. I put the gun away and trespassed my way back to Woldanski's house. The dog went on barking, but no doors slammed and no one called for me to identify myself.

The screen door's aluminum frame was bent but I hadn't left any of my face on the wire mesh. I picked up my hat and put back some of its shape and determined that my nose wasn't broken or bleeding and went inside when I couldn't think of anything else to keep me out. I had an idea what I'd find. I hoped I was wrong.

John Woldanski had done well for himself in the religious art business. The kitchen was stainless steel and the living room, two steps down at the end of a paneled hallway, was large and airy and full of crushed brown leather and cherrywood rubbed to a deep red glow like coals in a hearth. There was a circular fireplace with a funnel-shaped chimney in the center of the room and the walls were hung with Spanish oils depicting holy subjects, the faces angry and tormented, the brush-strokes slashes of bold color as in a bullfight poster. They were good originals, not the junk that converted Catholics and born agains hang all over like a gangster stocks his gallery, buying painted canvas by the yard and marble statues in case lots.

The bedroom off the hall was quiet, the walls pastel blue and the bed made. The top of the bureau was littered with coins and combs and brushes with white hairs caught in the bristles, man-clutter. A brown leather wallet containing a Social Security card, two credit cards, and sixty-three dollars in cash. No driver's license. A five-by-seven color photograph in a gold frame of a neat little man with white hair combed straight across a pink scalp, a large nose, and a small white moustache, holding hands with a plump pink woman with blue hair and glasses in octagonal frames. Three suits in three shades of gray hung in the closet. Two pairs of black brogues on the closet floor, a brushed felt hat on the top shelf. I didn't open any drawers. I didn't think Woldanski was that short.

The bathroom was burnt orange and chocolate. I stuck a foot inside and slid the plastic shower curtain open on its rings. There was a puddle of water on the brown tile floor, nothing else. I went looking for other rooms. There were no other rooms. It was a split-level house built on concrete without a basement or second story.

I stood next to the fireplace scratching my ear. When I got tired of that I went back through the kitchen and let myself out the back door.

The rear of the bigger house next door extended fifteen feet behind the ranch style. The buildings were so close they might have been part of the same lot. It had a back entrance close to the near corner. I smoothed a finger along the brim of my hat and stepped up to the door and rapped on the frame.

No one answered. The door was locked, but it was an ordinary spring lock and the place had been broken into recently or otherwise had the glass pane in the door broken and replaced with a square of plywood tacked on from inside. I pushed at it with the palm of my hand. The tacks gave. I pushed a little harder and reached between the plywood and the window frame and found the turning latch and turned it and set the button with my thumb. I opened the door and went inside.

There was only one window in the kitchen, a small one in the north wall with a checked dishtowel tacked over it, leaving the room in gray gloom. I tried the switch on the wall next to the door but no lights came on. The linoleum was badly scuffed, and when I stepped forward my toe kicked a loose tile and it slid a few inches. There were a bare table and some chairs and an unplugged refrigerator with a sofa cushion propping its door open from inside to keep it from growing mold while it thawed. I put a hand inside and touched the inner wall. It was cool but not cold and dry as the inside of a refrigerator that's been turned off for a while.

The dining room contained another table and chairs and a china cabinet with bric-a-brac behind dusty glass. There was a telephone stand but no telephone and a square hole in the wall over the baseboard where the box had been removed. After that came a living room with a worn rug and sheets thrown over the furniture. Just for the hell of it I lifted the sheets and looked underneath. I found the sofa that belonged to the cushion in the refrigerator. Another door opened on a steep bare staircase leading up to two empty bedrooms and a bathroom growing chalky mold in the bottom of the tub. I tried a faucet. It sucked air with a wheezing noise like an old man in an oxygen tent. I turned it off and went back downstairs.

The kitchen had another, narrower door in the wall next to the sink, held shut by a small bolt. I slid it back. Household tools on the wall over a landing and warped wooden stairs going down into blackness. I struck a match and started down, testing each step with a toe before trusting my weight to it. Nine steps down the glow of the tiny flame touched the scuffed sole of a man's slipper.

I blew out the match, which was burning down close to my fingers, struck another, and folding back the cover on the matchbook, set fire to the others. They flared bright white and burned down to yellow. The slipper was attached to a foot in a ribbed brown sock and beyond that was a patch of pale hairless skin and then a dark pantsleg and another leg bent under that and a ring of white shirt and a dark blue sweater with a roll collar and a head of white hair lying on its side on an earthen floor. One eye glistened in the wavering light, bright as a wet marble and seeing just as much.

He was sprawled head down over the bottom five steps with the upper third of his body on the hardpack dirt floor of the basement. Bracing my back against the cut stone of the building's foundation and holding the burning matchbook out like a torch, I stepped over him to the base of the stairs and bent down to feel the big artery on the side of his neck. He wasn't using it today. But his flesh was still warm and the scalp showing through the parted strands of his hair was as pink as in his picture on the bureau in the bedroom of the house next door.

I dropped the matchbook and stamped out the flame.

There was a little light in the basement itself, sliding gray as a toad's belly through the thick dirty glass of a rectangular window high in the stone foundation wall on the far end of the house. It was only a half-cellar, just big enough for an aging oil furnace like a steel octopus whose overhead duct-tentacles wouldn't let me stand up straight and some stored junk in dusty cartons and more objects under sheets. I nudged my hat to the back of my head and sat down on a carton full of old *National Geographics* and walked a Winston back and forth across the back of my right hand and tried to catch the dead man's eye.

"Mr. Woldanski, what are you doing lying with a broken neck in the basement of a house not your own?"

He didn't answer. He wouldn't even meet my gaze. His small neat white moustache looked as artificial as wax fruit. I stuck the cigarette in the corner of my mouth, patted my pockets for matches, then remembered and let it droop. I thought. I thought about an old woman whose grandson turns out to be dead just about the time she starts looking for him and I thought about an old man who may or may not know what became of a silver cross the old woman would like returned, and who gets dead just about the time someone makes up his mind to ask him about it. I thought about people who hit screen doors with other people's faces and don't stop to apologize. Mostly I just sat there sucking on a cold filter tip, thinking that I saw more stiffs in my work than a mortician who gives green stamps.

I had enough of that finally and got up and walked around the tiny basement. I lifted a corner of one of the dusty sheets, braced myself for rats, and tugged it free. I looked at a gold candelabra with nine curved branches and a Star of David on top and at some painted plaster saints with gilt flaking off the hems of their gowns and a stack of painted icons in frames like those I had seen in Stash Leposava's house, here standing on a rough shop table with a broken leg. I raised another sheet covering a pile of gold votive candlesticks and tiny silver crucifixes with chains attached. There was more of the same under the other sheets, paintings and carvings and ornaments in a holy motif. There were even a few glittering crescents and related Islamic items, although not many; their local market value wouldn't be as great. No big silver crosses with blue and red stones and Cyrillic lettering on the back.

It all had the look of money and lots of it. John Woldanski might not have died of old age, but he had died rich. I replaced all the sheets.

After a while I stepped over the body again and went upstairs and out and used the telephone in the house next door to order some law.

18

TWO DETECTIVES named Kowalski and Stamenoff got the squeal.

Stamenoff wasn't as big as Toronto. He was six feet three inches of hard fat in a brown suit and wide necktie with a hula girl painted on it, heavy lids and puffy lips in a flat face with blue jowls. He never spoke where I could hear him. Kowalski was as far from him as they come, a slim loose redhead with Grecian curls, blue eyes without brows, and a rubber mouth smiling in a long square jaw like a brake pedal. His suit was just a suit. The little basement got very crowded with them and me and the body on the stairs and the uniforms who had come in answer to my call. I doubted that there had been that many people in it since it was dug.

When Kowalski was through with the uniforms he came over to where I was standing next to the sheet-covered items and took my hand in a small hot paw. "Rental heat, huh? You dress like it."

I glanced down at my raincoat. "It's that kind of day."

Stamenoff got a pad out of his hip pocket and found a pencil and we got started. It didn't take too long to tell with Martha Evancek left out. I didn't touch on the search for Michael.

"This cross — valuable, is it?" Kowalski asked.

"Depends on what you call valuable," I said. "Melted down it wouldn't bring much, but a museum might pop for it if you caught them on a slow day. My client is offering five hundred dollars for its return."

"Not exactly worth trashing a guy."

"These days they knock you over for what's in your teeth. But they don't usually get cute for five yards, get an old man out of the house he lives in and shove him down the stairs of the place next door so it looks like an accident."

"Maybe it was an accident," Kowalski said. "Maybe you just surprised some of our local talent cleaning out Woldanski's place. We got looters coming in from the suburbs since they started tacking city paper to front doors in this neighborhood."

"Too much coincidence. Also his house is as neat as a bicycle clip and there's cash in his wallet on the bureau. It plays like the killer walked him in here and did the job and then went back to carve away everything that didn't fit the frame. Could be the job got done over there and the killer dragged the body here to make it look like he took a tumble coming to inspect his loot. But that's a lot of trouble to go to and there was a bare chance he'd be seen, even in a neighborhood as empty as this."

"You missed the license number?"

"I missed the car. I'd know its taillight anywhere." I thought. "It had a standard transmission. I heard the gears change."

"Swell. You get that, Dan? It was a stick."

Stamenoff nodded without glancing up from his pad or speaking.

"He didn't step on my face or you could have taken an impression of his foot off my forehead."

"It's a thought. The doors to both houses were open when you got to them?"

"More or less."

"More or less means what?"

"More or less means more or less," I said. "You're shouting down the wrong hole there. Everybody who could sign a B-and-E beef against me is spilled over those steps."

"We don't know yet that Woldanski owns this place."

"I didn't, until I saw what's under those sheets."

Kowalski looked hard at Stamenoff, who stopped writing and lifted the one covering the pile of candlesticks and crucifixes. Kowalski whistled.

I said, "Woldanski was a fence specializing in religious articles. You'll have a file on him downtown. It looks like when he retired out of his shop on Trowbridge he moved his inventory here. There isn't a lot of room for it in the house next door."

"I don't like that I don't know who you're working for," said Kowalski. "I don't like that more than I don't like anything else about this one."

"I'm in a confidential line of work. Like you. You don't give up your snitches without a fight."

"Yeah, and any night magistrate with a hard-on against cops can clink me for not sending mine over in open court. That works with doctors and lawyers and priests but you're not any of those."

I shrugged.

Kowalski scratched his long jaw. "Feed it to me again. What made you think of Woldanski?"

I fed it to him twice more. The second time was to see what holes showed. The third was just to remind me who was cop and who was suspect. In most murders the guy who calls the law is the guy who did it. It would be a statistic a cop like Kowalski would know and being a cop he would run with the statistics. He was back to asking the questions he'd asked the first time when the medical examiner came downstairs, followed by the fingerprint man and the photographer, as if they'd all arrived in the same car. We were jammed up against the walls now and Kowalski decided to adjourn to headquarters. He'd never looked at the body except to avoid tripping over it when he came in. Some of them don't, and solve those cases that can be solved just as quickly as the boys who peer under the deceased's fingernails and vacuum his pockets.

"You're driving what?" Kowalski asked.

"Silver-gray Olds Omega," I said. "It's parked out front."

"Keys."

I hesitated, then took the ring out of my pocket and dropped it into his palm. He handed it to one of the uniforms and told him to follow us in my car. "You don't want to leave it on this street after dark," he said.

I said that sounded all right. I hoped the uniform wouldn't find the Luger under the dash. Outside, Kowalski and I climbed into the back of a brown Pontiac and Stamenoff wedged himself under the wheel and we took off gently, no sirens or squealing tires. Real cops are dull.

Being a lieutenant, Kowalski had his own office in the detective bureau. It was a tight little room with a desk mounded over with file folders and pipe-smoking paraphernalia, a coffee maker on a yellow oak table, a three-drawer file cabinet, and cork walls tacked all over with curling color Polaroid shots of charred corpses in mangled cars with all the paint burned off and pieces of bodies caught in the limbs of trees. They reminded me a little of the death's-head pictures of Martha Evancek's late husband Michael in the back of her photo album. They were two of a kind, were Mrs. Evancek and Lieutenant Kowalski. He left me alone with Stamenoff while he went out to brief his detail. Stamenoff said nothing and stood at the window looking out into the squad room with his hands in his pants pockets jingling his keys and change. I found a pipe lighter on the desk and set fire to a cigarette. I finished that, lit another, and was looking at the pictures on the wall for the fifth or sixth time when the lieutenant returned.

"I took those when I was with County," he said, picking up a black blob of bulldog pipe from the desk and opening and closing drawers. "These city cops go out on shootings and stabbings and they think they see it all. You haven't until you've sponged a sixteen-year-old kid's face off the tree he's wrapped his little bomb around doing ninety-five on an icy curve with twelve beers under his belt."

"What's the gallery supposed to do, make men out of 'em?"

"No, that's strictly for the punks we pull in on Open Intox. Pictures don't work with police officers. The blood never comes out the right color, for one thing, and it's just not the same as when you're standing there in the middle of all that gasoline stink listening to some road patrol rookie tossing his crackers. Grabowska wants a piece of this one," he told Stamenoff.

The other detective grunted and went on jingling his keys and change.

The juxtaposition threw me until I remembered what Howard Mayk had said about his arrival at the Evancek house nineteen years before. I must have smiled, because Kowalski said, "You know the skipper?"

"Just by reputation. I hear he's got a glass stomach."

"I wouldn't give a nickel for a cop that didn't lose at least one meal on the job. But there's a limit. They called him Kid Puke around here until his last promotion." He gave up looking in the drawers finally and turned the scuffed brown leather pouch on his desk inside-out to fill his pipe. Then he flipped away the empty pouch and tamped down the tobacco with a stained thumb and started the complicated business of getting it burning. I've always admired pipe-smokers for their patience, but that's about all. At length he tossed the lighter back onto the desk and looked at me, puffing up thick gray clouds.

"Your story starts in the middle and quits before the end," he said. "I still don't know how you knew to look for Woldanski."

"I've got a place just west of the city. You hear things."

"I lived here all my life. I never heard of Woldanski."

"Is that my fault?"

We stared at each other. I didn't blame him; it sounded funny without Howard Mayk. But Mayk knew I was working for Martha Evancek.

We were still staring when the captain came in without knocking. He was younger than expected, about forty, with hair the color of wet sand, worn just long enough to cover the tops of his ears, and tan eyes with a curious dead kindness in them and a neat soft moustache that drooped a little over the corners of his mouth. He wore a sharp buff-colored suit that went with his eyes and hair and a red tie with a knot the size of a softball. He didn't look at me until Kowalski introduced us, and then he might have been looking at a door. He didn't offer to shake hands. "What've we got on the house?" he asked Kowalski.

"Fine, thanks," I said. "And you?"

He looked at me again, differently. His lips were stuck in a perpetual pucker, as if he were always getting set to say something. "You don't talk until I talk to you," he said.

"Then do I get a biscuit?"

"I've got a man in the clerk's office going through the plats," Kowalski put in quickly, slapping me down with his eyes. "Woldanski looks to have had the run of the place if it wasn't his."

"So I heard. Get someone from Robbery in here."

Kowalski glanced at Stamenoff, who left the office.

"When the M.E. gets through putzing around he'll say Woldanski left us on account of a broken neck," said the lieutenant. "He could have fallen, but it wasn't all that far to fall and he almost had to be pushed to hit that hard. Walker might have surprised the guy that did it coming out of the old man's house after either frisking the place or making everything look kosher. He didn't get a good look at him. I've got uniforms turning the neighborhood for an eyeball, but the pickings are plenty lean."

"Not lean enough," Grabowska said. "The old man should have cleared out as soon as the property was condemned. We can't protect them if they won't obey the law."

I said, "He had until the end of the month. You owed him protection till then."

He turned his mild dead eyes on me again and pursed his

lips. "Communist, huh? You stand four-square against progress and finding jobs for people?"

"If it means turning other people out of homes they took jobs to pay for in the first place."

"My kid sister's husband's out of work, Zorro. They're living with his folks because he can't afford any kind of house."

"Why don't you give him a job here?"

"You don't just walk into police work. It takes a special breed."

"Also a strong stomach," I said.

He spun on Kowalski. "Anyone laugh?"

"Not me, skipper."

Grabowska turned back, smoothed his moustache. "Who's your client, Hot Wit?"

I smoked. He rubbed his hands.

"Withholding, is it? Maybe some time in soak will take the starch out."

"I've been in jail, Captain," I said. "I didn't like it, but I was there long enough to find out you don't die of it, and I'll be out on a writ days before I feel like rattling my head against the bars to hear music."

"Oh, tough guy. We see a lot of that. They come in that door hard as boiler plate but they don't go out that way. They slink out like the yellow rats they are."

I had to grin. "I saw this one," I said. "Bugs ties a knot in Elmer's shotgun in the end and he blows his face off."

Kowalski snorted. Grabowska looked at him quickly. The lieutenant coughed and took his pipe out of his mouth and made a face and waved smoke from in front of it.

Stamenoff returned then, with someone I recognized. It was a tall, slender black man, loose-jointed like Kowalski, in patched and faded denims and a black T-shirt. He had his officer's ID pinned to the front of his ragged jacket, but I knew the big Afro and the way his cold cigarette dribbled from one corner of his mouth. He was one of the two men I had spoken with in John Woldanski's old shop on Trowbridge. He looked at me sleepily, without showing surprise.

I said, "What's the matter, they don't pay you enough here?"

The corner without a cigarette in it turned up slightly.

Grabowska looked from one of us to the other. "You met?"

"He was in DePugh's place asking about Woldanski," the black cop said. "I've been moled in there three weeks."

"Oh yeah, fence detail. How's it look?" Grabowska squinted at the ID. "Foster, is it?"

"Forster, sir. It looks sweet. I rang up a thousand in hot tape decks once when DePugh was busy out front hassling a meter maid."

Kowalski said, "Brother, are we in the wrong business."

Forster lifted the free corner again. The captain asked him if he knew Woldanski.

"Not to talk to. But when I was getting ready to go under I saw his name a lot on old reports. I never heard of him when DePugh was looking," he told me.

"Never mind that," Grabowska snapped. "You know he got spliffed today."

"The sergeant said." He tilted his bushy head toward Stamenoff.

"DePugh say anything about Woldanski after Walker left?"

"No, sir."

I said, "His flesh was still warm when I found him. He couldn't have been dead more than half an hour. What was DePugh doing around four-thirty?"

"Counting his money, maybe. It was a slow day. He closed up at four and I came here."

"Maybe you'd better talk to DePugh," I told Kowalski.

"What a sleuth. I never would've thought of it." He ground his teeth on the pipe-stem.

Grabowska puckered. "These monkeys don't retire. Could be they were laying some things off through each other that were smoking too much for one man's mitts. DePugh got rattled when a guy came around asking about Woldanski like a detective and powdered him to keep him from squawking."

"Except he's not the get-rattled type," Forster said.

"Everyone is, if you shake hard enough." The captain looked at me. "Who else knew you were looking for the old man?"

"Lee Horst. You know him, maybe."

"Horst?"

"Answer man," said Kowalski. "We kept stubbing our toes on him at County. You want it, he knows it, for a fee. Unless you're on the square. Then he's dumb as a baseball bat."

I shook my head, killing my stub in a copper ashtray full of glistening black plugs from his bulldog. "He's square. Maybe not all his customers are, but he's in a legitimate business or Detroit Metro would have turned the key on him ten years ago."

"For a guy who wouldn't tip over his client, you sure gave *him* up without a struggle," Grabowska said.

Kowalski said, "Horst is a wall. Throwing cops at him is like whacking tennis balls off a board fence. Lend me the riot detail and half of nightside, give us two days, and maybe he'll tell us his telephone number, that being listed. He's bigger than Stamenoff. No one's bigger than Stamenoff."

The mountainous cop grunted.

A telephone rang. Kowalski swept a dozen file folders off the instrument and barked his name into the mouthpiece. He listened for several moments, then said "Okay" and hung up. He turned to Grabowska.

"That was Wasylyk from the clerk's office. The empty house was Woldanski's. He built the new one eight years ago and moved into it after his wife died. Wasylyk called the morgue at the *Free Press* for that part."

The captain rubbed his hands in that way he had. "Okay, run with it. Crank DePugh in here and run a check on that stuff in Woldanski's basement, see is any of it on the hot sheet. Foster here will help with that —"

"Forster, sir," the black cop corrected. "And, sir, I don't

think we should lean on DePugh just yet. It'd blow three weeks under cover."

"Homicide takes front seat," Kowalski reminded him. "Sorry."

"Yes, sir."

The captain looked at me, and I was a door again. "You get this scroat's statement?" he asked Kowalski.

"Not yet."

"Get it and get him out of my building. Don't think we're cutting you loose, keyholer. You're still our Number One if we crap out on DePugh. And whichever way it winds up hanging, I'll remember you."

"I'm flattered. Who'd you say you were again?"

"Keep it up. I don't want to take the slightest chance of ever liking you." He left.

Kowalski made another face and knocked out his pipe into the ashtray. "Damn generous of Captain Cookies to show us how to conduct a homicide investigation. You married, Walker?"

"Not lately."

"Kids?"

I shook my head.

"Don't have any," he advised. "Sooner or later every married man with kids gets the Grabowska he deserves. Okay, Forster, thanks for coming in. Sorry about the stakeout."

"I'm used to it, Lieutenant." He opened the door.

I said, "Funny, you don't look Polish."

He smiled the tired crooked smile without disturbing the cigarette in his mouth. "That's good," he said. "That's the first time I heard that one today." He went out.

Stamenoff jingled his keys and change and grunted.

19

IT WAS DARK when I got my car out of the police parking
lot. The Luger was still there. I drove straight home without
thinking about Eric Rynearson's shop on Jefferson. His telephone recording had said he closed at seven, and anyway I
didn't feel like leaning on anything harder than a mattress,
not even for someone like Louise Starr. I bought myself a
drink in the kitchen while my supper was heating up, and I
bought myself another afterwards while listening to one of
the hourly news reports on the radio for a mention of the
murder in Hamtramck. There was none. There probably
wouldn't be, unless the cops tipped the press about the merchandise in the basement. You have to dress up murder these
days if you want air time. I bought a few more and then went
to bed, expecting to lie awake a while. I didn't. I didn't even
dream. I slept as deeply as I ever do, but it wasn't the sleep of
the dead. No sleep ever is.

I woke up with something heavy and hairy sitting on my
face clanging a bell next to my ear. The noise continued
while I got the thing's sharp feet off my eyelids, but the thing
crawled to the top of my head, balancing there with its claws
sunk in my scalp. One of its hot smelly paws had been inside
my mouth and all over my tongue. It went on clanging the
bell. It was trying to pretend it was the telephone ringing in
the living room, but I knew better. Its weight was dragging
the skin tight over the bones of my face and making my eyes
start.

I stuck my feet inside slippers and fumbled into my robe

on the way out of the bedroom. The bell rang and rang. I leaned my forehead against my great-grandmother's clock. 4:01. I got the telephone receiver in both hands finally and the silence when I lifted it was so sudden and sharp it hurt as much as the noise. My hairy thing snickered in my left ear.

"Amos? Hello?"

My demon reacted to the voice as if someone had waved a crucifix in its flat ugly face. A silver cross. It leaped off my head and scampered into whatever dark corner its kind lives in, leaving only dull pain and a faint stench of brimstone behind. I hoped it hadn't laid any eggs.

"Second." I rested the receiver on the little table next to my only easy chair and went back into the bedroom. When I came out and sat down and picked it up again the voice said:

"You just lit a cigarette, didn't you?"

"No." I blew smoke.

"Uh-huh."

"Am I awake at this hour for a message from the American Lung Association?"

"I earned that," Karen said, after a beat. "Sometimes my work gets in the way of the rest of me. You know what that's like."

"I've heard stories."

"You sound hung over."

"It's the connection. A lot of people think that when they call me at four A.M."

"Amos, are you all right?"

"Yeah."

"That's good." She sounded unconvinced. "I wouldn't want you not to be."

I let smoke trickle noiselessly out my nostrils and said nothing.

She said, "I'm sorry about this afternoon. Yesterday afternoon, that is. I guess you got to me with that crack about the gorgeous blonde more than I wanted to admit. I'm sure it's true, but no woman likes to be reminded there are prettier women."

"I thought maybe it was because you didn't want to talk about Young Dr. Kildare. Tim."

"That wasn't it. Why do you keep bringing him up?" She paused. It was very quiet on her end. "Listen, my shift just finished. I'm sort of on overdrive and I know I won't be able to sleep. Is it too late to come over and unwind?"

"I thought you were going sailing tomorrow. Today."

"Tim cancelled. He's studying for an exam."

"It's quite a hike over here. Why don't we meet at your place?"

"No, I'm too keyed up for home. Besides, I'm the one who got you out of bed. According to Emily Post that carries certain responsibilities."

"I'll dig out the tea cozy." I gave her directions and we spent a couple of minutes saying good-bye.

After hanging up I sat there and finished my cigarette. Then I went into the bathroom and stripped and stood for five minutes under a shower of icicles. I shaved, admiring the pinkish cast in the whites of my eyes. I made the bed and broke a fresh shirt out of the bureau and put it on with the pants to the blue suit. I finished dressing, went into the kitchen, plugged in the coffee maker, and washed the supper dishes I'd left in the sink, then got the carpet sweeper and went over the rug in the living room. I dumped ashtrays and dusted. By that time the coffee was ready. I had time for two cups and another cigarette and then the door buzzer sounded.

"You are hung over," she said.

She was still wearing her white nurse's uniform under a brown leather car coat that glistened wetly in the light from the lamp behind me, but she had undone her hair, which glowed softly reddish, like a good painting in the right illumination. Her face was roses and milk. Looking at her, I took in some air and let it out.

She put her arms around my neck and we kissed. I drew

her inside and kicked the door shut, setting the lock with my elbow. When we came unstuck she said, "You've done this before."

I made the diplomatic response and helped her out of her coat.

I hung it in the closet and we walked into the living room with an arm around each other's waist like school kids in the hall by the lockers. She looked around. "You're a pretty good housekeeper. I thought bachelors always had empty beer cans lying around and socks that needed darning."

"That's one stereotype. The other is a gourmet cook with a different kind of hanger for everything he wears and one of those dimmer switches on the wall."

"Which one are you?"

"When my socks get holes in them I throw them out and buy new ones. But only if the holes show outside my shoes. And when my lights get dim I know I forgot to send Detroit Edison a check that month." I sat her down in the sofa. "Coffee? No powdered creamer, sorry. You'll have to take milk."

"In that case I'll have a drink."

"Scotch okay?"

"With water."

I went into the kitchen and splashed water into a pair of small barrel glasses and colored it with Hiram Walker's. When I carried them into the living room she was standing by my cheap stereo, leafing idly through the record albums in the open cabinet.

"You have an interesting collection. I've never heard of some of these singers."

"Some of them have been dead longer than you've been alive."

"Could I hear one?"

"Take your pick."

She did some more leafing, slid one out and studied the picture on the cover. "She's pretty. Such a delicate profile. I think someone must have hurt her."

It was Helen Morgan. I said, "What makes it she was hurt?"

"She just has that crushed-petal look. This one, I think." She tapped the cover.

"Go ahead. That spike goes through the hole there in the middle."

"Thanks," she said dryly. She slid the record out of the inner sleeve and spindled it and found the ON switch. The Morgan started warbling.

"Plaintive." She accepted the glass I held out.

I lifted mine. "Voices from the grave."

"Voices."

We drank. She moved toward the sofa again, swaying a little to the music, hugging herself with the glass in one hand. I watched her with frankly carnal interest. She sat down and crossed her smooth legs. Louise Starr got the same effect by just crossing her ankles. But there are times when you want rich chocolate and there are times when nothing but sharp peppermint will do.

She looked at me for a while, and then she said, "What did you and Martha talk about today? Yesterday, damn it."

"Michael."

"That's all?"

"Mostly. Some other stuff, about who's tough and who's not and what makes them one or the other. Why?"

"I don't know. She seemed — furtive when I visited her later. She was quite willing to talk about anything but your visit. Whenever the subject came up she changed it. I thought maybe —" She shrugged and nibbled at her drink.

"Maybe what?"

Her gaze got direct. "Amos, did you talk her into hiring you again to investigate Michael's death?"

"I don't try to talk people into things. I'm generally too busy trying to talk my way out of this or that. Trying to persuade Mrs. Evancek to do something she didn't want to is not my idea of time spent constructively."

"You're right. I'm sorry. I should know better. It's just —"

"That they can be such children at that age."

"Well, yes" — she put starch in her glare — "they can. You don't spend as much time with them as I do, you don't know the games they play, their simple and touching deviousness."

"I've worked with them and for them. A lot of my business comes from people who are getting ready to die and want to see the sons and daughters they let go of years ago before they do. I've spent more time in nursing homes than a Spanish-American War veteran. Old people aren't cute. They're mean and kind and petty and impressive and pathetic and sometimes nice, just like the rest of us. The only difference is they've outgrown the rules you and I have to live by. Everything they do is serious because death is sitting on their shoulders and blowing in their ears."

She lowered the level in her glass some more. Then she set it down on my scratched coffee table and sat up straight with her hands on her crossed knee, looking at me. "You have a preoccupation with death this morning. What's wrong? No snappy lines, please."

"Mornings I think about death," I said. "I'm a little closer to it each time I roll out of bed, as who isn't? Also I stumbled over another stiff yesterday."

I watched her face work, and then she asked the question.

" 'Another'?"

"It's my hobby. Whenever I find one I throw up my hands and call it out like an out-of-state license plate. So far I'm way ahead of the pack."

"And who did this one belong to?"

"An old fence named Woldanski, in Hamtramck. He found a broken neck at the bottom of the stairs in an empty house on his lot. You'll read about it in the H section of today's paper unless war breaks out or the mayor buys a new suit."

"Was he murdered?"

"Probably. In my hobby they don't count if they weren't."

"Do you have to joke about it?"

I drank some Scotch. Listened to Helen Morgan.

"Dumb question," Karen said. She rubbed the back of her neck. "I'm strung like a guitar. Not thinking straight."

That seemed to be my cue. I set down my glass next to hers and moved behind the sofa and worked my thumbs in the hollows of her shoulders. Her hair smelled like fresh air. She made little purring noises.

"That's nice. Where did you learn to do that?"

"I used to strangle chickens for the Kiwanis Broil."

Her knotted muscles loosened grudgingly under my thumbs. She was all taut sinew under smooth flesh like a silken sheath.

"Did this Woldanski know something about Michael?"

I got my hands away from her neck. She turned her head a little, bringing one eyelash into profile. I said, "Listen closely, there will be a quiz later. I'm not looking into Michael's death today. I wasn't looking into Michael's death yesterday. I won't be looking into Michael's death tomorrow. Michael is as dead as Caruso, as dead as last summer's grass, as dead as this conversation. I just got through saying I don't have to look for dead things. They throw themselves at me like ale-wives fighting to reach shore."

The record played. Helen was asking someone to give her something to remember him by, but it didn't sound as if she expected anything to come of it.

Karen said, "It's just that there seems to be an awful lot of Polish names cropping up in your vocabulary lately. What am I supposed to think?"

"That this is an ethnic city. And that when I say I'm not doing a thing, the chances are I'm not."

She turned that over for a moment. "What are you going to do about the murder?"

"Nothing."

"Nothing?"

"I have aches and pains when I get up in the morning that a man my age shouldn't have because I thought that murder was somebody's business but the cops'. It took a lot of lessons but I finally got all the notes down pat. Woldanski may have been killed for the thing I went to see him about. The odds say it had to do with one of a thousand other things I never heard of. I don't have the time and the person I'm working for doesn't have the money to spend sorting them out. The trail ended at the base of those stairs."

"Your client won't be happy."

"Happy is a dwarf in a kids' movie."

"Cynical."

"No," I said, "just tired. Tired as hell."

"I can tell. I've been here twenty minutes and you've only kissed me once."

I bent down and took her chin and turned her head and fixed that. The needle came to the end of the record meanwhile and the arm swept back and the machine turned itself off with a discreet click, like a bellhop letting himself out of the honeymoon suite.

20

THE SUN WAS UP when she left, driving a big rattletrap Plymouth the color of dusty gold and towing a shadow as long as the block. The house smelled of her afterwards, and when I reheated the coffee and drank some it tasted of her. There are women that can be had and there are women that can only be borrowed. It was hard to picture anyone ever having Karen McBride. I took another shower and put on another clean shirt and the blue suit and drove through spreading sunlight to the office. It was going to be a nice day. The sidewalk was dry and warm and the shade of the building entrance touched the back of my neck like cool water.

Louise Starr was standing in the hall outside my little reception room. The theme today was gray, gray pinched jacket and matching high-waisted slacks and a light blue satin blouse. Her blonde hair was up, young-woman-executive fashion, but the light liked it anyway. She was clutching a black patent leather purse with a silver clasp. When I showed up she glanced down at a watch pinned to her lapel and smiled approvingly, with a trace of mockery around the edges.

"You keep early hours," she said. "I have a nine o'clock appointment with the Information Services director at Wayne State and I thought I'd stop in on the off chance of seeing you. I was about to leave."

I said, "Yours are early enough. It's only seven-thirty." I unlocked the door and pushed it open and stepped aside, holding it. I hoped she wouldn't hit me with her purse for that.

She didn't. She entered ahead of me. "Well, perhaps I was counting on that off chance more than I let on."

I liked her style. She didn't wrinkle her nose at the Devil's Island bench in the waiting room or the low chipped table holding up some magazines too old even for a dentist's office. I let her into my private sleuthing parlor, where a bar of dusty sunlight lay on the desk and carpet and file cabinet, all gone the same color with age. The wallpaper was fairly new, brown stylized butterflies trapped on a field of amber.

"I'd sue your cleaning service," she said.

I hung up my hat. "Go sue the little guy who turns off your car radio when you drive under a bridge. I don't think the service exists."

"Those Venetian blinds scream for dusting."

"I did that Tuesday."

"You might try standing a little closer next time."

"So clever, so early." I waved at the customer's chair. She sat, bending one knee over the other in her gray slacks, and wedged the purse between her hip and the arm. I opened the window and took charge of the swivel behind the desk. We looked at each other. She made the wallpaper look cheap.

She said, "You ought to get a new sofa and some easy chairs and a coffee maker and do business there in the corner. Sometimes desks get in the way."

"I could greet the clients in a caftan. Play bongo music and read their palms and sock them ten bucks a finger."

"Don't laugh. Our last book on psychic phenomena sold six million copies."

"Which as an editor and watchdog for culture you don't appreciate."

"What I appreciate has very little to do with it. People are reading less and less. They're all out running and getting themselves fulfilled and they wouldn't know good writing if you tied them down and read it to them aloud. Or care. A book has to weigh five pounds new or it's not worth the cover price."

"Like Mexican Brown," I said.

She raised delicately penciled eyebrows. "Is that a book?"

"It's crude quality heroin. The good stuff is pure white when refined. But the local addicts have been mainlining Brown so long they're suspicious of the other, and when the distributors do lay hold of the white stuff they have to step on it and tint it brown or it won't sell."

She nodded. "I think that's a fair analogy. You seem to know a great deal about drugs."

"If I worked in Akron I'd know a great deal about tires. I'm a drunk, not a head."

She laughed. Music played. When things got quiet again I opened a fresh pack and offered her one. She shook her head, smiling, and I lit one for myself. I launched the exhaust away from her. "What brings Publishers' Row clanking down my street this A.M.?"

"I was wondering if you'd talked to Eric Rynearson yet."

"I meant to last night. I got distracted."

"Are you still distracted?"

"A little. Not diverted. But Rynearson's store is only open three hours a day, and these aren't them."

"You have principles against" — she hesitated — "*warning* people in their homes? Like the Mafia?"

"I'm entitled to a few, like editors. But that isn't one of them. I don't know where Rynearson lives. He isn't listed. I could find out, but it would cost you seventy-five bucks. Probably a hundred now that I've sicced the cops on that source. I figure it's cheaper all around to see him at work."

"Oh, but he lives above the store. Didn't I say that?"

"No," I said, "you didn't."

"He lives above the store."

"Thanks."

She smiled again and smoothed the crease on her slacks between thumb and forefinger. Her nails were pointed and perfect and glossy-clear.

"It's straight," I said.

"What?" She looked startled.

"The crease. And if it weren't straight there's not a lot you could do about it now. Why else are you here bad-mouthing my fixtures?"

"Fedor Alanov's suite was broken into last night," she said.

"Is he all right?"

"He's fine. It happened while he and Andrei were addressing a library gathering in Warren. I was in my room reading manuscripts. Crimes in themselves," she added archly. "Fedor discovered it when he returned."

"Anything taken?"

"He says no. Whatever they were after, they were very neat about it. But Fedor is a meticulous man and noticed some things out of place. Shirts returned to bureau drawers in the wrong order, pages of notes not lined up properly, little things like that. But too many to overlook. Whoever did it had to have a key."

"The maid?"

"Hotel maids don't clean rooms at night unless specifically requested. Also they have no business going through drawers."

"They don't," I agreed. "But they do. You talked to security?"

"A tall young man with a floorwalker's manner. He walked around the suite and touched his moustache and insinuated that Mr. Alanov must be mistaken. Absentmindedness is often the culprit, or words to that effect. Fedor thanked him — you know that way of his — and said he'd never been called crazy or a liar in such refined terms. The security man offered to notify the police. I needn't tell you how Fedor replied."

"House dicks. They've come a long way from the old tobacco-spitters that wore their hats indoors. I don't think. You suspect Rynearson?"

"More likely it was one of the people working for him. Who else could it be?"

"Hotel thieves. Larcenous maids. A bellboy with a habit. A gossip columnist looking for a scoop. Someone who had the suite before and kept the key. Those things float all over the place, no one knows how many copies there are, and anyone with a buck can get an extra one made at any hardware store. But let's just for now say it was Eric Rynearson or his help. What would he be after in Alanov's suite?"

"Why, the *Asylum* manuscript, of course. Fedor had it with him in his briefcase or it would be lost."

I killed my stub. "Excuse it, please, but I'm having trouble following the plot. I thought it was Alanov this KGB stooge was after, not his book."

"Ideally, he would want the brain behind the words, but failing that he would seize the existing script as a stopgap."

"There's only one copy?"

"Fedor won't allow copying until it's finished. He won't even let anyone read it in its present form. I've only seen an outline. That's not unusual among writers. Their prejudice against showing unfinished work sometimes carries all the mystical ritualism of a pagan superstition." She smiled primly, like a missionary. She was as much like a missionary as I was like Billy Graham. I drew a pencil from the water glass on the desk and tickled my ear with the eraser. Scratching my brain.

"How come no one who looks like a cop believes Alanov when he reports this kind of thing?"

She lowered her lashes. They didn't come anywhere near her chin. "All publishing houses aren't as scrupulous as ours. There have been publicity stunts in the past to promote book sales. The Hughes autobiography didn't help matters."

"That's all?"

"No." She looked at me again and settled back in the chair with her hands on the arms. "There was an incident shortly after Fedor came to this country from the U.S.S.R. He reported that a Russian agent had been following him everywhere he went since he landed. Federal agents put him under surveillance and eventually apprehended a man who turned out to be an admiring reader from Baltimore who wanted Fedor to autograph his copy of *The Window on the Baltic.* The press caught wind of it and branded Fedor a paranoid. I guess in the eyes of the law that makes him like the hypo-chondriac who won't let his doctor tend to those patients who are really sick. But hypochondriacs get sick too. And some-times paranoids really are in danger."

"And wolves eat little boys with big mouths. I remember the flap now. It bothered me without my actually remember-ing it. What makes him not just a nut this time?"

"Andrei was with Fedor that night they tried to grab him. A nut he isn't."

I looked at her with new interest. She colored a little. "As I said," she explained, "Detroit is a long way from New York."

"Longer than I thought." I played with the pencil. "What's this do to my end of the patch? Do I still sweat Rynearson or what?"

"No, you buy him off."

"Buy him off how?"

She looked puzzled. "With money, of course. How did you think?"

"It isn't thinking work. I was supposed to do it with brass knuckles —"

"Oh, no, I hope you weren't planning on using anything like that."

"Figure of speech," I said. "Hard guys like me don't need them. That was the way I was supposed to do it, and now I'm to do it with sugar on top."

"That's about it. Yes, that's exactly it. I've been in touch with the brass in New York. To put it mildly, they weren't satisfied with the way I planned to handle the situation. We're an old firm, and so respectable we can hardly stand ourselves. The mossbacks in the front office can't forget we published Thomas Paine. They're anxious to avoid publicity that would reflect unfavorably on what they term to be the company's in-tegrity. They aren't interested in hearing that any integrity we might have had went down the air shaft when we started publishing diet books and hacked-out biographies of minor television talents."

"You got burned."

"To a crisp. I'd be on the street now if I weren't almost the only editor they could trust with a lot of cash."

"How much is a lot?"

She opened her purse and flipped a packet of crisp new bills onto the desk. It landed with a thud. There was a C-note on top and the band said there were forty-nine more underneath. There couldn't have been room for anything else in her purse, not even a paper clip. I poked my pencil at the packet. It moved reluctantly.

"Everyone's throwing these things on my desk lately," I said. "It don't hardly speak to the file cabinet no more. What would your mossbacks say if they found out you kicked their five long ones over to the arm-buster that got you in Dutch to begin with?"

"They'd say I had until tomorrow morning to come in and clean out my desk. But I'm no courier. There's more to being a good editor than rearranging paragraphs and putting in and taking out commas; the job requires a knowledge of people. I think that you are a man who can be trusted. Also I called your bonding firm and they gave you a clean bill of health."

"So for trying to snatch the stud of your stable and breaking into his suite, Rynearson gets five grand and you get — what?"

"His assurance that both Fedor Alanov and his book are let alone while he's in Detroit. It stinks, doesn't it?"

"It depends on whether Rynearson snaps up the bait, and if he does, whether his word means anything. If so you've got your blockbuster cheap."

Something dented the smooth expanse of her forehead. "I — can't offer you any more for the job than I already have. The company drew its purse-strings after wiring that money."

I twitched a shoulder. "It's the same job. Maybe a little easier because I don't have to make faces at anyone. If it goes sour it's meat for the cops. I know a detective in Homicide who could not quite be called a friend, but who if I say please

with the right whine in my tone might whisper into the ear
of someone who can help."

"Let's hope it won't come to that," she said. She seemed to
want to add something, then sat back again.

I said, "I'm not on staff at your firm. If Rynearson swallows
this candy I mean to make him see I'd consider it a personal
favor if no one's back gets stabbed."

"A personal favor. I see." She smiled. After that she relaxed
visibly.

I locked the five thousand in my joke of a safe, wrote out a
receipt and tore it off. Our fingers touched as she accepted it.
She didn't withdraw hers right away.

"This is a fascinating city," she said. "Not at all like New
York. I'm flying back Monday without having seen anything
of it but what's on the way from the airport to the hotel and
from the hotel to here. Are you free this weekend?"

Her blue eyes had a smoky look. Her soft collar was open to
the second button and there was a thin creamy line along the
top of her collarbone where the sun hadn't reached. The air
in the office smelled faintly of jasmine, the way the atmosphere
inside a crowded bus freshens when a messenger boards carrying a bouquet with dew still on the leaves.

I said, "I'll call you."

"Do that." She took away her hand finally with the receipt
in it and put the paper in her purse. Nodding a little, she rose.
"Yes, do."

I got up and let her out.

21

THE RIVER FLASHED like leaping trout between buildings along East Jefferson, where shirtsleeves and bare midriffs had begun to blossom on the sidewalks in the morning warmth. A stiff breeze was blowing from Windsor. When I climbed out of my crate I could smell the river, a fresh green smell like rain on new grass.

Rynearson's Eastern Imports wasn't in a commercial building at all, but a private two-story frame house painted white with red shutters and trim, with a square of lawn in front that had been clipped by someone with a nail shears in one hand and a micrometer in the other. The bugs in that lawn would line up for inspection twice a day. The building, narrow and high-peaked, looked like one of those Henry Ford had had thrown up for his employees, but any others that might have been on the block had come down for brick apartment houses and office complexes, giving the house that last-leaf-of-autumn look that always precedes an empty lot. A sign pegged in the lawn identified the business in fussy script.

"The shop is closed, young man. Come back this afternoon."

I stepped back off the porch and looked up in the direction from which the voice had come. A silver head and a smear of face looked down at me from an open upstairs window. It was in the shadow of the cornice and the features might have belonged to a man or woman. The voice was barely masculine.

"I'm not a customer," I called back. "I'm here to see Eric Rynearson."

"Who is here to see Eric Rynearson?"

It sounded polite enough, almost elaborately so. I gave him my name.

"I don't believe I know you, Mr. Walker. What's your business?"

"It has to do with Fedor Alanov."

The silver head turned away from the window. Low voices murmured inside. It turned back. "Wait one moment, Mr. Walker." The window got empty.

Not knowing how long one moment was, I lit a pill. I had a third of it smoked when there was some bumping inside and then someone worked a series of bolts and latches on the other side of the door with a noise like a convention of click beetles. I dropped my cigarette and crushed it out on the concrete stoop just as Alley Oop opened the door.

The back of his head came to perfect point, from which dull brown hair like a beast's coat grew straight down the shallow slope of his forehead and made a stiff shelf over his eyes, glistening wet plums without whites set well back under his bony brow. Dark beard matted his face from just under his eyes to his jaw, with an underdeveloped embarrassment of a nose so pink it might have been false poking out of the forest of hair and looking vaguely obscene. His shoulders extended beyond the doorframe and his chest was broad and deep under a square-tailed blue shirt that buttoned up one side like a tunic and hung outside his white cotton slacks. He was a few inches over five feet tall, but he looked much shorter, almost dwarfish, because he was so wide. And he smelled. The stink came rolling out when the door opened and slapped me in the face like a moldy towel, a thick, sour mustiness as in a kennel or the gorilla cage at the Detroit Zoo. It almost drove me off the stoop.

"Upstairs," he said. He moved to one side and I went in past him, breathing through my mouth.

The store proper was on the ground floor: delicate yellow Japanese tables with legs you could snap between a thumb and forefinger, translucent china and thick clumsy crockery, Malay walking sticks, silk screens with embroidered dragons, gold-handled scimitars and varnished Tartar bows, painted figurines, landscapes made of patches of flat color — tables and tables of the stuff neatly arranged on white lace cloths under a pair of crystal chandeliers fixed to the ceiling, all washed in gray from the shaded windows. The floor was bare polished hardwood. The place was spotless and would have made me feel dirty except for B. O. Plenty standing behind me. When he closed the door the stink got worse. He relocked the locks.

A spiral staircase Henry Ford wouldn't have recognized wound straight up from the middle of the floor through a hole in the ceiling. As I went up I felt my escort's weight on the metal stairs below. I climbed with one hand on the brass rail and the other pressed against my lower back, as if the effort strained it. The butt of the Smith & Wesson felt good under my palm.

"You should be flattered, Mr. Walker. I allow very few up here where I keep my private collection."

The speaker was not tall but looked it, as he was very slender and his burgundy-colored velour smoking jacket matched his trousers in a long thin sweep of rich maroon. His hair was not silver at all close up, but bluish, parted an inch to the right of his widow's peak so that a lock broke over his left eyebrow. The eyebrow, like its mate, was very black and his face was tanned so evenly that at first I took him for a Hispanic. He had a thin nose that you might call acquiline if you wanted to be polite, but if not you would say it hooked. He had ordinary cheekbones and his face was beautifully shaven, almost feminine in its hairlessness. His eyes were no color at all. His brown throat was bare and he had on red slippers with gold dragons on the toes and between the first and second fingers of his right hand tilted an ebony cigarette holder with an oval butt lisping smoke out the end. That was a first for me. You hear about them, but how many of us have actually seen one in use outside of old war movies?

Smelling Mr. Hyde behind me, I shifted position to take him in without seeming to. He was breathing a little heavily, whether from the climb or because his malformed nose didn't work so well I wasn't sure.

What I saw here was more of the same, only doubled. The furniture was a little more fragile, the squat vases gleamed a little softer with greater age, the painted canvases on the walls were thinner, almost to the point of transparency. The rug was thin too but lovingly needled by a hand that was dust on some Persian plain by now. The furniture that was made for sitting in and otherwise using was much newer but designed along the same exotic lines and arranged in a living room setup. There were doors leading to other rooms and books with cracked and flaking spines on shelves behind glass. The windows — including the one the blue-haired man had hailed me from — were shaded, as were those downstairs. A globe like a crystal ball lit the room with a milky glow from a bandy-legged table in the center of the room.

"Cute." I gestured with my hat toward a folding bamboo screen standing in a corner. "Does Dr. Fu Manchu make his entrance from behind there?"

The noise of amusement the blue-haired man made was as delicate as the décor, and fluttered like a hummingbird trapped in his throat. "I'll treat that as a compliment. Humor is often used to conceal awe. Paul, take Mr. Walker's hat."

The Neanderthal in the tunic took a step forward. I said, "I won't be here that long. I just came to deliver a message to Rynearson."

The blue-haired man tapped ash off the cigarette in the holder into the mouth of a ceramic ashtray fashioned after a laughing skull and straightened without raising the holder to his lips. "I am Rynearson. Who are you, besides a man named Amos Walker?"

"I'm a private investigator. Fedor Alanov's publisher hired me to deliver this message I'm here to deliver." I paused. The room smelled of cigarette smoke and incense and Paul. Mostly Paul. "Show me you're Rynearson."

His colorless eyes flicked to the other man, who turned and took himself out through one of the doors, lumbering from side to side like the chimpanzee someone had meant him to be.

The blue-haired man and I killed the time looking at each

other. His ash grew and he got rid of it and the cigarette never got higher than his waist. After a minute or so Paul returned carrying a flat leather wallet with gold corners. The blue-haired man slid a driver's license out of one of the compartments and held it out between two fingers. I took it and looked at the picture and read the legend and gave it back. "It's expired," I said.

"I haven't driven in years. Paul is my chauffeur, among other things."

"I'll bet. Does he do it to you or do you do it to him?"

Paul made a sound in his throat that was not amusement and started toward me.

Rynearson transferred the wallet and license to the hand holding the cigarette holder and grasped Paul's arm in his free hand. He moved swiftly and apparently without effort. But the skin went white around his fingernails and the bearded man's face twisted in pain and he stopped.

I admired that. Rynearson could pass for sixty but I figured he was closer to seventy, and Paul was at least thirty years younger and built like a piling.

When it was obvious the wide little man had been subdued, the hand was withdrawn. His hairy features betrayed no relief and he made no move to rub the arm, but the sleeve held the cast of Rynearson's fingers and there would be purple marks on the flesh beneath.

Rynearson said, "I think that you're being deliberately unpleasant, Mr. Walker. It seems to be the latest step in Fedor Alanov's campaign of harassment against myself and my business."

He spoke with an American accent, but his language was careful and his pronunciation of the writer's name was subtly different from Louise Starr's.

"Alanov's publisher sees it the other way," I said. "The way I heard it, you tried to snatch him once and when that didn't work you frisked his hotel suite looking for the manuscript of his new book."

" 'Frisked'?"

"Tossed. Rifled. Ransacked. Burglarized. Broke into the place and defiled the man's personal and intimate possessions with your vile Bolshevik paws."

"I see. You have a melodramatic, if sarcastic, bent. When did I do this — frisk?"

"Last night, while Alanov and his translator were in Warren."

"Impossible. I was downstairs in the shop from four to seven, and after that I was up here entertaining the owner of a rather fine K'ang-hsi bottle that I have my eye on. He declined to sell," he added bitterly,

"He have a name?"

"Not for you. He will for the authorities should you choose to make this a police matter."

"Giving you time to cook up a story with him, if he exists," I said. "What about Paul? Was he entertaining too?"

"He had the night off."

I looked at Paul. He wasn't spitting out any answers today. His plum eyes glittered hard as wet river stones. Back to Rynearson. The blue-haired man had on a cat's smile.

"What's funny?"

"That I would have any interest in Alanov or his book. I read *The Window on the Baltic* twice. The man has an interesting style. You almost don't notice that he has nothing to say. If he had been born here he would be considered one of the better second-rate writers, nothing more. But because some bureaucrat behind what is laughably called the Iron Curtain had difficulty understanding his convoluted epigrams and decided that he was writing in some kind of dangerous code and should therefore be ridden from the country with trumpets, he is considered a patriot and a sensitive artist and feted by political and literary groups whose members have never read so much as a newspaper from start to finish. No, Mr. Walker, I assure you I have no designs either on that poor man's Pasternak or his *Asylum*."

I jumped on it with both feet. "Who told you the title of a book that hasn't been written yet?"

He was still smiling. "Dear boy. Alanov, of course. Each time he's interviewed in the press he makes certain to mention the project at least once. He's an incorrigible publicity hound, as who wouldn't be, given his opportunities?"

"You said he was harassing you. Harassing you how?"

"It's difficult to operate a legitimate enterprise under the best of circumstances. Well-nigh impossible when police and federal agents are continually prowling the premises, looking under tables and lifting the lids off six hundred-year-old teapots to peer inside."

"Suspected spies should expect such inconveniences."

"Oh, yes, that KGB rot. I'd hoped that was laid to rest finally. I suppose that's the risk every honest businessman takes who makes numerous trips abroad and is seen meeting in public with opposite numbers from the so-called captive nations. I would make a singularly inept spy, Mr. Walker. I have no access to government secrets and the gentlemen with whom I meet are similarly handicapped. If any of them happens to be in the pay of the U.S.S.R., it has no bearing on our talks, which rarely concern themselves with subjects more current than the early seventeenth century."

"Then why was a car with the name of your shop stenciled on the side involved in an attempt to kidnap Alanov?"

"That is the easiest of your questions to answer. It wasn't."

"Someone says different."

"Someone is either mistaken or a liar."

"You're making it hard to deal, Rynearson."

His very black eyebrows slid up without disturbing the smooth brown skin of his forehead. "Deal? Oh, spare me the colorful synonyms this time, I'm familiar with the word. Its use in this context makes me curious."

I slid the thick packet of bills out of my inside breast pocket and tossed it onto the tea table between us. The light coming from the globe lamp waggled a little. Paul's mouth opened slightly, a black inverted crescent in his matted beard. Rynearson glanced down at the packet briefly. Smiled.

"Five grand to forget the name Fedor Alanov and his book

until he's out of reach," I said. "But since you say you're not interested in either of them I'll just take my little bundle and split." I stepped to the table and bent down.

Rynearson laughed.

It rocked me a little. His laugh was almost noiseless, a broken hissing off the roof of his mouth, and it wasn't the reaction I was after. I straightened with the packet in my hand, tapping the edge against my other palm. Waiting.

Showing very white teeth against his dark skin, the blue-haired man removed the stub from his holder, put it out in the skull, tipped back the hinged lid of a heavily carved mahogany box nearby, selected a fresh oval cigarette with elaborate care, and fitted it into the holder. From a pocket of his smoking jacket he drew a lighter whose smooth green case might have been jade and played with it. He said:

"Look around you, Mr. Walker. The carpet you're standing on cost fifteen thousand dollars. I paid cash for it. There is nothing in this room worth less than a thousand. I'm a wealthy man. If I were engaged in some nefarious plot to keep the Russian out of print, do you really think that tiny bit would make me waver? An unimaginative idea at best, and whoever had it did you no favor. Very well, Paul."

Paul was faster than he looked. He came in low and hard in one of those diving tackles that turn pro quarterbacks into commercial spokesmen in less time than it takes to describe it, but I wasn't there when he expected to make contact. Dropping the money, I pivoted aside like a door and he rocketed past. I crossed an ankle in front of one of his but his reflexes were too good. He hopped over it and, with the momentum still behind him, he spun on a dime and launched himself shoulder-first sideways at my chest. I danced again and he struck me a glancing blow that knocked air out of my lungs. That made me mad. I scooped a four-foot black vase off a fluted wooden stand and brought it down on his head with both hands. Pieces flew all over.

Someone groaned, mortally injured, but it wasn't Paul, out cold on his face on fifteen thousand dollars of Persian carpet.

The groaner was Eric Rynearson, staring at the curved shards of black porcelain littering the room.

"That was a Ming!" His voice cracked.

"Take it out of Paul's salary. He broke it." I got my gun out and held it on him while I bent a knee and scooped the packet of bills off the floor. My left bicep stung when I returned the money to my coat. I figured I'd pulled it maneuvering the heavy vase. "Hands high, Rynearson. Like in the movies."

He lifted them to his shoulders with the lighter in one hand and the cigarette and holder in the other. His expression was still dazed. I stepped over the unconscious man on the floor and around the tea table and patted down the shopkeeper. I felt the flat wallet in one of his pockets, nothing else. I stood six inches in front of him, looking into his dishwater eyes. The room felt close after my exercise, and the stink of incense and Paul were oppressive. My chest hurt where I'd been struck. My left arm tingled.

I clapped the gun sideways against the side of Rynearson's blue head. He cried out and reeled.

"That's for paying someone to be hard for you. Swishes I can take or leave, but swishes that buy muscle I don't like lots."

He stood with his head bowed and one hand to the side of his skull, glaring up at me through the hair in his eyes. I said, "What do you want with Alanov or his book?"

He started to shake his head. I hit it again. He whimpered.

"Talk it up, Cary. I've got a big mad on and the whole day to get rid of it." I raised the gun again.

"Don't!" He crossed his hands in front of his face. He'd dropped the jade lighter on the first blow and the cigarette holder dangled, empty and forgotten, between his fingers. "Please! I don't want them. I'm a collector, not a spy. Please, I'm telling the truth."

I'd done some more threatening business with the Smith & Wesson. The room seemed smoky now, and very hot. His features swam. I talked a little faster.

"Your car was seen. The feds have a file on you. Too much

coincidence is bad for the system. What are you after?" I cocked my elbow for the backhand.

"Not the book. An object. A silver ornament, very old. A religious item."

The words came out faster than his lips formed them. It was like watching a movie with the sound out of synch. I could barely make out his face now, though we were as close as lovers. I was sweating from my hairline to my toes. My left side was numb and the gun was slippery in my right hand. It seemed that Rynearson was watching me closely, but out of curiosity, not fear.

"A religious item," I echoed. The words were a long time getting out. My tongue was as thick as a tire.

"A cross," he said. "With a blue stone at the axis, a lapis lazuli, and garnets at the points. It dates back to the reign of Sigizmund Augustus of Poland. There is an inscription on the back —"

Suddenly the voice was Martha Evancek's. I turned from him, almost falling, did fall over the tea table, landing hard on my dead left shoulder and losing my gun. The light in the room wobbled crazily, I hoped because the globe lamp had fallen and rolled when the table went over, but I wasn't sure enough to be relieved. I got up and stumbled towards the stairs. The way was clear and I was glad of that. Then I wasn't. It shouldn't have been, there should have been something on the floor between me and the stairwell. What? Think about it later. I felt good. I felt warm, cozily insulated, and deliciously drowsy, a man in flannel pajamas under a thick comforter in a room icy with winter. My foot found the first step. I dragged the other, the numb left one, over the edge of the well and set it down next to the first. It was wearing a lead boot. I grasped the rail. It squirmed in my hand like a snake but I held on. I found the second step, the third, rounded the first turn going down. My hand skidded along the rail. I let go, mopped my palm on my pants, started to tip forward, grabbed again for the rail.

The rail wasn't there . . .

22

"GIVE ME YOUR LEFT ARM, Amos. No, your left. That's a good boy."

I smiled. The blue-haired man smiled back and that made me feel good. He had traded his burgundy jacket for a white coat like doctors wear and he looked very professional with a hypodermic needle in his hand and I liked that. I liked everything about him. I couldn't understand how I could have not liked him before, but I didn't want to think about that; it made me feel ashamed. He had a nasty bruise on the left side of his head that closed his left eye a little. It looked as if some nasty person who didn't like the blue-haired man had done it and it made me very mad at the nasty person, but not mad enough to hurt him. I didn't want to hurt anyone. I just wanted to go on lying in that comfortable bed that was like a cloud and do things the nice blue-haired man asked me to do so he would call me by my first name and tell me I was a good boy. I thought then that I must have been in heaven. I didn't even feel the prick when the needle entered my wrist.

I dreamed. The nice blue-haired man was my father and we were at the carnival, the one that used to come to our town every summer until someone died when a rusty cable snapped on one of the rides, and then narcotics agents busted the man who ran the shooting gallery for awarding the same winning contestant his third identical panda stuffed with cellophane packets full of white powder. But this was an earlier summer, a deep blue July night with the midway lit like a Christmas tree and so many small brown moths fluttering about in the light that you had to be careful when you opened your mouth that you didn't swallow one. Canned music clanked and wheezed from the merry-go-round and the Ferris wheel creaked as it turned and the loudspeaker over a peeling booth invited visitors to come see the Two-Headed Baby and the Giant Mummy and the Goat with Its Head Where Its Tail Should Be, the same message over and over in a tinny voice, so that it seemed as if it would go on forever just as it had been going on before we came and would continue after we left. I thought I understood infinity then. My blue-haired father kept asking me questions to find out how much I was seeing and how much I would remember of what I saw. Most of his questions had to do with a huge silver cross that towered over the midway where the main light pole usually stood, deep blue light shining from its center and less dramatic red lights glowing at the points. There was writing on the back in strange characters, but I found that I could read them quite easily.

" 'Glory and Eternity,' " I read aloud.

Father Blue Hair became excited. His smooth tan face moved very close to mine, close enough to show the hairline fissures at the corners of his eyes and the pouches at the ends of his mouth. His eyes were as devoid of color as puddles on asphalt. They were nice eyes for that, brimming with kindness.

"You know the inscription," he said, and I felt his breath, warm and sweet as a kitten's on my face. "Do you see the cross, Amos? Do you see it?"

"Pretty cross." I smiled when I said it. The words tickled my lips. I said them again and giggled.

"Yes, yes. But where is it?"

"Shiny. I can see my face in it."

"Where?"

I started to cry. Hot tears left molten tracks down my cheeks and puddled in my ears.

"There, there, Amos. Daddy's sorry he yelled. Rest, now.

We'll talk later." A towel made from the same cloud-stuff as the bed stroked my face gently, mopping up my tears. I slept.

More dreams. The carnival, a rowboat on a green pond where I used to fish and tangle my line in the eel-like superstructure of the calm lily pads, a stroll along a familiar rutted clay road where ancient snapping turtles used to cross like great dusty gray beetles with the moss thick on their humped backs. The silver cross showed up in those places too, soothing places with nothing worrisome crouching in the bushes or among the reeds or behind the booths where cotton candy was sold, just the kind brown face with blue-rinsed hair breaking over one neutral eye, its lips shaping gentle questions about the cross. I decided definitely that I was in heaven, but that I was undergoing some sort of catechism that I had to pass in order to stay. I cried whenever the blue-haired man's reaction to my answers told me they were wrong. More than anything I didn't want to have to leave.

A troll entered my paradise. I smelled him first, a foul animal stench, and then his misshapen shadow swam across the fluid of my eyes and crockery rattled and then the shadow swam back the other way, leaving its odor curling in the corners. It was the first smell I'd smelled in years; my olfactory sense had been on vacation, but it was back. I lay breathing poisonous air and looking at the stars overhead. There shouldn't have been stars. Wherever I was, and I was becoming less sure that it was paradise, it felt like indoors. I closed my eyes tight and snapped them open. The stars remained. They were pale blue on a background of turquoise, spaced regularly, and formed no recognizable constellations. I moved my head left and right. The stars didn't move with me. They were painted on the ceiling.

I turned my head sideways. The corner of a foam-rubber pillow in a cotton slip blocked my left eye. My right saw a wall with more stars on it. I turned my head the other way. Stars on that wall too, and before it, next to the bed, a nightstand with a stainless steel tray on it with a white cloth spread on the bottom and six disposable plastic hypodermic needles lined up neatly on the cloth. A small glass brown-tinted bottle stood on the corner of the tray. That explained the rattling I'd heard.

What I did next was very hard. I pried myself up on one elbow and peeled aside the thin yellow fuzzy blanket covering me. I slipped off my elbow the first two times and the blanket was heavier than it looked, it was made of woven iron with steel reinforcement, but I puffed and sweated and strained my eyeballs and finally lay unencumbered on the sheet, naked except for one of those thin white cotton hospital gowns that fasten in back. My head was heavy and sloshed when I moved it. I tried not to. My left arm was sore. I looked at it without trying to lift it. The underside of the wrist was dotted with blue holes. Someone had been using me for a dartboard and there was a fresh set of darts waiting for another game on the tray on the nightstand.

Light found its way into the room through green curtains drawn over an ordinary window in the right wall. The semiopaque fabric diffused the light and I couldn't tell if it was morning or afternoon. My watch was gone with my clothes. I didn't know what day it was, and then I felt the cold touch of terror that comes to a man who isn't sure what month it is either, or what year. Psychiatrists would have a name for that. The smug bastards have a name for everything. They would probably call it the Van Winkle Syndrome.

I heard footsteps muffled by a wall. They had a familiar cadence, sort of a thump-thump with a beat between the thumps, like someone walking a piece of furniture that was too heavy to lift. They grew louder.

I moved as fast as a man who has been kept drugged and locked up in a room for days or months or years can move, which is not fast. I pulled myself to the edge of the mattress and leaned on my right shoulder and reached out with both hands until I had the brown bottle between my palms, and then I pried at the plastic top. I was lucky. It wasn't a child-proof cap and I had it off in five minutes, or it seemed that long anyway.

A key rattled in a lock. I sobbed audibly, snatched at the needles, scattering them and pricking my hand, finally got hold of one and got its point inside the mouth of the bottle on the second try. I pulled back the plunger. It made a greedy slurping noise and colorless liquid filled the hollow plastic handle. I didn't know how good a dose it was. Maybe it was fatal. Whatever it was it went well over the top measuring mark. Air stirred in the room. I smelled Paul. I fumbled the bottle back onto the tray without its top and let my left arm drop to the floor. I had the needle in my right hand pinned under my body. I hoped I wouldn't stick myself or lose sensation in the trapped arm.

Paul's footsteps were a long time thumping into the room. I was afraid he'd seen what I was doing. Then the cadence started. I lay with my eyes closed and felt his shadow pass over me on his way past the foot of the bed to the nightstand. Lord, he stank.

"Kicked off your covers, huh? Guess you're ready for another helping."

There was a two-foot space between the bed and the stand. He sidled along it and turned his back to set down a smaller tray containing a blue plastic pitcher and matching cup. My eyes were open now. His back muscles tensed. He'd seen the disarray on the nightstand.

I came up off the bed in a kind of slow-motion, but I must have been faster than I seemed because he was just turning when I got my left arm across his throat and stuck the needle into the carotid artery on the side of his perfunctory neck and rammed home the plunger.

It didn't work. He shrugged out of my grip like a bull bursting through a ribbon of crepe, roaring and clawing at the thing that stung him. He looked at the needle in his palm for a stupid instant, then dashed it to the floor and forearmed me in the throat. But I had lost my balance and was already falling backwards across the bed, missing much of the blow's force. I wheezed anyway. I landed on my back on the mattress and bounced and then Paul was on top of me, hot and heavy and spraying my face with spittle through his bared brown teeth and stinking like a slaughterhouse in July. He wrenched my right arm up and back and I yelled and he got the fingers of his other hand inside my mouth and tried to tear loose my jaw. I bit down hard, tasting the stink of him on my tongue. He whined keeningly through his teeth from the pain of it but he didn't let go. I had shot my assailant through with vitamins or something equally counter to my welfare and was going to die with my mouth gaping horribly. Rynearson's laughing-skull ashtray flashed to mind. My strength was going. I was beating the back of his head with my left fist, but it was like pounding a tire. I couldn't get any force behind the blows. We might both have been underwater. My jaw muscles creaked.

Suddenly my right arm was free. I felt his grip slipping and threw off his hand just like that. Panicking, he tried to regain the hold, only to grasp empty air as I got my palm against his ugly face and shoved. His fingers tensed mightily on my jaw, but it was only a spasm. They slid out of my mouth, smearing my chin with blood from the knuckles my teeth had torn. He stopped resisting the pressure of my hand on his face and lay like a sack of iron on my chest.

We were like that for a while, reconstructing a depraved frame from a Fellini movie, and then I pushed and slid and finally rolled out from under him and went down on my hands and knees on a spongy green carpet, panting and dry-retching, spitting out blood and the taste of Paul. I wondered if I would ever eat again. I wondered if I would ever care. I wondered what I was doing on my hands and knees in a strange room with the breeze fanning my bare backside.

I pulled myself to my feet, using the bedframe and leaning against the star-papered wall. The headboard was six feet of dark oak, very old, and carved all over with fruit and braided vines showing the marks of the chisel. I looked down at Paul, snoring on his face on the mattress with an arm like a bent log hanging over the edge. If someone didn't turn him over he could suffocate. Yes, he could. I moved away from the bed.

The blue plastic pitcher still stood on the nightstand. I lifted it in both hands and sniffed its contents. No smell. I tipped it up, took some of the liquid in my mouth, and sloshed it around, not swallowing. Water, with an added metallic taste that took me back to my college boxing days. Liquid protein. I swallowed the mouthful and waited five minutes with the wall holding me up. When I didn't fall asleep or feel like running up the ceiling fixture I drank some more. I set down the pitcher and snatched the white cloth off the other tray, scattering the rest of the needles, and mopped Paul's blood off my face. My flesh stung. I explored my features with cautious fingertips. I had a scab on my nose and my right eye was tender and a little swollen. My front teeth moved a little when my tongue touched them from behind. I was lucky. I could have been seriously hurt if I hadn't broken my fall downstairs with my face.

The room had two doors. One would belong to a closet. Clothes are kept in closets. Trouble was, the one that looked most likely was clear across the room. I took some deep breaths and squared my shoulders and started pulling myself along the wall the long way.

It wasn't much of a hike. Guys with one leg and cancer eating their insides make lots longer ones for the research foundations. I leaned against the wall until my breath stopped whistling and my heart got through whacking my breastbone, and then I tried the knob. Of course it was locked. I worked my way around the rest of the distance, which brought me back to the bed, and went through Paul's pockets. Of course they were empty. I leaned against the wall and felt my brow wrinkle. Then I grinned. I reversed directions and went back past the closet door, moving a little faster now. About crawling speed. I bumped the wall from time to time for reassurance. I grasped the knob on the other door and pulled. It came open. A ring of keys wobbled from the key in the lock.

The fourth key opened the closet, where my clothes hung among a dozen suits in muted colors with tailor's labels sewn inside the jackets. My wallet was in my inside breast pocket where I'd left it, contents intact. The packet of hundred-dollar bills was not. I found my wristwatch in another pocket. The battery was working. The hands read 7:10. The calendar said it was Sunday. I'd entered Rynearson's house on Friday.

My shirt was on the hanger — it was a wooden one, I hoped I'd remember to thank Rynearson for that — and I took off the hospital gown and got dressed. I found my shoes on the closet floor with my socks rolled up inside and put them on. Just for the hell of it I went through all the pockets in the tailored suits. I found two silk handkerchiefs and a book of matches. I wondered what a man with a jade lighter would want with matches. I put everything back and walked around the bed to where I'd started. I was doing fine now. I felt like a one-legged milking stool. Paul snored.

The drawer in the nightstand was empty. I left it open and looked at the two needles left on the tray. Selecting one, I filled it from the brown bottle and held up the point and squirted a short thin stream, testing it. I was ready to talk to someone.

23

OUTSIDE THE ROOM was a short hallway paneled in yellow, with a door standing open to an unoccupied half-bathroom across the way and at the far end a square of strong sunlight. I locked the door to the room with Paul in it, dropped the ring of keys into my pocket, and crept toward the light, holding the needle underhand with the point forward like a knife. The hall opened into a room I knew. It was the one in which Rynearson kept his personal collection of eastern art and antiques. The light slanted in through an unshaded window in the east wall and lay solidly on the fragile canvases and paper-thin stuff of the ornate rug, probably for the first time since they had taken up residence. I didn't like that. The pieces of the Ming vase I had shattered on Paul's head had been swept up, but I found them still lying in a wicker wastebasket in the kneehole of a fey teak desk with an onyx pen set on top, and I didn't like that either. A man who wears a smoking jacket should be more careful about his things.

The desk drawers were locked. I selected a likely looking key from the ring and it worked. All the drawers were empty except the top one on the left side, which contained my Smith & Wesson in its holster. I unleathered it, swung out the cylinder, said hello to the brass cartridges, snapped it back in place, strapped the holster to my belt, dropped the needle into the drawer and locked it. When in doubt go with the weapon you know. With it in hand I went through an open door into the next room.

It was an office, with only a dark tapestry that Christ might have seen hung on one wall to speak of Rynearson's weakness. A glass cabinet held more needles and two small brown bottles like the one in the bedroom. The place looked untidy for a man of his habits. Three empty file drawers were stacked crookedly, one atop another, on the big modern desk. Two of the desk drawers hung open with nothing inside. I slid out the others, and also those still in place in two tall file cabinets in the corner. The same. The air had a charred smell. There was a fireplace in the corner near the window, with a heap of ashes in the grate. I touched them with a poker and they broke apart. It was a funny time of year to build a fire.

I tried the handle of a gray steel safe set in the floor behind the desk. Whoever closed it last had either forgotten or hadn't bothered to spin the dial. The door hinged open and I reached down inside and lifted out a familiar-looking packet.

I counted the bills; they were all there. The safe was empty otherwise. I stood there with my lips pursed, riffling the bills. Then I put them away inside my jacket and got back to work.

At the end of the hall opposite the living room was a dressing room in a five-foot space between walls, containing an upright hickory bench like a church pew, its curved seat polished by contact with many rumps. A wardrobe too cheesy for show held a couple of camel's-hair overcoats and a white lab coat and some empty hangers. Rynearson's burgundy-colored lounging outfit was draped over the bench, the slippers with dragons on the toes kicked underneath. The trousers had no pockets. In the pockets of the smoking jacket I found the ebony cigarette holder and the jade lighter. I flicked open the lighter's lid and spun the wheel. An invisible seam popped open in the side and a thin steel rod two inches long licked out. There was a hollow in the end of the rod. I placed my thumb against it and pushed. The rod telescoped back into the lighter with some resistance and the complaint of a tiny but feisty spring concealed inside. I kept pushing until something clicked and then closed the little doors in the side.

The lighter had no flint and there was no reservoir inside for fluid. Yet the last time I'd seen it he'd had it in his hand to light a fresh cigarette in his holder. Not long afterwards my system had started shutting down. I remembered the stinging sensation in my left arm, that I'd blamed on a pulled muscle. I thought about the hollow in the end of the spring-loaded rod.

I pocketed the lighter and went back toward the main room, stopping along the way to unlock the bedroom door and look in on Paul. He still lay on his face on the bed, his snores shaking the frame. I locked up again and took the spiral staircase to the ground floor. I holstered the Smith. I was pretty sure now I wouldn't need it soon. The rail stayed put this time, it was just cold brass after all, but my ankles wobbled and I leaned on it plenty. I was sweating again by the time I reached bottom. I rested against the banister for a moment before continuing.

There was nothing for me there. The shop didn't look any different. All the windows were shaded. I punched NO SALE on the cash register on a glass counter with moderately expensive carved jewelry on black felt inside and looked in the cash drawer. It was as clean and empty as a TV minister's head. There was a kitchen with a breakfast nook, a full bathroom, a storeroom containing packing crates and a cot with rumpled bedding on it and artistic odds and ends on shelves and in boxes that there was no room for out front. No basement. No Eric Rynearson. My hat decorated a peg near the shop door as if I'd hung it there. That was a nice touch.

I climbed the stairs again, stopping to rest twice on my way up. Paul's snoring was inspired. I stood between the bed and the nightstand looking down at him for a moment, and then I grabbed a fistful of the thick matted hair on the back of his head and lifted his face and dashed the contents of the blue plastic pitcher into it. He gasped and spluttered and went on snoring.

This would take a while. Well, it was Sunday and I was too late for church anyway.

I let go of him and carried the pitcher across the hall into the half-bathroom and filled it from the tap and went back and did it again. This time he stopped snoring long enough to spit curses. I made two more trips. Puddles collected on the sheet and the mattress squished when I let his face fall. After the fourth dousing he said something indecipherable, but which was not a curse. I held on to him and slapped his face — loud, stinging smacks that burned my palm. He gurgled and lunged. But there was nothing behind the lunge and I pulled my head back and his fingers skidded off my throat and his momentum almost carried him off the bed, depositing him over the edge. He started making familiar deep sumping noises. I stepped back just in time. I walked away from the racking and splattering and wrenched up the window to let in sweet air.

When it was over and Paul lay moaning with his head hanging off the mattress and his chin dripping, I reached across the bed from the other side and got another fistful of hair and yanked him over onto his back. He was conscious enough to yell. But his pupils had shrunken to pinpoints, and if the same stuff Rynearson had fed me was pumping through his veins he was in a carnival or a rowboat or some other childhood memory of a time of peace. Assuming he had a childhood. As ugly as he was now he must have been a fascinating little gargoyle when he was small.

"Where's Rynearson?" I asked.

"Rynearson?" His tone was shallow, not at all the deep volcanic rumbling that normally originated in the hollow of his enormous chest.

"Right. Where is he?"

"Rynearson?"

This wasn't working. If it was the same stuff, scopolamine

or Sodium Pentothol or some bastard hybrid of the two, Rynearson had probably combined it with some kind of hypnotism in my case. I was too old to learn the trick. But whatever lights of knowledge were glimmering in the little ape's shrunken brain wouldn't shine out through a broken head. There was too much Paul even in that stupid shell to give up an inch that way.

I played nurse. I fluffed his pillow, I used the white cloth the needles had rested on to wipe his face and mop up the worst of the mess on the bed, I sat on the dry side and patted a knobby hand that had hair like barbed wire on the back and called him by name and asked him about Rynearson. He spoke in broken sentences with long pauses between, and sometimes snoring, and when I woke him gently he'd forgotten what we were talking about and we had to go back to the beginning. After an hour I had my sticky hands on just two pieces of information: 1. When Paul had been getting set to retire to his room above the garage the night before, Rynearson had told him to come in first thing in the morning and set out the needles and serum, which Paul called "the junk." 2. Rynearson had said he'd sleep on the cot in the storeroom downstairs just as he had the night before and meet Paul in the bedroom in the morning.

Paul had risen at 6:30 as always and gone to the cabinet in the office and gotten the stuff as directed, assuming his employer was still sleeping or else getting ready in the dressing room down the hall. What Paul made of the mess in the office could only be guessed at. Maybe he'd thought Rynearson was reorganizing his files. In any case the assistant had come in expecting another day of dope and questions for the P.I. in residence. When I tried to get him to go back further he started jabbering about beaches. I figured they were his carnivals. Questions about the cross skidded off the sloping bone of his forehead.

"So where'd Rynearson go," I asked rhetorically, "and why'd he burn his files?"

"To avoid dragging in the kind of associate nobody wants to have mad at him."

I looked at Paul. It didn't sound like something he'd say. It wasn't even his voice, doped up or otherwise. He lay with his mouth scooping a round black hole in his beard, snoring fit to bubble the paper on the ceiling. I looked at the hallway door, through which two men in dark tailored suits were coming with automatic pistols in their fists.

I placed the man who had answered my question right off. He was the older of the pair, with steel-gray hair cut very short and the kind of flat tired eyes I would know if I saw them floating all by themselves in a jar, in a face running to fat and freckles, millions of freckles. He had a handsome leather folder open in the hand that was not holding his Army Colt.

"FBI, friend," he said in that same conversational tone. "You look like a man who knows the position. Show me."

24

"HE RABBITED. His car's still in the garage so he hooked a cab. My thought would be around midnight, when the shift was getting ready to change outside. That's when these kids start looking for the relief instead of what Uncle pays them to look for. Like smoke coming out of a chimney on a warm night in May."

On *kids,* the gray-haired agent glanced at his companion, a reedy youth showing a lot of Adam's apple above his Arrow collar. This one looked a little like Kirk Douglas' son in *The Streets of San Francisco,* with graphite-rimmed aviator's glasses and crisp black hair combed straight back and cut off square at the nape of his neck. His face didn't flicker.

The older man's name was Gervais. He called his partner Tommy, but I'd seen his ID too and none of his names was Thomas. Officially he was Special Agent Mulholland. We were sitting in Eric Rynearson's museum of a living room, Gervais in a cruel-looking clawfooted chair with my gun and the contents of my pockets spread out on the table holding up the skull ashtray at his elbow, including my credentials, Rynearson's jade lighter, the ring of keys I'd taken out of the bedroom door, and the five thousand dollars. After Gervais had pulled my fangs I'd told him what I was doing there and for whom and as much as I knew of what had gone on since Friday. I left out the cross. I wasn't sure why, and I was beginning to wonder if Rynearson had mentioned it at all or if I'd been hallucinating. None of it made sense anyway.

I said, "You've been watching the place?"

Gervais nodded. His face had a kind, mildly amused look that didn't fool me for a minute. "You were seen going in but not coming out. We ran your license plate and I've been dying ever since to know what a private star would want with Rynearson. City cops towed your heap away, incidentally. Yesterday morning."

I made a face and lit a cigarette from the crushed and wilted pack in my shirt pocket. I had to hold the match in both hands to keep from shaking out the flame. It was an effort just to remain sitting up. I envied Paul out cold in the bedroom. "He really is a Russian agent, huh? I thought that was smoke."

"Maybe yes, maybe no," Gervais said. "We've been on him like shit on a statue because he's been smuggling art treasures out of Europe against their laws and without paying duty. Today's the day Tommy and I were fixing to arrest him. Imagine our surprise when we walked in and found just you holding hands with Mighty Joe Young in the bedroom. There could be something for Detroit Vice in that."

"We're just good friends," I said. "Rynearson knew you were coming. That's why he powdered."

"Looks that way, doesn't it?"

"Maybe not." Mulholland gripped the arms of his chair. "He might have felt the heat and got out just under the wire. Lucky for him."

"We've got a leak, Tommy," Gervais said quietly.

"We don't know that."

"We don't know," he agreed. "But we know."

I said, "I thought you G-men were untouchable."

"G-men." Gervais smiled. "No one's called us that since Machine Gun Kelly. We're about to move on some feds who have been peddling stolen Lincoln Continentals in Mexico City for two years. They won't touch anything but new Mark IVs. Bring them a Marquis with fifty miles on the speedometer and they'll spit in your face. We're untouchable, all right. Like Mae West."

"Am I supposed to know this?"

"Who cares? I'm leaving the Bureau end of next month. I've got my thirty in."

I switched back to the main line. "So Rynearson got a telephone call, or a heliograph, or a note strapped to a pigeon's leg, probably sometime between when he and Paul turned in last night and midnight when the guard changed. He burned his files to protect himself from getting hanged in some cell or shivved in a shower room in case he didn't get clear, and went south. He'd need cash. Why'd he leave the five grand behind?"

"He thought it was marked," Gervais suggested. "Any clerk with a black light under the counter could get him slammed. He'd have had plenty green he could count on in the safe for case dough. What I'd like to know is what all this has to do with Russian writers."

"Me too. It seems like one too many holes for one old queen to have his nose in."

Gervais picked up the jade lighter, sprang the little rod. "Some things don't change. You'd think a guy with his money could afford a better way to get that little dart under your skin."

"You don't tamper with something that works," I said.

"That's another thing I'd die happy knowing. What he thought you could give him that was worth juicing you and keeping you juiced."

"Maybe he wanted to find out how much I knew about his operation. Panic."

"Five foreign government agencies didn't panic him. The FBI and the CIA didn't panic him. One local snooper with a toy badge panicked him. Interesting."

I got the weak look on my face and knocked some ash off perversely onto the Persian rug.

Mulholland said, "He's jerking us around. Let's take him down."

"It's a thought."

"First let's get some cops," I said. "I've been assaulted and held against my will for two days and pumped full of drugs. I've got charges to prefer."

"Against who?" the gray-haired agent wanted to know. "Sweetness there in the bedroom?"

"Him to start. Rynearson when you get him."

"Get him how?"

"You're the one with the Washington training. Put him on your Most Wanted list."

Gervais smiled. "They don't go on that list until we know where they are. Keeps the record tidy."

"Whatever. I want cops."

"I don't think so."

"Am I busted?"

He patted his breast pocket. "We've got warrants for all occupants of this address. Untangling the mess could take a week. Meanwhile you'll be in federal custody. Incommunicado."

"At the end of the week I talk to the press. I hear they get nasty in D.C. when they read about clandestine operations on the comics page. Nasty enough to forget thirty years of loyal service to the Bureau."

"Don't do it, Walker. You're a kid and I'm a book of matches. They don't go together."

"It's a two-fisted fed," I marveled. "I thought that got buried with J. Edgar."

"Hoover." He wrinkled his freckles. "I bet I blew two weeks in Bermuda on snap-brim hats on the off chance he'd pop in or I'd get my picture in the papers and he'd see it. He was a twerp, but at least he knew how to throw a blanket over a thing so it would stay. When the press came sniffing into his office he tossed them releases and they went out wagging their tails. Then the wimps took over and now we've got to worry about what the papers and TV are saying. Tommy can have it, I'm getting out."

I rested my head against the tall back of my chair and

closed my eyes. "Whatever beef the feds have with Rynear-son, I'm a vegetarian. We can't help each other."

"You're saying it. I'm hearing it. So far that's all."

"Call Louise Starr at the Westin."

Gervais jerked his chin at Mulholland, who rose and started down the spiral staircase.

"He'll be a good field man when they get him away from the idiot box," Gervais said. "He feeds suspects their rights even when no one else is around to hear."

I said nothing, got another Winston going off the butt of the first, and flicked the stub into a silver saucer with Arabic writing on the bottom. I swallowed some smoke, coughed. It burned my stomach wall and I remembered I hadn't had solid food in forty-eight hours.

After a few minutes the young agent returned. He bent his head next to his partner's and murmured.

"Well, you gave it your best shot, Walker," said Gervais, when Mulholland straightened. "The lady doesn't know you."

"Like hell. I figured you to be ahead of stunts like that. Cops don't whisper when a witness' story goes sour. They laugh in his teeth."

"Think you know us, do you?"

"I've got barely enough gray cells left to know my name, Gervais. I came here two days ago expecting to stay ten minutes. I got the full Frankenstein treatment. Anything you and Uncle can do to me can't start to compare with how I spent this weekend. You've got my key out of here. Maybe you'll let me use it, maybe you'll lose it in the system and I'll be appealing a false arrest beef into middle age. All we'll wind up doing is burning each other's daylight."

He still had the trick lighter in his hands. He fiddled with it, pressing the sprung rod back into the case and letting it snap out again. Finally he put it down on the table.

"You talk a good talk. I'd like to catch you when you're a hundred percent. Put this stuff back in your pockets, shamus. The money too. It makes my fingers burn."

I got up and did that, leaving the keys and the lighter for evidence or whatever. The weight of the gun on my belt corrected my shaky balance. "How about a lift?"

Gervais glanced at Mulholland's stiff face and laughed. "I can't figure out whether this son of a bitch has more sand in him than a camel's udder or he's still doped. I have to go in and stand on someone's carpet for all this anyway. Downtown? Police impound's closed until tomorrow."

"St. Clair Shores. If it isn't too far out of your way."

"Anything for you. Maybe you want to stop someplace for a bite?"

"I don't know. How hard do you bite?"

"It's never been measured." His face now didn't look as if it would support a smile.

He got to his feet with none of the noises a fattish man usually makes in the process and told Mulholland to hold the fort and watch Paul while he was gone. Turning to me: "Unless you'd rather have Tommy for company."

I considered the young agent's stony expression, then shook my head. "I'm afraid he *would* bite."

Downstairs I put on my hat. It felt tight around my swollen skull. "Why do you call him Tommy?" I asked Gervais.

"I had a no-good dog by that name once."

The car was an unmarked green Granada. He drove with one thumb on the bottom of the steering wheel and never missed a light. As he drove he made chewing motions with his jaw. I figured I knew what he was chewing.

"I could pin a tail on you or tap your phone, but that never buys anything from guys like you," he said. "I could make a call and get your ticket yanked—"

"Been done," I said.

"—but all that would buy me is someone's yanked ticket. All I can do is slam doors. Someday you'll have so many in your face you won't be able to investigate the inside of a Dixie cup. Uncle has a bad disposition and a long memory."

"Every P.I. walks that tightrope." I sat on my spine in the

passenger's seat with my knees up and my hatbrim resting on the bridge of my nose.

"Not without a net or a balancing pole, like you."

"No one's going to dance or cry if I fall."

When we were past the city limits I directed him to a street two blocks over from Karen's place and had him let me out on the corner.

"Shamus."

I bent and looked in at him through the open window.

"Aw, fuck it," he said, and drove off, almost taking my head with him.

It was a long walk. It was the Trail of Tears, the Burma Road, the Selma-to-Montgomery march laid end to end. It was two blocks. I leaned on corner lightpoles while my knees wobbled to a standstill, looking all ways to make sure Gervais wasn't shadowing me. The gun got very heavy behind my hip. The noise of cars swishing down the street hurt my ears. The bright sunlight hurt my eyes and the odor of the lake was sharp in my nostrils. I felt torn from the womb. I opened a door and climbed another set of stairs — the world was full of them — and finally I stood on the narrow runner in front of Karen's apartment. I was the soldier returning from the front, Ulysses back from his cruise, Moses casing Jerusalem. I squashed out the cigarette I'd been chewing and used the little brass knocker. It sounded loud enough to wake King Duncan.

Karen came to the door in curlers and a fuzzy pink bathrobe. She was a more beautiful sight than the Statue of Liberty. She took one look at me and said eek.

"You're making me blush," I said, and fell on her.

25

HER BEDROOM LOOKED DIFFERENT by daylight. The bay window was very bright and the colors in the room were cheerful and a stuffed rag doll with yarn for hair sat on a chair next to the bureau staring at me with the unblinking fixity of someone's brat watching someone else eat in a restaurant. It was the only thing little girl-like about Karen and I didn't like it. But the bed was comfortable and the eggs I was cleaning off the tray balanced on my lap had been laid in heaven.

Karen occupied a chair beside the bed with her elbow propped on her knee and her chin in her hand. She had taken out the curlers and changed into a scarlet blouse and black skirt. Without make-up she looked sixteen.

"But why didn't you tell the FBI about the cross?" she asked.

I put down my fork and studied her. "I guess someone's been talking in his sleep."

"I couldn't help overhearing with you lying on top of me like a load of bricks in the doorway. I won't ask about the carnival."

"Don't. The cross had nothing to do with why they want Rynearson. It would have led to questions my client doesn't want answered. You have to know where to stop when you're talking to cops."

"To me too, apparently. I don't know anything about this cross other than that you're looking for it. Is it full of diamonds or what?"

"I was told it wasn't worth a lot. Not enough to do what Rynearson did to me to try to find out where it is. It isn't even why I was there. That was a different case. I thought." I sipped coffee and reached unconsciously for a cigarette before I remembered I wasn't wearing a shirt.

"Here." She tossed my wrinkled pack onto the tray.

"I'm okay," I said. "Just habit. Who helped you drag me in here?"

"Not you, that's for sure. You were looking for the cross when you found that man dead in Hamtramck, weren't you?"

"Yeah."

"What's it mean that it has something to do with this other case too?"

"Beats me. I'll have to throw everything I know about both of them into a bucket and shake it and see what comes out. What'd you use, a block and tackle?"

"For what? Oh, that. You keep changing the subject. I've helped bigger men than you into hospital bathrooms. I thought you were drunk until I got your shirt off —"

"Sex fiend."

"— and saw those marks on your wrist. I still think I should make an appointment for you with our toxicologist."

"Thanks, I've seen enough white coats for this lifetime. Speaking of which, when does the old lady get sprung?"

"Tomorrow, why?"

"I don't want to waste a trip when I go to visit her."

"I didn't know you'd hit it off that well."

"Little old ladies love me. It's my honest face."

She studied me. A question fluttered around the corners of her mouth. She shooed it away. She reached out and stroked my cheek. "It can use a shave."

"I'd cut off an ear trying to scrape my chin."

"Just stay put." She got up and went out. I finished my coffee. She came back carrying a razor and a shaving cup and brush. I said, "I hope you borrowed that from a neighbor."

She pasted my mouth shut with lather.

Later she brought in my clothes on a hanger and hung it on the back of the chair she'd been sitting in. "I pressed the suit and rinsed your shirt. Don't expect that kind of service on a regular basis. Your gun's in the living room. What are you doing?"

I had peeled back the blanket and swung my feet to the floor. "It's called getting out of bed. I'm starting to be pretty good at it. Next week I plan to try walking."

She stood between me and the clothes. "You've had only six hours' rest. You'll run out of gas before you get outside."

"Lady, I've been running on fumes since I got away from Rynearson's." I tickled her. When she squealed and jumped I got my pants off the hanger.

"Don't call me lady, you lunk. It makes you sound like a taxi driver."

"I've driven taxis." I put on the pants. "You don't see many ladies through that little window. It's not a word I throw around."

"Are you paying me a compliment? I can't ever tell with you."

I scooped her up. We kissed. She said, "I guess you are."

I brushed her cheek with my fingertips. "I'd stay, but the meter's running."

"I'd ask you," she said. "But Tim's coming by in a little while."

"Is there a Tim?"

"There's a Tim." She paused. "Last night he asked me to marry him."

I could see my reflection in her brown eyes. "What'd you say?"

"I wasn't very original. I said I had to think."

"Are you thinking?"

She looked at the floor to the right of me and nodded jerkily. It was a way she had. I took her chin and turned her face toward mine. We brushed lips and she said, "I've been asked before."

"I don't believe it. An ugly thing like you."

She didn't smile. "I couldn't picture myself married those times. I can now. Maybe not married, exactly, but part of some kind of commitment."

"With Tim?"

"With someone, not him necessarily. I'm sick of Saturday night movies and restaurant dinners you don't taste because you're busy wondering if you're going to ask him in afterwards. I'd like to try a different rut. Sometimes I think I'll scream if I don't."

"Don't tell me about ruts. I wrote my dissertation on them."

"Is everything funny to you?"

"No."

"I think you're wonderful," she said. "I also think you're a man of many secrets, mostly other people's. I don't mind that I don't really know you. But people who make a habit of keeping confidences have a hard way about them. Their eyes look bleak and when they smile or frown it's just their faces moving. It's like they've drawn a black confessional curtain between themselves and the world. When they talk you can see them turning over every phrase first to make sure something important isn't stuck to it."

"I'm like that."

"You try not to be, or not to show it. You try to park your secrets on sidings, but the ends stick out and you have to step carefully around them. Talking to you is like tiptoeing through a minefield."

"Three different metaphors in a row," I said. "Or are they similes? I can never get that straight."

She passed it. "At first I liked that. It made you mysterious. But it's a side of you I could grow not to like a lot. I don't want there to be anything about you I couldn't like."

"Are we saying good-bye?"

"You could change."

"No one has since Lot's wife."

"It doesn't have to be good-bye good-bye," she said. "Secrets don't harm a friendship the way they do, well, love."

"It doesn't work like that. It's not something you can go back from."

She said, "I'm sorry you feel that way."

"It's not the way I feel."

I finished dressing and she walked me through the living room to the door, holding hands. The way you hold on to something you've borrowed for a while and it's time to give back. As if it might break before you return it. I stopped to snap on the gun in its holster. On the threshold we faced each other again.

"Thanks for taking care of me," I said.

"I was about to tell you the same thing."

"You don't need taking care of."

"I know," she said. "It's a bitch."

Her eyes glistened on the edge of something. An edge of something I will never be in a position to push someone over. We kissed again, and it tasted the same as always. Everything was the same except one thing.

She said, "We're always kissing in doorways."

"I'm always going through them. Mostly out."

I let go of her hand very slowly and went through one more.

The weather looked warm, but I couldn't tell. I felt anesthetized. I could stub my toe and not feel it till Christmas. I caught a cab to the office. The driver, who had looked at me without speaking as I got into the back, adjusted the mirror to keep me in it. I glimpsed my reflection as he did so. I couldn't blame him. I climbed stairs again, resting on the landings, and let myself in through the waiting room. No one was waiting in it, but that was okay, it was Sunday. I didn't have any mail. I counted the money again and locked it in the safe. Crumpling the pack with two stale cigarettes in it, I bonged it into the wastebasket, got a fresh one out of the carton in the top drawer of the desk and sat down and propping my feet up on one corner I laid the hot-radiator smell of tobacco smoke over the mustiness in the air. After five puffs I put out the weed and hauled the telephone over by its cord, hand over hand like a swabby weighing anchor. There was no answer in either Louise Starr's room or Fedor Alanov's suite. Out hustling Great Literature.

I looked at the blonde in the mini-misdemeanor bikini on the advertising calendar. She was standing in the classic S-curve, bending forward a little to rub suntan oil on one slick brown thigh so that a soft V of petal-white showed just above the brass ring that held her top together in front. I had stood in every corner of the office and had not been able to see down any farther under the bright material. Her smile was glistening white against the deep, deep tan of her skin.

The walls were bellying in. They had been doing that in every room I had been in since coming awake in Rynearson's bed. I stood up slowly with my head sloshing around like a water balloon balanced on my neck. I walked carefully up to the calendar and just as carefully tore off the page and doubled it over and balled it up and chucked it across the room into the basket. There was a redhead in an even skimpier outfit underneath, and six more girls under that.

26

THE MAIN BRANCH of the Detroit Public Library on
Woodward is set back from that incredibly long boulevard
that begins in the posh communities north of the city and
stabs straight as an icepick down through the tattoo parlors
and street-gang hangouts and all-night jiggle shows and bars
and bars and bars of downtown, ending at the docks where
the painted wheezing triple-decked anachronisms of the
Boblo boats load passengers bound for the only United States
island amusement park in Canadian territorial waters. The
colonnaded marble-faced library building stands alone in its
own square of grass and asphalt like a handsome senile em-
peror anointing himself with cologne against the animal
smell of his subjects. All the knowledge that can be stored
between covers is sheltered under its flat roof, but the lads
dealing peanuts and white powder on the front steps could
add something.

My business today wasn't with them. I paid off my cabbie,
who looked from my battered pan to the elegant columns
behind me and said, "Library's closed today. It's Sunday."

"I have an indulgence," I said.

"Huh?"

I smiled in my saintly way and blessed him with two fingers. He blessed me back with one and took off with a yip of
tires. An agnostic.

I walked through the parking lot around to the back door
and rapped. It was opened almost instantly by a black ex-
boxer of middle height with thick sloping shoulders under

his uniform shirt and a neck like a leg. Balloons of scar tissue crowded his brows and his modest Afro was blazed white on one side as if he'd been struck by lightning — which, if you believed in stories, was the only thing that hadn't been thrown at him in eleven years in the ring. He recognized me and grinned with just his lowers.

"'Afternoon, Mr. Walker. It's been months. You look every day of it, too."

"Count on you to say just the right thing when I'm low, Rupp," I said, stepping in past him. "I've been using the front door lately, when the library's open. But this won't wait."

"Microfilm room?" He drummed broken-knuckled fingers on the keytainer next to the revolver on his belt.

"Humanities section. Art history."

He clucked his tongue. "To think I knowed you when it was Archie comic books."

"Like hell. I was translating the *Arabian Nights* back into the original Sanskrit when I was six." I handed him ten dollars.

He tucked the bill into his shirt pocket, buttoned the flap, raked a glance any detective would trade his gold shield for over the closed-circuit television monitors above his desk, and led the way through the maze of corridors and varying levels that I hoped one day to know from the palace at Mycenae. He walked noiselessly on the balls of his feet with one shoulder turned forward like a fighter coming out of his corner at six-forty-five with dinner reservations downtown at seven. He had this job because I'd erased a smudge from his sheet at police headquarters. The department computer had had him mixed with another Damon Rupp pulling twenty to life in Jackson for Robbery Armed, and it was just a matter of sending a case of Seagram's Seven to an overworked punch clerk in Records and Information, but Rupp had me down as the Al Kaline of fixers and so far I hadn't gotten around to setting him straight. I probably never would as long as the library closed Sundays and holidays.

When he left me alone in the stacks I took notes from the card file and selected nine likely titles having to do with the religious art of eastern Europe. They proved to be big volumes and it took two trips between the shelves and the nearest reading table before I had them all in one place. I sat down and peeled my hat off and hung it on the divider and started with the indexes. I was the only thing stirring in the glossed vastness of that room lit by sunlight coming gray through the narrow, grilled shatterproof windows. The sound of pages turning was like small avalanches.

After an hour I had read enough to mark the useful sections with leaves torn from my notebook. Then I settled down to study. I learned everything anyone would ever want to know about the art of the Catholic and Eastern Orthodox churches and the lost-wax process of casting holy impedimenta in gold and silver and bronze. I could deliver a lecture on the subject anytime I felt like clearing a room. A hand the size of a switch engine shook me by the shoulder.

"You can't stay here past dark, Mr. Walker. It's the job if my relief catches you."

I blinked at Rupp's heavy features. They were indistinct in the gathering gloom.

"You should've let me sleep another five minutes. I was about to be crowned Pope."

"Must of been something you read," he said dryly.

It was dark when I got back home. I walked through the place, turning on lights as I went and seeing everything through new eyes, the way you do when you get back from jail or the hospital. I had been to both at the same time. There was enough Scotch left in the bottle in the kitchen cupboard for two drinks and I used that without bothering to hunt up a glass. As the heat scaled my belly I realized two things: that I was hungry enough to eat a typewriter and that I was too whacked-out to turn on the oven. I found half a loaf of bread and a jar of stale peanut butter. It beat liquid protein clear to Grand Rapids and back.

The telephone rang in the living room just as I was starting on my second sandwich. I unstuck the roof of my mouth with water from the tap and threw a leg over the arm of the easy chair and picked up the instrument on the fourth ring. The caller was Louise Starr.

"I tried to reach you earlier at your office. Why did the FBI call me?"

"It's a long story," I said. "It's a novel. A Russian novel."

"I thought we had a date this weekend. You stood me up."

"You wouldn't believe for who."

"You sound like a record winding down. I can barely hear you on this end."

I said, "When's your plane tomorrow?"

"Two o'clock. But I'll be tied up all morning. I've been putting off reading the rest of those manuscripts too long."

"Need a lift to the airport?"

"Andrei's driving me. But that could change." She sounded a little less cool.

"No, I want to talk to him too. I'll ride along if I don't have to share the back seat with trunks or anything."

"I travel light. Two suitcases and a briefcase. Has something happened? Is this to do with Eric Rynearson? Did you deliver the five — the package?"

"We'll talk. One o'clock at the hotel?"

"Better make it twelve-thirty," she said. "I don't want to get hung up in traffic."

"Traffic's pretty low on the list of things to worry about in this town."

There was a pause on her end. "Well, that's properly enigmatic."

"It's in character, Mrs. Starr. I'm a man of many secrets." I said good-bye and broke the connection.

27

I SLEPT A DRUGGED SLEEP crawling with soft sinister men in white coats with big needles and gamey apelike assistants and corpses in cellars and rumpled professional men moving in and out like worker ants with the same tired look on their faces and behind them tempered steel. I got up several times during the night to grope my way into the bathroom and draw cold water into a glass and watch my reflection in the mirror over the sink while waiting for it to fill. I was getting the look.

"She smiled like a monkey," I told the face. "Who needs that?"

In the morning I stepped out of a cold shower into the imitation seersucker and ate breakfast and took a cab to the impound to bail out my car. The tow chain had scraped chrome off the front bumper, but that was the extent of the damage. I drove to the office. Obese white clouds lay beached on a sky the color of blue chalk. Once upstairs, I opened the window to let the flies out and got the Underwood down from atop the file cabinet and spent an hour typing up the main facts of the Evancek and Alanov cases from my notes. With the articles and adverbs left out they still filled three pages, and they didn't make any more sense in black and white than they had in my head. It was like trying to match two torn pieces of paper with a third strip missing from the middle. Finally I filed the works in the drawer where I kept my change of shirts and put my heels in the hollow worn into the desk top for that purpose and ignited a Winston, working on my rings. This was one for Baker Street.

The mail came at ten. Two bills, one of my own statements returned for lack of a forwarding address, a circular advertising a martial arts course for hotel dicks and private investigators, and a coarse Manila envelope carrying a La Paz postmark. I tore it open and stared stupidly at the top handwritten page of the sheaf for a moment before I realized it was in Spanish. Several pages in, a translation into bastard English began and continued for ten garbled pages. The last was signed "Luis Esteban Cristobal, *Sargento, Policia de Cabo San Lucas.*"

I read the report twice, consuming three cigarettes in the process. By then it was time to meet Louise Starr. I lined up the edges and tipped the papers back into the envelope and filed it with my typewritten scenario. Before leaving I broke a fifty-dollar bill out of the safe, folded a piece of blank paper over it, sealed it in an envelope, wrote Sergeant Cristobal's name and the address of his station on the outside, stamped it, and put it in my breast pocket for mailing later. Then I locked myself out of the office a wiser man than I had been going in.

The clerk in the lobby of the Westin, an Arab with a moustache like a mascara line, rang Mrs. Starr's room, got no answer, tried Alanov's suite, spoke briefly to whoever answered, cradled the receiver, and told me to go on up. It was probably as much work as he had done on his shift.

Andrei Sigourney met me at the door to the suite. Today he was wearing a light blue suit contrasting the slightly olive sheen of his features and dark feminine eyes. His Nantucket beard interfered not at all with the square lines of his face. The scar on his brow looked less vivid now, but I was used to it. We shook hands briefly and he stood aside to let me through the unused room into the main part of the layout. Fedor Alanov was sitting on the same humpbacked sofa as if he had never left it except to change his clothes. He now had on a plain yellow short-sleeved shirt with a square tail hanging outside his slacks. A descendant of the bottle I had seen him kill off last visit was dying the same quick death into the glass in his other hand. His beard was no grayer, his shaggy black hair was no thicker, the bridge of his nose was no more nonexistent. Glaciers had come and gone since I had last stood in that room, but Alanov was still Alanov and Cracker-jacks still offered prizes.

"How's the book coming?" I asked. "Or do writers get sick of hearing that?"

"It's coming. And we do."

"Save it for the reporters, Fedor. Mr. Walker's a detective. He sees right through that irascible pose."

I turned toward the new voice. She wore the brown tailored suit and cream blouse I had seen before, but the outfit would have been to the cleaners and back since. Her hair was down and sunlight coming through the doorway behind her haloed her head. Rooms changed when she entered them. They always would. I lifted her proffered hand and said, "No one else shows you the sights next time you're in town, right?"

"Right." She smiled. It was strictly for business associates. "But I doubt I'll be back. The bean-counters in demographics don't consider this a high-sales area. It's too bad." Her smile changed a little and it didn't seem to have much to do with book sales. Then I decided that that was more than you can get out of a smile.

"What happened to your face?" she asked then.

"I ran into a floor. Luggage?"

"In the car. I just have to check out at the desk. We can go anytime you're ready."

"I came ready."

She hesitated. "Fedor —"

"You'll have the book when the book's done," he said, topping off his glass. "We did that. The good-byes too. So get out of here and let a man work."

"I don't like leaving you here alone," she said. Then she

looked hopefully at me. "Unless the Rynearson situation has been dealt with."

I said, "You ended that sentence with a preposition. And no, it hasn't. Not in the way you wanted it to be."

"I don't understand."

"It's a big club."

"Club?"

"B. B. B. B. and B.," I said. "The Benevolent Brotherhood of the Bothered, Befuddled, and Bedraggled. Also Bludgeoned. I'm hoping to dissolve it after we get through with our ride."

Her deep blue eyes glinted like waves catching the sun. "I'm not very good at riddles. But if Fedor's still in danger someone should stay with him."

"He isn't."

"But you said —"

"He never was." I offered her my arm.

After a moment she took it. We left, trailing Sigourney. Behind us Alanov's bottle of wine gurgled.

An elderly couple shared the elevator with us and we didn't speak on the way down or in the lobby, where a crowd of conventioneers was being checked through. In the covered driveway leading from the hotel garage, a teenage attendant in a uniform with a stripe on the pants hastened to open the front door on the passenger's side of a black Mercury for Mrs. Starr. She was a lady a lot of men three times her age would move fast to open doors for. She shook her head slightly and said, "I'll ride in back. This gentleman and I have business to discuss."

He glanced at me, measuring me, swung that door shut, and opened the one behind it. I walked around the trunk and got in on the other side. Nobody opened my door. Sigourney got into the driver's seat and started the engine and we got rolling.

On West Jefferson Louis Starr watched me light a cigarette. The flame jiggled in my fingers. I still didn't have any feeling in the tips. She said, "You look terrible."

"Thanks. I feel horrible."

"Did Rynearson — ?" She left the end dangling.

"Not alone. He had help. He sicced his Man Friday on me and got a needle into me and kept me for two days. I think he wanted to preserve me for his collection. I'll take my receipt back." I handed her the five thousand dollars.

"He didn't take it?"

"He couldn't see it from the pile of cash he was standing on. Tell your bosses the next time they set out to buy someone to find out his price first."

She counted the money, put it in her purse, found my receipt, initialed it, and gave it to me. "What's this about needles?"

"Your frightened old shopkeeper has a personal gorilla and some drugs the FDA has never seen." I stuck the receipt in my wallet and put it away. "Also he's a hypnotist. These are not tools listed in government pamphlets on the operation of small businesses."

"Then he is a Russian agent."

"Maybe. On the side. Mostly he's into smuggling national art treasures past Customs. Anyway, he's the FBI's meat now. So your boy Alanov is safe to write an exposé the world needs like it needs another Elvis impersonator. Not that he hasn't been all along."

We were heading north along the unlimited access stretch of the John Lodge toward the Edsel Ford, with buildings crowding in close on both sides and the sky only a narrow rectangle between the roofs. Sigourney drove in silence with both hands on the wheel.

"Right, Michael?" I asked him.

28

WE STOPPED for a light. He said nothing. I got some ashes into the tray in the door handle at my elbow without losing any fingers to the spring lid.

Louise said, "Michael?"

"Andrei Sigourney's real name," I said. "Michael Evancek."

The translator's slightly tilted dark eyes looked at me from the rearview mirror. "How long have you known?"

"Just since now, when you told me. But I've suspected it since this morning, when I read the report of your drowning off Cabo San Lucas. Michael Evancek's body was never recovered, which wasn't unusual. Eighteen months later somebody not his family showed up there asking about the accident, which was.

"It cost me fifty bucks, but it was worth it," I continued. "My contact down there was thorough and kept records of everything connected with the accident, including the man who came around asking questions about it, introducing himself as a friend of the family. The cop he talked to had a good eye. The man's description matched Paul, Eric Rynearson's gofer. There can't be two who look like him in civilization.

"He hangs around the police station the better part of a day, then leaves with some answers, but he's seen here and there in the vicinity throughout the week. Six months go by, and then men in the employ of Eric Rynearson make an attempt on a car carrying Fedor Alanov and his translator Andrei Sigourney near Detroit. No one's ever heard of Sigourney, so naturally it's assumed Alanov the famous and controversial Russian writer is the target. Only he's not. Michael Evancek is, because he came out of the Pacific with a new name and nationality."

The car behind us tooted its horn. Sigourney glanced up at the green light and started forward. "That's a long leap to make on a description," he said.

"Not so long. Some things Paul said about beaches when I was questioning him under drugs confirmed it, though they didn't make much sense to me at the time. Also you looked familiar to me from the start. You have a little of your grandmother in you. I'd put it down to your coming from the same racial stock, but what with Paul and Rynearson's interest in the cross Martha Evancek gave her son the coincidences got too deep to wade through. I saw your picture too, and some features don't change from childhood, though the scar and beard threw me off for a while. Rynearson must have made pretty much the same connection. You look a little like the pictures of your father, except you're not as wide."

"I've never met Rynearson."

"But he saw you. What about publicity? Ever have your picture in the paper?"

"When *Baltic* appeared we set up some speaking engagements for Andrei as translator," Louise offered. "We blanketed the area fairly heavily."

"Rynearson burned his files before ducking the FBI," I said. "There were a lot of them. The so-called drowning might have been covered in some newspaper up here and the account might have found its way into those files. He would collect everything to do with his interests, and the cross was one of them."

Louise said, "I'm lost. What cross?"

"A family heirloom a woman named Martha Evancek hired me to look for after I told her her grandson was dead. A thing of little value, she told me, other than sentimental. Only I did some digging in the library and found out that anything commissioned by the court of King Sigismund Augustus of Poland not now in the museums is worth a small country to the collector interested in such things. Rynearson would know the cross's history, and at least suspect that it came here with Joseph Evancek, Michael's father. Not being an investigator, he would lose track of it at the time of the shooting in Hamtramck. When luck dropped the surviving Evancek into his lap he wouldn't be able to resist trying to kidnap him to pump the cross's whereabouts out of him. Failing that he might rifle the suite Michael was sharing with Alanov on the off chance it was hidden there."

Sigourney said, "I have an apartment in town. Someone broke into it a few weeks ago. Nothing was stolen. I never put it together with the kidnap attempt. I don't know anything about the cross beyond what I remember of it from my childhood. I don't have it."

"Why'd you play dead?" I asked.

"I didn't start playing until a few months ago. I split my head open on a rock or something off Cabo and was washed ashore a mile north. A Mexican fisherman scraped me off the beach. He took no newspaper and didn't own a radio or TV set and never heard about the swimming accident. He was a kind old man who had read *War and Peace* four times, and when he'd brought me around and found out I didn't remember who I was he named me after Tolstoy's Prince Andrei because he thought I looked Russian.

"You wouldn't think that you could get used to not knowing your own name, but you can. At first it was like that nightmare you have about having to be somewhere far away and not knowing just where or how to get there, and of time rushing past while you're wandering aimlessly. Then I just stopped thinking about it. When I was well enough to earn my keep I started going out on the boat with old Julio. I got to be a pretty good small-craft boatman. I left after ten weeks and made my way north, taking work with charter boat operations. You need a last name to work above the border, so I took Sigourney. It went with Andrei. Andrei Sigourney swabbed decks in Long Beach and drifted, stopping in YMCAs and cheap hotels. Nights I wrote. I don't know how I got started on that, except that it seemed natural. Maybe something was trying to tell me I once wrote catalogue copy for a cereal box manufacturer in Dayton. Some months later I had a book. I had it typed and submitted it to a publisher in New York. Two publishers later it wound up on Louise's desk."

"It was a fine first novel," she said. "With a seafaring background, all about a young man's learning to cope with a past that was a mystery to him. But I never dreamed it was true."

"By then it wasn't." He watched the road. "I'd discovered an understanding of Polish and Russian, though I hardly knew it was my father who had taught it to me. When the book was rejected I asked to translate Fedor Alanov. Something — it might have been the very act of writing — had jarred a hole in the blank wall in my skull and I had started remembering things. My friend Fred Florentine. Ohio. My Aunt Barbara, who raised me. She scared me when I walked in on her in Dayton. She took one look at me and screamed. She really thought I was a ghost."

I said, "She told me you were dead."

"I asked her to, if anyone ever came around asking."

I waited. The Michigan Avenue overpass slid overhead.

"Not many of us get a chance to start over fresh," he continued after a moment. "Like every other copywriter in the history of advertising I'd wanted to do some serious writing, and like almost all the rest I was afraid to walk away from a steady paycheck. The amnesia wiped away that fear. I was on my way toward becoming an important novelist and I didn't want to take the chance of slipping back into that old secure, wasted life. I wanted Michael Evancek to stay dead. Even Fred couldn't know the truth. It wasn't a hard decision; Michael had never been happy. I'd acquired all the papers you need to get by these days, and it was really easier to go on being Andrei Sigourney than to go back to being that bright young advertising talent."

"So of course you came back to Detroit, where Michael Evancek lived the first eleven years of his life," I said. "Is there something wrong with that logic, or am I still suffering from narcotic poisoning?"

"I wasn't running away. I felt the need to revisit old haunts, or get the horrors every time someone mentioned Detroit. No one there would remember Michael, or if someone did, the odds were he wouldn't recognize him as the boy who left almost twenty years ago. I didn't count on Eric Rynearson. Who would? Tracing me all the way from Cabo must have cost him a fortune. My aunt moved here to be near me. That was a mistake too, but you've met her. You know she's as easy to persuade as a flash flood."

"She let your subscription to the coin magazine run until she moved. That's how I found her."

"Son of a bitch." He pounded the steering wheel with the heel of his hand. "I told her to cancel it."

"You found out from her I was looking for you?"

He nodded, meeting my gaze in the mirror. "That's why I got Louise to call you in after Rynearson made his move in Ypsilanti. I wanted to find out how much you knew. The strange thing is, I really thought it was Fedor he was after. I barely remember the cross and I never knew it was valuable. You mentioned my grandmother. Are you working for her? Is she in this country now?"

"She wants to see you. Or she did until I told her you were dead."

"I don't see that it would accomplish anything."

Louise said, "I really feel as if I've started reading a manuscript in the middle, and one I wouldn't buy. To begin with I can't believe anyone would go to such lengths to avoid going back to a life he never wanted in the first place."

Neither could I.

* * *

We made the rest of the trip in silence. Sigourney pulled the Mercury over to the curb in front of the American Airlines terminal and climbed out to get Louise's bags and briefcase out of the trunk. She and I stood on the sidewalk with sky-caps bustling all around. A jet roared hollowly overhead, un-rolling a thick layer of noise over the jabbering and traffic sounds on the street.

"I've got jet lag already," she said, raising her voice above the din. "I haven't known what's been going on since you showed up at the hotel."

Her face looked stiff. I remembered then that she and Andrei were not just an editor and a writer. "Maybe he'll write a book about it someday," I said.

"I wish I knew what to say when I get back to New York."

"Tell them the truth. Your boy Alanov's in the clear."

"They're going to ask why I still have the five thousand."

"Tell them Rynearson had a change of heart. Or don't tell them anything and keep the money."

She looked at me. The scent of jasmine seemed stronger here than in the car. "You know I won't do that. I hope you know."

"Yeah."

"I'm sorry to be missing that tour," she said wistfully. "I have a feeling I'm missing more than I know."

"Maybe not. According to some informed sources."

Sigourney finished arranging the luggage on a skycap's cart and handed her the briefcase. I wandered to the curb with my back to them and lit a fresh cigarette and watched a bus unload a gang of chattering Japanese tourists with cameras strung around their necks. I wondered what they'd found to take pictures of in Detroit. When I turned back Sigourney was standing there alone, watching Louise Starr switch her hips through a glass door held open by a gray-headed man carrying a suithanger over one shoulder. The writer-transla-tor turned back, touching his lips with a folded handkerchief. We got back into the car.

"A man named John Woldanski was murdered in Hamtramck last week," I said, as we glided around the long looping drive that led back to Edsel Ford East. "He fenced religious articles at the time of the Hamtramck shooting nineteen years ago. Whoever killed him wasn't looking for the cross, because neither of Woldanski's two houses had been searched. He was taken out for the sake of silence. You wouldn't know anything about that."

"I never heard the name until just now." Sigourney accelerated into the stream of traffic on the expressway. "Or maybe I did and don't remember it. There are still gaps in my memory."

"They come in handy sometimes."

"Meaning what?" It came out too quickly.

"Meaning that you remember as far back as Dayton, but Detroit stays a blank order."

"I was pretty young when I left. I've been to doctors and they tell me I may never remember all of that part of my life."

"You saw the shooting. You remember it, because you didn't ask 'What shooting?' when I mentioned it just now."

"I didn't see it. I got home after it was over." His eyes were bolted to the road.

"That's what you told the cops a couple of days later, after your Aunt Barbara had a chance to tell you what you saw and what you didn't. A witness saw you come home before the first shotgun blast."

"I didn't see anything."

"It's over," I said. "No one who can do anything about it cares who shot who. Michael Evancek is legally dead. I couldn't prove otherwise if I wanted to, which I don't. We're just two guys talking. You'll park this car at the Westin and we'll get out and go two separate ways and probably never see each other again. I think you'll have to tell someone someday or split down the middle. Why not me?"

We drove. A jet, possibly Louise Starr's, strained against

gravity going over the freeway, its silver belly flashing in the sun. "I killed them."

"What?" I didn't think I'd heard him right over the whooshing of the engines.

"I killed them!" It was a shout. "I killed my mother and my father and my sister.

"I came home and found my parents screaming at each other for the thousandth time and I went into their bedroom and got my father's shotgun and shot them both and when my sister came running in I shot her too. Or Michael Evancek did. I'm Andrei Sigourney. Andrei Sigourney, who writes books and translates Russian authors into English and never shot anyone."

As he spoke he lowered his foot against the accelerator. We were coming up on eighty now, and snaking in and out between slower-moving cars and trucks, the slipstream buffeting the Mercury's sides like a high gusty wind. I felt my fingers going white on the dashboard. I didn't remember putting them there.

"You didn't kill them," I said.

"The police said my father did." His hands were locked on the wheel, his profile drawn tight with scenery blurring past on the other side. "That's what Aunt Barbara wanted them to think. It's what she wanted everyone to think, including me. But I know. It's the reason she refused to discuss it with me afterwards."

"You didn't kill them," I repeated. "And neither did your father. There's only one other way it clicks."

I wasn't getting through. We had run out of speedometer and were still winding up. I tried again.

"It was your mother, Jeanine Evancek. Barbara's sister. She pulled the trigger."

29

WE WERE PASSING a green van with blue side-curtains. Sigourney dropped the left front wheel off the pavement, grinding gravel and spitting dust behind us. He wrenched it back the other way, overcompensated, and we fishtailed wildly across two lanes to avoid sideswiping the van. I had a brief glimpse of a blur of face through the window on the driver's side with a mouth working in it, and then it was behind us. Sigourney eased back on the pedal and we drifted back into the slow lane.

"My mother never killed anyone," he said. "She couldn't."

"Anyone can, given the right — or wrong — circumstances." I pried my fingers loose from the dash and worked them, forcing circulation past the knuckles. "She was found lying next to your sister. That didn't fit the way the cops wanted to figure it, so they just put it down as one of a million variables that come up in the course of a homicide investigation. Your sister had to have died first. It explains the position of the bodies, why she didn't run the other way after the first shot was fired. All the months of pressure from your father's unemployment and drinking erupted suddenly and your mother got the shotgun and cut loose at the first thing that moved. It happened to be her own daughter, but she would be too far gone to know that. What I think happened next is your father wrestled her for the gun and it went off, killing her. That saved your life, because you would probably have been the next victim. Then when the full force of the situation hit him, he went into the kitchen and blew out his own brains."

"You don't know any of this."

I said, "It clears up a lot. Like why your aunt kept the cops away from you for so long. She hated your father and loved your mother and couldn't bear to have the world know her sister had turned into a crazed killer at the last. You were in shock and so your impressions were malleable. She coached you until you were ready to swear you weren't there at the time of the shooting. Most of the other witnesses' testimony was on her side in that. In time you probably came to believe it yourself. But part of you knew different, and the guilt of your secret turned into a worse kind of guilt, and you came to suspect yourself of the murders. The pressure of that suspicion may have helped bring on the amnesia after you almost drowned; it was too much guilt for one man to bear, and so you just stopped being that man. Even now you're still shutting out the whole episode.

"Or not. But that pop-shrink stuff has its uses in my line."

We drove. The indicator hovered around sixty. He chewed his lower lip.

"What makes you think it wasn't me?"

"Your father's body was found in the classic suicide position, with the shotgun between his legs. The blast caught him square in the face, which is unusual but not impossible. It bothered me for a while. But if he hadn't killed himself, the killer would have had to make it look as if he had. That means premeditation, and this was not that kind of killing. Everyone in that house was a victim that day."

"I wish I could believe you. I've thought otherwise too long."

"That was your aunt's fault, for making you see something you didn't and for not talking about it ever again in your presence. I wouldn't be too hard on her, though. She was protecting her family and she thought she could protect you by selling you on an idea the way she sells artificial siding over the telephone. That may be the worst crime of all, the murder of memory."

"I need time to get used to the idea."

"Take it. There might be a book in it. Who knows?"

"That's a hell of a thing to say!" he rapped.

I rested my head on the back of the seat. "It's the drugs talking. Work it out your own way. I'm sick of the Evanceks and the Sigourneys and the Alanovs. Every time I put the case down it springs back up at me. Here's where I walk away from it."

"What about the cross and this man Woldanski?"

I said, "I take care of that today at four o'clock."

He looked at me sideways but said nothing.

The uniformed teenager at the hotel garage accepted Sigourney's keys with indifference — Louise Starr was long gone — and we shook hands at the entrance to the building. The writer's grip was warm.

"Your grandmother wants to see you."

"I don't know her," he said. "I don't know that I want anything tying me with Michael Evancek."

"Sure you do. You have since before I came in. You knew damn well your grandmother was in this country. I took Louise Starr's first call less than an hour after leaving Barbara Norton's place the first time. There wasn't time for her to tell you I was looking for you and for you to make the decision to hire me and then get Louise to do it. You had to know I was working for your grandmother before I ever talked to your aunt."

He breathed some air and looked away from me.

"I read my grandfather's obituary in the *News* some time ago," he said after a moment. "Evancek isn't that common a name. I've been paying the people on the other side of the duplex ever since to look after my grandmother, without letting her suspect it or why. Her phone is just an extension of theirs. They overheard her when she made her first appointment with you. As soon as they told me I looked you up through the state police. I had to know what you'd found out."

"See her. It's easier."

"I wouldn't know what to say to her."

"Try the truth. She's heard and seen stranger things, believe me."

We said good-bye. The revolving door sucked his trim frame inside.

Gallagher was relatively quiet. If you closed your eyes to the clouds of granite dust roiling to the south you could pretend that the rumble of heavy equipment rendering wood and brick was distant thunder. Neither the red Bronco nor the blue Pinto was parked in the driveway that the house shared with the place next door. The neighbor's green Camaro was there. Leaving my Olds at the curb, I climbed the concrete stoop, opened the screen door, glanced up and down the street, and used my hat to protect my fist when I pushed in the glass in the storm door. It made no more noise than a dog shaking itself and I reached in and turned the latch. It was quarter to four.

At ten past, a high-pitched engine wound down nearing the driveway, gears changed, and heavy tires kissed the pavement, coming to a stop. A door slammed, keys jingled on the way to the stoop. Then silence. He had spotted the broken window.

"It's me, Mayk," I called in a normal voice. "Walker. Come in and make yourself at home."

His Colt Python entered first, its nickel plate glittering like cheap costume jewelry in the sunlight coming through the window over the sink. Then he came in, big and square-shouldered in his gray uniform, broken glass crunching under his shiny black Oxfords. His mud-colored hair swept back like a mane from his wide face with the lines etched deep in the ruddy flesh. There were dark circles under his tired cop's eyes and beads of moisture on his long upper lip. He saw me sitting at the kitchen table facing the door and he saw what was on the table and he closed the door and leaned his back against it. The gun was a growth in his fist.

"When'd you put it together?" he asked quietly.

"A few hours ago. When I finished the rest of it and found parts left over. Four people knew I was looking for John Woldanski, but only one knew it was the cross I was after. One took over the old man's fencing operation on Trowbridge. One was a Hamtramck cop working undercover. Neither knew Woldanski personally. The third was just an information broker I use from time to time. He's got his own racket and it pays very well. That left you. You knew Woldanski; busted him, in fact. You investigated the Evancek shoot. And you knew I was looking for the cross, because I told you."

"Pretty flimsy."

"You of all people should recognize a judgment call," I said. "It made me curious enough to invite myself in and frisk the place."

I had removed the large crucifix that looked as if it had been carved out of a single block of wood from the hallway wall leading into the living room and placed it on the table. With one hand I lifted the top half free. Tarnished silver shone dully in the hollow, its blue and red stones gleaming.

I said, "It disappointed me. Edgar Allan Poe didn't know anything about the way the police work or he'd never have considered hiding the purloined letter in plain sight. As a cop you should have known better."

"It wasn't a matter of hiding it, exactly. Just putting it somewhere where I wouldn't have to look at it." He sounded as tired as he appeared.

"It needs polishing. It didn't nineteen years ago or it wouldn't have tempted you."

"It was that bastard Bill Mischiewicz," he said harshly. "He was on the pad since the academy. He bragged about it. You couldn't stay straight and spend much time with him without feeling like a chump. It was wrapped in a blue cloth in the top drawer of Evancek's bureau when we tossed the place after the shoot. I didn't even think. I smuggled it out under my jacket and never told Bill or anyone else about it. If the

Nortons or someone else asked about it I'd of given it back, said I was just holding it for safekeeping. But no one ever mentioned it. I didn't even know for sure it was worth anything, but it looked like it was. Hell, I didn't need money. I mean, I wasn't hurting. But it was like finding a hundred-dollar bill on the sidewalk."

"You tried to sell it to John Woldanski?"

"I felt him out about it. I backed out of the deal. We busted him soon after and I was scared he'd talk, but he didn't and I patted myself on the back for being so clever about the way I approached him. But by then I was sorry I'd ever seen the cross. My record was clean, I mean *clean*. What was I going to do, give it back? I stuck it away and forgot about it. I thought."

"A cop who's basically honest never forgets his one moment of weakness," I said. "When you found out I was looking for Woldanski to talk to him about the cross, you panicked. You knew damn well where he was, but you sent me the long way around the block to keep me busy while you dusted him to keep him quiet."

"I just meant to scare him, rough him up a little so he'd stay forgetful. It was an accident. He fell downstairs and broke his neck."

"Save that for a jury of your peers, Mayk. You were still a cop when Woldanski's wife died and you would've been keeping tabs on him in the line of duty and known when he closed up his old house and went to live in the new one next door. You knew it would look more plausible if he was found dead in the place where he kept his stolen merchandise. Fence dies gloating over booty. So you marched him over there from the house he was living in and gave him a shove. He was old, his bones were brittle. If they didn't cooperate you could always bash his head in afterwards."

"You don't know any of that."

"I know that after icing Woldanski you went back to the other house to make sure everything jibed with your scenario, turn off running faucets and put out smoldering cigars or whatever. I showed up sooner than expected and you knocked me out of the way escaping. But I heard that Bronco of yours changing gears during the getaway. That and the cross are material for conviction. Men have been hanged on less."

"You're forgetting this." He waved the shiny Colt.

"You won't use it."

He smiled, a tight, tired smile.

I said, "You broke a long-standing rule nineteen years ago and swiped something that didn't belong to you. You've been living with it all this time, and when it looked as if the rest of the world was going to find out about it, you overreacted and killed an old man. But you're not the kind to keep on climbing from crime to crime. I think you'd rather have it over."

"The cross belonged to a dead man. And Woldanski was a crook. The world smells sweeter without him."

"You don't believe that."

"You think you know everything there is to know about me, huh?"

"I used your telephone to call Lieutenant Kowalski after I found the cross. He's on his way."

Mayk said nothing. The house got very quiet. Just to relax the tension I lifted my right hand from my lap and rested it on the table. The Smith & Wesson clanked on the sheet-metal top.

He said, "I guess you don't leave much to chance."

"Neither do you. It's our police training."

"Twenty years a cop," he said. "One mistake."

"Two."

"No, one. It's still happening. But it stops here."

And before I could move he put his gun in his mouth.

30

WE WERE SITTING in the almost-dark, Martha Evancek and I in her lacy mausoleum of a living room, with no lights on and dusk thickening outside the windows. I could make out the highlights of her patrician face in the depths of her over-stuffed chair and the orange tip of her cigarette that glowed fiercely whenever she brought it to her lips, her hand covering the lower half of her face. The ruby ring glistened.

"Do you think Michael will come to visit?" she asked, wrinkling the long silence.

"I don't know. He has a lot to get used to first." I knocked some ash into the tray on the arm of the sofa. None had grown on my Winston since the last time.

"I want very much to see him."

I concealed a yawn. The smoke in the room burned my eyes and I always felt wrung out and slung over a line after a long session with the police.

"I should not, but I feel sorry for this man Mayk," she said. "That theft must have been eating at him all these years."

"He killed an old man guilty of nothing more than laying off some stolen property. That takes him out of the class of people I feel sorry for. Anyway, his troubles ended when he put that bullet through his brain."

"According to my faith they are just beginning."

I let her have that one.

"I still don't understand how you came to doubt the police version of the shooting," she said.

"The bodies didn't fall right, for one thing. If Jeanine had died first the way the cops had it figured, little Carla wouldn't have died in the same room. No normal child would have hung around after that first deafening blast unless she was the recipient. Ninety-nine times out of a hundred in these cases, the mother will kill the children first, while the father will start with the mother. It's a maternal thing, a twisted belief that by removing the children she's protecting them. That Michael didn't die next indicated that Joseph stopped her. Joseph was powerfully built and if he'd had the gun, she wouldn't have been able to prevent him from killing the boy too. The cops didn't give that any thought because they believed the confused witnesses who said Michael didn't get home until after the excitement. Also Joseph's blood test didn't show enough alcohol in his system to put him over the edge. Because of his history of unemployment and drunkenness the cops took the path of least resistance. That's understandable, if not forgivable. Two minutes after the first detective was invented, he was given a dozen cases to solve and only enough budget to solve three.

"Plus, Barbara Norton, Jeanine's sister, was too anxious to wipe out all memory of the incident from Michael's mind. That lady's sense of family takes less dents than armor plate. At all costs Jeanine had to be made to look like the victim rather than the killer."

"What about Eric Rynearson?"

"Just another mugger, but with a hypodermic needle instead of a switchblade, and more expensive tastes. Someone will recognize him from his picture in a post office someday and the feds will snatch him from behind a cash register in some junk store. Or they'll scrape him off the floor of an alley after someone in a delicate position gets to worrying about what's in his head that couldn't be burned in his fireplace. His fuse is pulled."

"You've suffered so much for so little," said Mrs. Evancek 'The drugging. Trouble with the authorities."

"It's the way I work. You paid me to take risks. I could have laid it off on the cops when it started bending their way, but I wouldn't have been earning my fee. The bad will it bought me is a thing I live with. I'll bill you."

We smoked in the dark. After a while she said, "Karen confides in me. I know what happened between you."

I said nothing.

"She's a foolish girl," she went on. "I told her that. You are like my late husband Michael. I had thought he was the last of the kind."

"Karen will always do what's right for her. She'll marry her med student and have three kids and they'll all grow up solid. None of them will wind up a bushed P.I. running a one-man show in a depressed area."

"She would not know a solid man if one fell on her."

I felt a grin forming. "You've been spending too much time with me. Next you'll be spouting dirty limericks and picking your teeth with a stiletto."

She made a hoarse sound in her throat. Her cigarette-tip came up and flared, casting orange light over her high cheekbones and thick curved nose.

I read the luminous dial on my watch and got up. "It must be coming on your bedtime. I'll be missing when Karen comes in to help you." I put on my hat. "The cops are hanging on to the cross. You should get it back after the inquests on Woldanski and Mayk."

"I care nothing for it now," she said. "Michael is alive."

She asked me to turn on the light on my way out — Karen scolded her for sitting in the dark — and we said good-bye. I stepped out into the early-evening cool. My clothes felt clammy on my frame. I felt the cold dried sweat on my back and under my arms and in the bends of my elbows. The lights of St. Clair Shores glittered like stars fallen from the brushed black sky. There were no blanks as there would be in Poletown, where the lights that had drawn so many pilgrims from the tired Old World had been extinguished by bulldozers and iron balls and men with wrecking bars and sledges.

My crate was parked on the street. I climbed under the wheel and pulled the door shut, but I didn't start the engine right away. I lit a cigarette and sat there and smoked it and put it out and lit another. After a while a dusty-gold Plymouth rolled past and swung into Martha Evancek's driveway. The taillights went off and Karen McBride stepped out, wearing her white nurse's uniform under a light topcoat, and walked up to the door leading into the back half of the duplex and rapped and waited and then went inside without once looking in my direction. Something tiny and bright glinted on the back of her left hand.

In a little while I ground the starter and it caught and I drove home the long way around Hamtramck.